West

A History Interrupted Novel

Lizzy Ford

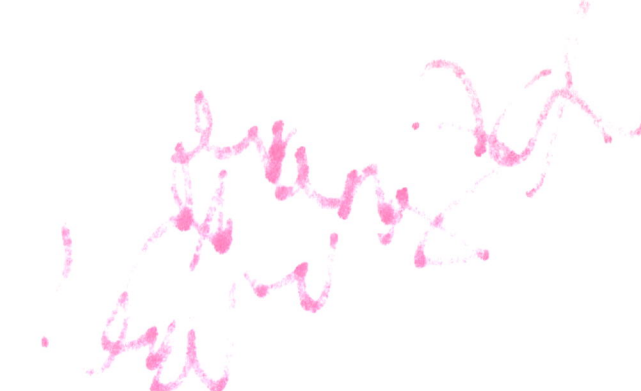

Copyright © 2014 Lizzy Ford
http://www.LizzyFord.com

Cover art and design copyright © 2014 by Eden Crane Design

Photography copyright © 2013 Cathleen Tarawhiti

Cover model: Georgia Stanwix

Fleuron © spline_x - Fotolia.com

Excritura Pro font © 2014 by Linotype

Published by Kettlecorn Press

All rights reserved.

No part of this book may be reproduced in any form or by any electronic or mechanical means including information storage and retrieval systems, without permission in writing from the author. The only exception is by a reviewer, who may quote short excerpts in a review.

This is a work of fiction. Names, characters, places and incidents either are products of the author's imagination or are used fictitiously. Any resemblance to actual events or locales or persons, living or dead, is entirely coincidental.

ISBN-13: 978-1-62378-161-3

FIRST EDITION

Dedication

For anyone who's dreamt of disappearing into a book.

Chapter One

Take a survey while you wait!
Only three questions!
Free $50 gift card!

FIFTY DOLLARS WAS A LOT WHEN MY BANK ACCOUNT WAS CLOSE TO zero.

I stepped out of the stream of tourists strolling along the covered wooden sidewalks of Tombstone, Arizona, and paused before the table with an iPad laying next to the propped up sign. It was over a hundred and twenty degrees in the shade and even hotter in the brilliant midafternoon sun. The stores were packed. The beverage sellers at each corner of the tourist district wore heavy period clothing that made me feel sorry for them, as evidenced by the collection of overpriced water bottles weighing down my purse.

The first page of the survey was pulled on the iPad's screen, just waiting for someone to stop and fill it out.

"Why isn't this place crowded?" No one even glanced this way. Either it was my lucky day or I was the only person wondering how I was going to pay off student loans after graduating college. "My lucky day!" I placed my purse down on the table, picked up the tablet and glanced at the window of the store behind the survey.

It wasn't a souvenir or jewelry shop or western-themed eatery like every other business lining the sidewalks of the popular tourist spot. The pictures in the window were sad – of Old West pioneers burying their dead and Native Americans being marched in chains while flanked by cavalry members on horseback. It was a stark reminder of how gritty life back then had been.

Every kid who was ever forced to take an American History class knew how the Old West was won and the natives suppressed, and I had read every book about the era I was able to find when I was in high school. I wasn't certain why this store was in the heart of a tourist trap, unless the city was trying to keep things more authentic than the Old West souvenirs made in China.

Seeing the photos made my heart hurt for the long dead people.

"Are you interested in the history of the Wild West?" asked a male voice.

I looked over, not expecting the stranger to be as stunning as he was.

He smiled. Tall, trim and sexy, with sparkling blue eyes and dark hair, he wasn't much older than I was, maybe the age of the Masters students in the university where I had recently graduated with my Bachelors in a field unrelated to the Old West: modern languages. He had charming dimples in both cheeks that gave him a boyish appearance, exotically high cheekbones and a tilt to his almond-shaped eyes.

Déjà vu. I knew I'd never seen him before, but the sense we had met at some point was strong. Never one to pass up talking to a man stunning enough to be a Hollywood A Lister, I lowered the tablet and smiled.

"I'm not really into American history anymore. I was obsessed with the Old West when I was in high school, but I grew out of it," I answered. "I minored in European History in college."

"So you do like history?"

"Yeah. Civilized history, I guess."

"Civilized?" He laughed. "Tell that to Genghis Khan when you meet him! I mean … if you meet him." He blushed. "If you go back in time and …"

He reminded me of my youngest cousin, a super brain who was awkward around women. It didn't seem possible this man had issues with women, though, because he was absolutely *hot*. The fact I resembled the perfect blond haired, blue eyed, bubbly cheerleader drew all kinds of attention from men, but none had blushed quite like this.

"It's okay if you want to try that again," I said, struggling not to laugh.

"Thanks." His cheeks were almost purple with embarrassment. "I meant to say, I don't think there's such a thing. If we were to go back in time, I think we'd find the past anything but civilized."

"Good thing we're in the here and now." I glanced at his nametag. *Carter, History Interrupted, Inc.* "You're the one doing the survey?"

"Yeah. It's nice to meet you, Josie." He stuck out his hand.

"I'm …" I trailed off, realizing he'd already said my name. "… not wearing a nametag."

"Oh." He turned red once more. "You look like a … Josie."

"No one *looks* like a Josie," I said with a laugh.

"Fits the period." He appeared relieved I wasn't freaked out, his smile large and dimples larger. "Lucky guess."

This is strange. "Nice to meet you, Carter, I think." I picked up the tablet again. "Is this one of those surveys where you try to sell me a timeshare before you give me my gift card?" I was cute, petite and quick to smile; it was how I always managed to get away with talking to people the way I did.

"It's an absolute honor to meet you, Josie. And no, there's no timeshare involved. Can I at least give you my pitch?" he asked hopefully. "I've always wanted to talk to you. To someone like you. To someone who …" He was flustered again.

"Wait, stop there! Let me put you out of your misery." I smiled, taking pity on the socially awkward man. "Tell me about the survey or your project or whatever it is you're doing."

There's something odd about this guy. Not in a bad way, just like a lost puppy that clung to the first human to show it kindness. The combination of Hollywood looks – but no clue how to talk to women – and his over the top enthusiasm about meeting me were endearing. I liked him almost immediately.

"What if I told you that all this," he waved at the pictures on the window, "could've been prevented? That one man started a chain of events that ended with the near destruction of the native peoples of North America?" His eyes glowed, and he became animated, his hands complementing his words with flourishes. "Just one man. Someone who may not have known the impact of what he did? Maybe he made one tiny choice, like you did this morning when you put on black yoga pants instead of jeans."

I wasn't able to stop my smile. His passion was apparent. "I'd say that's an amazing discovery. But … does it matter now?" I asked, puzzled.

"Have you ever seen Doctor Who?"

I laughed. "Yeah."

"Just … pretend I'm the Doctor and you're my companion and we can go back to any point in time. Okay?"

I nodded.

"One man in the eighteen forties made a single choice that forever changed the landscape –"

"His pants," I said, grinning.

"– right or something else. Whatever it was, he did it on September twenty fourth, eighteen forty-two. So he does this one thing, and bam. The lives of nearly a million Native Americans and tens of thousands of pioneers are lost over the course of a century."

My eyes returned to the pictures. This ... speech, if it could be called that, was a bit morbid. I understood his point, even if I didn't really get why we were playing this hypothetical game.

"What would you do if you could go back in time?" he asked. "Would you stop him if it saved a million lives?"

"Yeah. Who wouldn't?"

"There are some people who think history is chiseled in stone, that it shouldn't change, even if we could."

I shook my head. "I don't agree with that at all. I mean, assuming we one day had the ability to time travel, why shouldn't we go back and help those who didn't have a chance? We could do so much good, save the planet from all the abuse we've caused during the globalization age, stop men like Hitler. Of course I'd change things."

He was smiling. "Good. You're very idealistic."

"My uncle says the same," I said and rolled my eyes. "I'm not totally naïve. I know there are bad people who might try to go back and change things to make themselves billionaires or get revenge on the Homecoming queen who rejected them or whatever. But I'd like to think humans are naturally good and if given such a power, we'd use it wisely."

Carter looked at me a little too long, his features glowing again. I was always friendly, especially since he was starting to remind me of the guys in *The Big Bang Theory*, who were uncomfortable talking to other humans in general. "Is that ... it?" I asked.

"Oh, yeah. Sorry. Didn't mean to stare." He shifted feet like an excited child on Christmas Eve. "Just if you could, take the survey, so

I get credit for something today. It's only three questions."

"What kind of research are you doing?"

"It's a relatively new discipline of history. There's a lot of psychology that goes into determining how our outlooks of our world have changed over the years. What we once viewed as moral and just is now barbaric, and so on."

"That sounds interesting," I said. *But not my thing at all.* Such a complex subject seemed right up the alley of the man I suspected was a genius behind all his blushing.

"It's so beyond fascinating, I could spend days … but I won't. I'll let you complete the survey." He moved way to give me space.

Amused, I turned my attention to the iPad, unable to shake the sense of déjà vu. After I filled out the portion for my name and age, I swiped to the second screen.

If you could go back in time to prevent atrocities such as the Trail of Tears experienced by the Native Americans, and the massacring of pioneers caught between native warriors and the Calvary, would you?

I glanced at the pictures on the windows, once more touched by the visible pain. The people gazed at me in silent desperation, suffering clear on their features. "Sure, why not?" I selected the green button on the survey and was taken to the second screen.

If you could save the lives of a hundred thousand people TODAY, would you do whatever it took?

"Duh. Who wouldn't?" Tapping the button, I read the next question.

If you could go back and change history, would you?

"Only if there's a modern sewer system, espresso and AC," I quipped and then sneaked a look at the images looking over me. "Sorry. I didn't mean it," I said to them quietly. "I'm hot and irritated. I would go back and save you all, if I had the power." I swiped to the last screen and entered my email address.

Carter was waiting patiently nearby.

"That's it?" I asked loudly enough for him to hear, perplexed by the simple questions. I replaced the iPad on the table.

"It is!" Carter beamed and joined me once more. "Well … except …" He cleared his throat, ears red. "Would you maybe want to … get a drink tonight at the Victorian Vittles Saloon?"

"Ah, I'm sorry, Carter. We're leaving in an hour or so."

"Oh." He appeared surprised. "I thought you were staying here."

"No, sorry."

"Okay. Thanks for letting me down easy," he flashed a dazzling smile. "If you change your mind or … decide to stay in town, I'll be there shortly. I'm packing up soon to leave."

"Sure. Sounds good." I picked up my purse and offered my hand. "Nice talking to you."

"Thank you. So much." He was nearly gushing as he clasped mine in both of his.

Overwhelmed by his enthusiasm, my cheeks grew warm, and I laughed instead of answering. Pulling away, I waved and started towards the direction towards where I was supposed to meet my aunt and uncle. The tingling instinct that I knew him lingered. Not one to ignore my intuition, I halted.

"Wait, Carter, can I ask you something?" I asked, turning.

"Of course."

"Have we met before?"

He looked like I'd agreed to go on a date with him. His unguarded expressions were something I expected from a kid, not a full-grown man. "Does it feel like we have?" he asked with hushed awe.

My brow furrowed. I gave another small laugh, uncertain how to take his strange reaction. "Sorta. Like déjà vu."

"We haven't," he said. "But I'm really glad we did."

"Me, too." And I was, without really understanding why. His innocent, boyish charm made me want to tease him the way I did my youngest cousin or maybe, to ask him if he needed help doing his homework. I couldn't explain it, except that it wasn't physical attraction per se, more of a sense of being kindred spirits. My aunt believed in past lives and how we met the same souls over and over again throughout our many lives. I could almost believe it about Carter. "Bye."

Hopping off the raised wooden sidewalk, I strode across the street and glanced over my shoulder. Carter, the table and survey sign were gone.

Then I realized I had left too quickly to get my gift card. "Broke for another week." I sighed. "Oh, well."

I spotted my aunt – a slender woman with bleach-blonde hair – and jogged towards the middle of Tombstone. My uncle was short and squat in comparison, a Beverly Hills plastic surgeon with a warm smile and a wife he turned from pretty into an ageless beauty.

"Great news, Josie," my aunt started. Her loud words were like her dress – exaggerated. From the obscenely wide-brimmed hat to the bug-eyed sunglasses and fuchsia cowboy boots, there was no chance of my over-the-top aunt fitting into the dusty, laid back environment of Tombstone. "We're staying here tonight!"

"Here? Where?" I asked.

"Your uncle won a drawing for a free night here in Old Tombstone!" she exclaimed.

"Oh, okay," I murmured. *Looks like I'll be able to meet Carter for a drink after all.*

My quiet uncle appeared proud of himself while my aunt beamed him an adoring smile. As different as they were, they'd always been a doting couple. I viewed a relationship like theirs as enviable, even though they used to embarrass me when I was younger.

"You have time to look at more rocks," my aunt added.

"Yes, because that's all a rock hobbyist is interested in," I said with a sigh. I had given up explaining why I became an amateur geologist. My aunt had never gotten past the fact I was more interested in rocks than jewelry and accessories. "I do love them, though," I added, excited about the multiple rock shops I'd visited already. I had too many interests. I barely had the credits to escape the dreaded, generic liberal arts degree to obtain one in modern languages.

"I'm sure there are some fascinating specimens in these shops," my uncle added. "They have a lot of dinosaur fossils here, too."

"And meteorites. Maybe there's some space peridots," my aunt said.

We stared at her, surprised she'd noticed something about a gem that wasn't a price tag or whether or not her wealthy neighbors already owned something similar.

"Come on!" she said, oblivious. "Let's find our bed and breakfast. It's supposed to be authentic!"

"I really hope that doesn't mean we're peeing in buckets," I said with a laugh, recalling the first tour we went on when we arrived to Tombstone.

"You and me both." My uncle smiled then led us down the road to an intersection. His warmth always melted my impatience with my aunt, a reminder of how much I had always wanted a real father when growing up. My uncle was as close as I had gotten, and he'd always been sweet and supportive – but not really mine. He had three other kids that called him *father* while I called him *uncle*.

Orphaned when I was young, I was grateful that my aunt and uncle had taken me in and treated me as family. None of my cousins were roped into this crazy trip across the southwest in search of some kind of rare turquoise my aunt had heard about. Of course, none of them were geological hobbyists who could help her find what she wanted.

My uncle guided us around one of the buildings to a three story, restored Victorian house that appeared to deliver on the promise of being authentic by its wooden façade. The ground floor was a saloon with a sign hanging in front that read, *Victorian Vittles Inn and Saloon.*

Another sense of déjà vu washed over me as I stepped onto the porch. I had never been here before, but like Carter, it was almost familiar.

Shaking my head, I followed my aunt and uncle into the foyer dividing the saloon from a more formal dining area. To my surprise, Carter was already seated at the bar. I looked twice, not sure how he managed to get here before us, but curious about him to the point I didn't really care.

"Hey, I'm gonna grab a drink," I said to my uncle.

"Here." He handed me a twenty.

I accepted it and walked to the bar. "Mind if I join you?" I asked and plopped down beside Carter.

"I thought I'd see you here," he said with another excited smile.

"You're kinda weird, Carter." I laughed.

"Well … I didn't mean … I'm sorry. I just …" He sighed.

"It's okay. I understand." He was flushed again, and I felt bad for embarrassing him.

The quiet was awkward. I ordered a beer and waited for Carter to say something. For having invited me, he was strangely quiet, staring at his bottle.

"How did your surveying go today?" I asked finally.

"Slower than usual."

"Hmm." I wasn't good at pretending to be interested in things that really held no importance to me. "So, uh, you like history."

"I like *changing* history. The idea," he added quickly. "Theorizing. Researching. That kind of thing."

"If you went back in time, would you change things?"

"Yes. I have it calculated." He pulled out a cell phone. "You could spend less than two weeks in the eighteen forties to stop a million deaths. You'd just have to find a Choctaw Indian named Running Bear and another man named Taylor Hansen."

"They caused everything?"

"Sort of." He glanced up. "Am I … weirding you out?"

"Not yet."

He perked up and began talking. He was a delight to watch, charismatic and exuberant. With little interest in history, I paid attention to him as much as possible while he began an epic tale about how one change could have prevented a million deaths. His detail and knowledge of the past was astounding, along with his passion.

Drinking beer after beer, I was more interested in watching him speak than in what he said. The sense we were friends in a past life or had met somewhere in this one grew stronger the longer he spoke, and I found myself laughing and enjoying his company.

Somewhere around beer four, more people trickled into the saloon for dinner, and the lantern-like lights went on around us. My uncle texted me what room I was in while my aunt mentioned a wine tasting bar they were headed to. I, however, liked being around Carter. Bubbly and cheerful, he had a natural, happy energy that compelled me to stay.

By beer number seven, the bar had grown loud, the televisions were blaring a college football game, and Carter and I were plotting how to change history.

The drunker we got, the more sense it made.

"So would you go?" he asked some time later above the noise of the evening crowd. "Like a two week vacation to the Wild West."

"Yes," I said with no hesitation. "All you have to do is figure out how to time travel."

"I can do that."

"I believe you. You're one of those geniuses aren't you?"

He grinned. "Yes, I am."

"I so knew it!" My words were slurred, and so were his. I couldn't remember the last time I'd had this much fun at a bar.

"You go back in time. I'll stay here so I can help you find the right people. We can text each other," he said.

We stared at each other for a moment before we both began laughing at the amazing yet ridiculous idea.

"But wait, Carter!" I exclaimed suddenly. "I can't speak Choctaw … Choctawan. Whatever. How do I convince him to wear jeans?"

"Oh I can fix that," Carter said. "I created a brain chip … I mean … micro chip for your brain and it'll let you understand and speak every language known to man. It translates everything into … American English and then everything you say is translated into the language of … whoever you're talking to."

"Seriously?" I gave him an astonished look. "I could've used that for French class."

He laughed. "You want to … to use billion-dollar technology to cheat on a French exam?" For some reason, that tickled him, and he laughed until he was crying.

I ordered us another round of beers.

Wiping tears away, he drew a deep breath.

The loud crowd was growing out of focus. After all the parties I attended in college, I knew where I was on the drunk chart: driving – no, stairs – only if necessary, another round – the last.

"I have another one that is like an internet. In your brain," Carter continued. "It has all of history on it and my research."

"Another what?" I asked, easily lost while drinking.

"Microchip. For your brain. Because there's no internet in the past."

"Oh, that's brilliant, Carter!"

He smiled. "I *am* brilliant."

"Do I need shots?" I asked him. "Because they had diseases back then."

"I didn't think of that." He appeared thoughtful. "That explains a few things."

We both giggled, even though I was beyond comprehending why.

"I can get you innoc ... ulations." He hiccuped then leaned forward. "Do you wanna know a secret, J... Josie?" He asked drunkenly.

"Yes!"

"I have a time machine."

"No way!"

"Way way."

"Why didn't you say something before?" With the line between reality and the imaginary blurred, I was so excited, I was barely able to get off my stool without falling. "Then why haven't we gone back? C'mon, Carter. The past is waiting." I took his arm and pulled him through the crowd to the warm night outside. "Where did you park it?"

Carter laughed and caught himself against a pillar on the porch. "I didn't *park* it! It's in my lab."

"Okay, then, let's go there. We can rescue people and come back by morning, right, like on Doctor Who?" I made my way down the stairs. A thrill worked its way through my drunken haze. The idea of saving a million people, of seeing what Tombstone looked like almost two hundred years ago, was the most incredible adventure my drunken mind had ever gone on.

"You need brain chips first."

I laughed, nearly collapsing. "Like potato chips in my brain!"

He tripped and sprawled onto the sidewalk. Quakes of laughter tore through us both, and we stayed on the ground until we were able to walk again.

Helping one another up, we started walking, arm in arm. "You … are amazing, Josie," he said. "They told me so and now I know."

I looked up at him, his handsome profile outlined in the moonlight. "Who told you?"

"Oh. No one."

"You're so weird, Carter."

"Josie, wait." He faced me, as serious as could be. "It really is an honor to meet you. A *great* honor."

"Thank you, Carter." I held out my hand and shook his rigorously. "It's an honor to meet you, too. Let's go to your lab."

"Yes, let's!"

Together, we half walked, half staggered back to the storefront where I took the survey earlier. It took four attempts before he was able to unlock the door and pushed it open.

Brilliant light spilled out into the night, too bright to see into the room.

"It's … there," he said proudly. "My lab. Your brain chips."

A tingle of awareness slid through me, one that warned me I was wandering around in the middle of the night with a complete stranger. It just as quickly fizzled, replaced by the comfortable warmth of being drunk and the idea of time traveling like Doctor

Who.

    "Let's go," I said and strode into the light.

    I squinted to see what was inside.

    And then the world went dark.

Chapter Two

I HAD A WEIRD DREAM, WHICH WASN'T WHOLLY UNEXPECTED after drinking so much. In it, I was unable to cool off. I stood in the hot Arizona sun, in the middle of Tombstone. The tourists were gone, and I was alone, except for ...

Carter. At least, I thought it was him. His athletic form was at the end of the street. Whenever I tried to walk towards him, he stayed the same distance away. In fact, it was like I was walking in place. Sweating. Craving a damn mocha. With a weird headache.

"Hey, Carter!" I shouted. "You forgot my gift card!" I paused to look around, then up at the sky. "What the hell?" I shielded my eyes with both hands to get a better look.

The sun was rapidly getting closer, larger and brighter.

"Almost time to go."

I whirled at Carter's voice, startled to find him standing behind me.

"I have to cover a few things before you leave." A tablet appeared in his hands.

"Where am I going?" I asked.

"More like, *when*?" He beamed a warm smile. "That sounded

better in my head. Anyway, let's get started."

"Oh, right. The eighteen forties. We're still doing that?"

"Yes! Your brain chips are in!"

"Cool." I smiled. It wasn't like I really cared. It was a dream, after all, and I liked Carter. "Shots, too?"

"Yep! You are immune to everything from the Black Death to diseases that don't exist yet."

"Awesome."

"Okay." He focused on his tablet. "First, you'll have headaches for a few days, the side effect of brain surgery."

"Naturally," I agreed.

"Second, you'll find over time that what we did is going to materialize rather randomly. We have mastered the *how* but not the timing yet," he said, eyes on the screen of his tablet. "Your language and empathic memory skills will hopefully emerge the first week. I'd really appreciate feedback on how they work for consideration of future travelers."

I shifted feet, half listening, alarm fluttering through me. "Are you worried about that?" I pointed up. The idea of the sun crashing down on us was more concerning than anything Carter said.

"It means I don't have the time I'd like to cover things," he said. "Third, don't go swimming for at least two days. I was going to say don't go flying, but there's no chance of that where you're going." He chuckled.

Frowning, I stared at him.

"Because they didn't have planes," he prodded.

"Oh, right. Cowboys and such. You sure that's not a problem?" The light was growing hotter, more intense and closer.

I willed myself to wake up, not liking the semi-lucid dream at all. I had never had one so real – or so bizarre – and my body was uncomfortably fevered.

"Fourth, you can always text me," he said. "Okay? I'll answer. Always."

"I don't have your number." My phone was in my hand. I started to unlock it when he continued.

"Fifth … someone out there is trying to prevent me from changing history and saving lives." Carter's tone grew urgent. "If they succeed in thwarting you, horrible things will happen. There's a man named Taylor Hansen. He might be dangerous. I need to know what he's doing back there to figure out his role in all this. So find him and let me know what he's doing. Then find the Choctaw Indian named Running Bear. Remember whatever happens on or around September twentieth fourth is what eventually results in a million deaths."

"I understand."

"Are you taking this seriously?" he searched my gaze.

"Yeah, sure. It'll be a piece of cake. Go back, find Running Horse and Taylor and –"

"Running Bear."

"Yeah. Easy."

He offered a smile. "Thank you for volunteering."

"No problem. When I get back, we can go drinking again."

An emotion I didn't understand flickered across his features. "Sure. I'd like that." The words weren't as warm as they had been, and he averted his gaze to the screen of his iPad once more.

Sounds a little bit ominous. I studied him. Or maybe, he was being himself – awkward.

"Sixth and most importantly, whatever you do, play along and don't panic. They have to believe you're the person they think you are," he added. "Oh, and the others might know you're coming, so be careful."

"Others?" I echoed.

"People who don't think history should be changed."

"Oh, yeah. They're pretty serious?"

"Very." Carter nodded solemnly. "You don't want to get mixed up with their kind."

"I understand." I didn't, but I was overheating, a sign I would probably wake up soon.

"Close your eyes. It gets bright."

The world around me was bathed in white-blue light so intense, it hurt my eyes. I found myself obeying out of necessity.

I was too distracted by the idea that the sun was getting ready to fry me alive to consider everything Carter and I had discussed. I pressed the heels of my palms to my eyes and began panting, unable to bear the heat. Sweat dripped down my body and soaked my pajamas and my hair. It grew too hot to breathe. The insides of my nostrils burned, and I choked then buried my face into my shoulder to try to protect it from the sun.

"Carter?" I rasped.

"Don't fight it, Josie. I promise – you'll be okay." *Eventually.*

Did he say the last word or did my drunk, sleeping mind imagine it? The light was too blinding for me to look.

In the distance, I heard what sounded like a sonic boom, and hot, dry air roared by me. I was no longer standing but floating, upright yet unable to reach the ground with my feet.

A second boom went off, followed by the strange crack of a baseball smacking into a concrete wall.

The heat was suddenly gone, along with the light.

Gasping for air, my eyes flew open, and I flung my arms wide, too fevered to touch my own skin.

Cold rain poured from the skies, shocking me at first. Lightning tore through the night, brilliant and bright, before it vanished and just as quickly plunged me once more into darkness.

The world smelled funny, like the area in Tombstone where a

man had been super heating and blowing glass by hand. Raindrops pelted my face. The surface beneath me was hard, cool, and smelled of dirt.

I was definitely not in bed, and the sensations were too real for me not to be awake. I was on my back, gazing up at a night sky. It took a moment for the fast moving clouds to take shape beyond the sunspots left over from the brilliant light.

Disoriented, I pushed myself up and looked around. I lay in the bottom of a steaming crater, right at its center. At first I thought I was surrounded by water, until I recognized the glassy, green rock.

"Moldavite," I recited. "Occurs when dirt and dust are thrown into the atmosphere after a meteorite hits the earth."

Moldavite was rare – and sold for a huge price. If I took some back to my aunt, I knew her jeweler could make me something from it and I could sell the rest to pay down my student loans. A thrill went through me at the discovery and I stretched towards the nearest pile. It was still soft. The weird sensation of malleable glass made me withdraw. Wiping my hand self-consciously on my wet yoga pants, I took a second look around.

How did I get to the center of a crater? Beneath me was earth, and surrounding me, moldavite. As if I had been there when the meteorite struck.

As if I *were* the meteorite. I touched the edge of a thick chunk of moldavite near one foot. It was still soft enough for me to push an indent into but cooling rapidly. No longer super heated, it had not yet frozen into its permanent shape yet, either.

This shit is worth a fortune. And there was a ton of it. If I weren't somewhere I shouldn't have been, I would have been calculating how to transport the rare rocks to the hotel before someone else found them.

More than the chilly rain caused the shudder that ran down my spine. Aside from feeling fevered, I was in the pajamas I normally went to sleep in. I seemed healthy or at least, uninjured.

Beyond the moldavite and patch of dirt were natural, rock-dirt walls about six feet tall topped by swaying grasses battered by the winds of the storm.

Had a meteorite hit Tombstone and flung me out of harm's way?

Confused, I shifted to my knees. I felt ... weak. As if my muscles were having difficulty remembering how to walk.

That makes no sense! Frustrated, I climbed to my feet. One pocket of my pajamas was heavy, and I reached in to see why. My cell phone was there. Satisfied I could call for help, once I was out of the crater, I ventured onto the moldavite.

My feet sank into the soft glass, and I grimaced. Wobbling, I caught myself twice as I made my way to the edge of the meteor pit. Rain quickly filled my footsteps, leaving behind an eerie trail. I made it up the slope and over the edge of the crater before pausing at my second obstacle: the dirt wall that was my height.

Fevered and tired with the mild throb of an alcohol-headache, I leaned against the earthen wall standing between the prairies and me. It was much cooler than I expected, and I pressed my forehead to a flat stone for a moment. The rain was cold, and it felt good against my burning skin.

How did I survive being flung out of the city into the grasslands? I wasn't hurt that I could tell. The last thing I really remember was staggering through town with Carter.

Had he been thrown out of the town, too? What if he was hurt? What if my aunt and uncle were?

Someone's hand stuck out over the edge of the crater. I blinked, uncertain if I was seeing things or not. It was a strong hand, with a wide palm and long fingers. Definitely a man's hand by its size. What looked like a thick bone and leather bracelet was around his wrist.

I had been talking to Carter and then …

No. I had been *dreaming* of talking to Carter when a meteorite hit and flung me out of the dream and Tombstone simultaneously.

I shook my head. The series of events that ended with me in a meteorite made no sense.

First things first. Get out of this hole.

The man waiting with his hand extended spoke, his low voice barely above a whisper. Engulfed in trying to recall what happened, I didn't catch what he said and moved away from the wall.

I took his hand. He gripped mine with both of his and deftly lifted me out of the crater. I swung one leg to the edge of the pit and then the other.

He released me.

I wobbled.

The stranger steadied me with his hands on my arms. Startled, I looked up, expecting to find Carter or one of the hotel workers holding me. Lighting illuminated his features.

He was a man I had never seen before whose face was hidden beneath a layer of dark paint that appeared impervious to the rain. He wore a combination of cowboy and tribal Indian period dress: workpants that might've been the predecessor to jeans with a gun belt slung low over narrow hips, and a leather vest and band around his forehead to keep medium length hair in place. Face paint over the upper half his features hid what he looked like.

Lighting slashed across the sky and lit up his eyes. They were pale green, a striking shade of mint I had never seen before.

My cold hands were against his warm chest, and I curled my fingers instinctively, uncertain if I should be touching him yet startled by how solid and muscular his lean frame was. Shivering, I huddled closer to him until I was pressed to him, not caring what he thought.

One of his arms went around me. He spoke, but the words warbled through my mind as if I hadn't quite awaken fully yet.

The man was confusing me, neither cowboy nor Indian, and dressed in the clothing of the eighteen hundreds when it was clearly past the tourist hours of Tombstone. On the plus side, he was built like someone whose lean strength was honed from daily use rather than the bulk of a gym. He had absolutely no body fat that I could feel.

This time when he spoke, it came out nonsense.

Or maybe, some Native American dialect. I had only heard it in movies and had no idea for sure. Had I been blown out of my hotel and into a nearby reservation?

Another voice answered him before his attention returned to me.

"English?" I murmured.

"Who are you?" he demanded in a gravelly voice. "What're you doing here?"

That I understood.

"J…Josie. Josie Jackson," I managed.

There was a surprised moment of silence, and then, "Not again!" He released me and spun, stalking away, leaving me alone in the cold.

What the hell does that mean?

I watched him join two other men dressed from head to foot like Native Americans, who were mounted and waiting on horseback. He flung himself onto the horse with no effort – and no saddle. They appeared to be unaffected by the downpour. Muscular thighs pressed to the horse's belly, and he picked up reins to a bridle much simpler than any I had ever seen during all my years of dressage.

"Let me guess. You're John's daughter." The man I had never met before was *angry* with me.

"Yes," I said. "How do you know that?" *My parents have been dead for twenty years!*

Ignoring me, he spoke rapidly to the two Native Americans waiting.

I experienced a sense of being disconnected, like watching myself in a dream, except that all my senses were painfully aware. Shaking from cold, I rubbed my arms to warm them while attempting to process what the hell happened that I ended up *here*.

It had something to do with Carter. I didn't quite understand the instinct, except that we'd been talking about going back in time.

An odd feeling washed over me, one that sat heavily in my stomach. I was awake and aware but nowhere I could recall ever being. The clouds above had slowed from their frantic movement. The thunder was growing distant, and the rain was beginning to subside.

Dressed like cowboys and Indians after hours. Riding horses bareback. Some random stranger claiming to send me to another time in a dream. Uneasiness went through me at the train of thought that was inching towards a possibility I didn't feel was remotely plausible.

"For only trade," one of the Native Americans said, motioning past me.

"Trade?" Unable to decipher his meaning, I watched him. "What do you mean?"

He held up a piece of the moldavite.

Understanding crossed through me. They knew it was worth something, which meant my plan to repay my student loans wasn't going to work.

I turned away. Walking to the edge of the crater, I stared into it. It still steamed, and there was a plume of dust hanging in the air, as if the meteorite had recently hit. Chunks of mossy, glassy moldavite glowed in the occasional lightning, giving the place an eerie appearance, as if it wasn't quite part of this world.

How had I ended up in the middle of a crater?

My skin was fevered but I felt cold inside, as if some part of me knew the world was no longer mine.

"We should go." The curt direction from the cowboy with green eyes jarred me, reminded me that I wasn't alone. He moved his horse close enough for me to feel its heat.

"So cold," I murmured and huddled next to the great animal's neck. "But I think I should stay here."

"You're trespassing on the Indians' lands, ma'am," was the calm if terse response.

"I'm on a reservation?"

"A what?"

Uh, oh. I didn't let my mind go down that path.

"You'll catch your death out here," he added, voice softening. "C'mon. I'll take you home."

"Really?" I asked. "You know where my home is?"

"Yes."

"You won't drag me off and murder me or something, right?"

He gave a surprised chuckle. "No, ma'am, I won't. I'm the local law. It's my job to make sure that doesn't happen."

After a brief hesitation, I took the arm he held out to me. With ease that hinted at his strength, he pulled me onto the horse to sit behind him. I settled between his muscular frame and the horse's rump, instinctively wrapping my arms around him.

"How did you find yourself out here, ma'am?" While polite, there was something in his tone that made me think he wasn't as surprised as I was to discover me in the middle of a crater.

The horse began walking, and I debated what to say. My teeth chattered almost too much to speak.

"Take my coat," my rescuer said. He pulled it from a saddlebag and handed it back to me.

I hugged it around me. The interior was soft from wear and smelled of the man it belonged to: leather, horses, rain, and his own dark, subtle musk. It was a natural, purely male combination with no trace of cologne or fruity soap like I used.

I rested my cheek against his back, absently breathing in his scent. It was oddly comforting, not quite familiar, but pleasant enough that it could be.

Like Carter. There was no such thing as a time machine, no way in the world I was in the past. I didn't even know why I considered it, except that being blown out of town by a meteor opened the door to other strange possibilities.

He waited until my shaking stopped before asking again how I came to be out in the rain.

"I don't really know," I said. I wasn't about to tell him what I suspected. It was hard enough for me to humor the idea without speaking it aloud and ending up humiliated when we reached my aunt and uncle. "What did you mean when you said *not again?*" I asked.

"I usually find the town drunk in a hole in the middle of a storm."

I frowned. He was hiding something. He'd uttered the phrase after I told him my name, not when he found me. Not about to lose my coat or ride, I didn't challenge him.

"Rare day when you rescue a pretty girl out in the middle of the storm. Your governess know you're out?" he added.

The man with amazing eyes called me pretty. I smiled. "Governess?"

He muttered something beneath his breath without answering.

Dressed in my usual pajama bottoms – an old pair of yoga pants – and a tank top, I hadn't gone to bed thinking I needed a coat in the desert when I awoke. I was soaked, though the rain had turned to a light drizzle. Without his coat, I would catch a cold for sure.

In fact, I didn't recall going to bed at all. I went to Carter's office and then … passed out? Then who put me in my pajamas?

I twisted, a sliver of panic working its way through my system at the idea of missing time. While not out of the ordinary for a long night of drinking, I wasn't certain why I didn't recall stumbling into bed at least.

The dust plume above the crater was still visible. It was impossible to tell directions in the storm. There was no glow on any horizon to indicate a city was close, and the rolling hills of grass was more representative of the fertile Great Plains than the desert southwest.

Was it possible to have been thrown miles and miles away from Tombstone by the meteor without so much as a scratch?

My cell phone vibrated. Adrenaline surged through me at the reminder I had a way to call home or for help. I yanked it out of my pocket.

There was one message.

Don't panic. It was marked from Carter, a contact I hadn't had in my phone earlier. It was possible I put him there when we were drinking, though.

A sense of the surreal was creeping up on me. It made my stomach turn and my insides shake.

I typed a response. *WTF happened? How did I end up in a crater?*

Tapping send, I went through my phone's contacts to call my aunt and uncle and make sure they were okay.

There was only one contact in my phone. All the other icons – those for internet, my apps, everything – were also gone. There was no content on my phone, aside from Carter's number, listed as *undisclosed*, and his message.

I examined the device. It had the dings and dents that I recalled, just none of the information. It had no signal and no bars indicating battery power, either, and yet, the phone was on.

My hands were starting to shake, my head spinning. His response was quick.

Doctor Who, remember? Two-ish weeks to change things? I'm in a meeting. Just hang in there and play along. I'll text later.

His message was accompanied by a smiley face.

"You're in a *meeting*?" I demanded of the phone with a startled laugh. And what the hell did he mean by the reference to one of my favorite television shows? He couldn't possibly be serious about …

"What?" The self-proclaimed lawman asked.

I have a time machine. Carter had said.

What if it was more than a drunken boast?

"Nothing." I pocketed the phone. My baffled thoughts tried to make sense of what had happened. I struggled to recall exactly what Carter told me in the dream.

Thank you for volunteering. But for what exactly had I volunteered? Time travel? How was that remotely possible?

"What year is it?" I asked cautiously.

The lawman didn't answer for a moment. "You know your name but not the year."

"Rough night," I said in what I hope was a cheerful voice. "Help a girl out?"

"Eighteen forty two."

"Of course." *There's no way.*

We reached the crest of one of the rolling hills and halted.

The idea Carter had somehow sent me back in time didn't catch footing until I saw the town nestled in the valley below. Lanterns glowed in houses and stores along a main strip while smoke curled out of squat, brick chimneys. The roads were dirt, the buildings wooden, the posts in front of each occupied by horses or wagons.

The tiny town was like something out of an old western movie, only worn, rustic and realistic, designed for function rather than as a tourist destination or movie set.

Authentic.

A stab of pain went through my skull. Carter's warning about having a headache returned. Did he really do brain surgery on me, too? Was that worse than being sent back in time? A vacation I could almost agree with but *brain* surgery?

Tunnel vision clouded my vision while ringing filled my ears. I slumped against the man in front of me.

"I'm not feeling so well," I murmured. "Might be … a brain … chip … issue …"

Chapter Three

A MAN OF FEW WORDS AND RARE EMOTIONS, SHERIFF TAYLOR Hansen twisted to catch the woman before she tumbled off his horse to the ground. All but dragging her in front of him, he shook his head when one of his companions, a seasoned Choctaw named Running Bear, asked if he needed help.

There's nothing you can do for this one, he replied silently. Unlike Josie Jackson, he understood why she seemed to magically appear in the prairielands near the natives' village.

"We shall not speak of the latest starman," Running Bear said, referring to the word the natives used to describe the people who came from the sky in a bolt of lightning. "That makes six, including you, brother."

"Five too many," Taylor grunted.

He jostled her until he was somewhat comfortable and balanced. He guided the horse with his legs and found himself once more looking down into her face.

Josie Jackson was flawless with large blue eyes and soaked blonde hair framing a heart-shaped face. Clearly lost, she was nonetheless a potential danger, one that he alone understood. He didn't believe her shell-shocked story about how she got to be in the middle of the grasslands. He knew better than to trust any word she ever told him, and hoped she came to her senses before it was too late, like it had been for many others.

Trained to observe first and act quickly to protect the natural course of history, his duty was to wait and see why she was there before he determined the course of action required.

"Let's get her home," he said.

"Again?" Running Bear asked with quiet humor. "Can you not tell your starmen to stop sending Josie Jacksons?"

"If I had any way of doing so, I would," Taylor said, eyes lingering on the beauty in his arms. "I can't keep buying coats like this."

"Our niece can make you one. Better than the white man's stitching."

"Blue Stream is growing up too fast." Taylor smiled at the thought of the thirteen-year-old girl. The first of six to fall from the skies, and the sole traveler with Choctaw blood, he had been found wandering a nearby field and adopted by the mother of Running Bear. His adopted brother taught him everything he knew about hunting and tracking. Ten years older than him, Running Bear remained his confidante and friend, a solid bridge between the often-tricky relations between the settlers in the area and the natives inhabiting Indian Territory.

The distant growl of thunder drew his attention to the woman in his arms once more, and unease replaced his amusement.

She may not have been the first Josie Jackson to magically appear out of the sky, but if he had anything to do about it, she would be the last.

Chapter Four

I STRETCHED LUXURIOUSLY BENEATH THE WARM BLANKETS. THE crackle of a fire almost put me back to sleep if not for the sunlight streaming through a window onto my face. For a moment, I was back in the dream where I had been blinded by a ball of light.

Weird.

I cracked my eyes open and recognized what I assumed was the tray ceiling with ornate crown molding of the historic hotel where I had fallen asleep. I lay still. All I needed was a mocha, and I would be set for the trip back to California.

Excited to be home, I tossed off the covers and swung my legs over the side of the bed.

And stopped cold.

My heart turned over in my chest, and a chill went through me.

I wasn't in the hotel. This room was large with a hearth, tall windows and a sitting area. The period furniture looked new and was of high quality, the quilts, rugs, and blankets all brightly embroidered. The drapes had been pulled back to let in the sunlight.

A quick assessment of my clothing revealed a long, loose

nightgown of homespun cotton. It was plain, soft and comfortable, covering everything from the top of my feet to my neck.

I crossed to the window, praying I would look out over the cars parked along the street near my hotel.

My chest tightened so fast, I gasped. Outside my window was a sea of rolling grassland beneath a wide blue sky. The tall grass was punctuated by a herd of fluffy white sheep I would squeal over, any other time.

The night, and the reason my hair was still damp at the roots, returned to me.

Carter had sent me back in time. "He really did it." Butterflies churned in my belly. Where was I?

"Miss Josie."

I turned. A middle-aged woman in period costume resembling that of the women I had seen in Tombstone stood inside my doorway. She wore an apron over a dress that was apricot in color. Her leather shoes were worn and well kept.

Starting to smile, I marveled at how well she fit in with the surroundings.

"I didn't expect to see you awake," she said, scrutinizing my features. "Are you warm enough?"

I nodded.

The woman closed the door. "Are you well?" The words were a whisper.

I didn't respond.

"Can you remember me now?"

"I'm sorry but no," I replied. "Who are you?"

The older woman's severe features softened into pity. She went to the bed and patted it.

"Lie down, child," she said. "They say you're taking on this illness to avoid a certain obligation." She moved across the room to add wood to the fire as she spoke.

I listened, brow furrowing. I went to the bed and sat on it, curious to explore the world Carter sent me back to.

"I say you cannot remember a blessed thing. It's true, isn't it?"

"I'd say so," I replied.

A look of disappointment crossed her features. "I'm Nell. I've been your governess since you were but a babe."

"Why do I need a governess? I'm like, twenty two."

The woman's face fell even more, and I felt bad, even knowing I shouldn't.

"Miss Josie," Nell said, tilting her head to the side. "Would you tell me if you knew me?"

"I would," I assured her.

"Swear on the Bible?"

"I'll swear on a stack of them. I don't even know where I am. Where am I, Nell?" Fear fluttered through me. *Short vacation.* I told myself. Then I returned to my own time. *This is an adventure – nothing more.*

"Indian Territory, where you been raised your whole life." Nell sighed. She appeared haggard suddenly, tired and worn. "I prayed to God every night when you were gone."

From what I recalled, Indian Territory later became Oklahoma and northern Texas. Astonishment bloomed within me. Carter really was a genius. Realizing Nell was staring at me, I blinked and returned to the conversation at hand.

"Gone where?" I asked. "I can't remember living here at all."

"Of course you did, child," Nell said, concerned. "Your father knew you on sight when them savages and that sheriff brought you in. I did, too. You been gone for a year, but we knew you."

Hmm. So I have a father. I wasn't sure how else to ask about who Nell thought I was. Carter had said to play along. I just needed a few notes on who I was supposed to be, and then I could probably manage it. He had clearly placed me in a safe environment, or so it seemed.

"Look." Nell pulled a photo off the mantle and crossed to me, sitting beside me on the bed. "You haven't changed a bit."

The girl in the photograph did look a lot like me. Long, flowing blonde hair, a small frame. There was no color in the photograph, but her eyes were light, her skin ivory. The differences were subtle: the girl in the picture appeared a little taller than me, if the chair photographed was the same one by the window. Her lips were thinner, her hair straight where mine was wavy.

We could've been sisters, I acknowledged silently. *But this isn't me.*

"I expect there are some changes. Frontier life is not easy on us," Nell said, before I was able to speak. "But your father ... he came back to life when you were brought to his door." Her eyes sparkled with happiness. "As did I."

Play along, Carter had said. Thinking of him made me stretch for the pocket that wasn't there.

"Nell!" I exclaimed. "Have you seen my phone?" At the blank look she gave me, I racked my mind for an explanation. "A small, silver box that was in my pocket when I came here."

"You mean the devil's box?" Nell's voice was hushed. "I have it. I did not let your father see it, Josie."

"Right. Where is it?"

Nell hesitated then got up and went to a jewelry box on a vanity near the window. She opened it and pulled out the phone.

I almost sighed with relief.

Nell put it back quickly, closed the box and kissed the dainty golden cross she wore on a thin chain around her neck.

"So I am the daughter of John," I began. There was no easy way to figure out who I was. "I've been gone for a year because ... why did I leave?"

"A certain obligation," Nell whispered, as if I should know. "Do you remember?"

"No."

"You were to marry a man your father chose."

I started to laugh then stopped at Nell's confused look. I hadn't thought twice about the status of women in the Old West. Recalling that the women's rights movements didn't start for another almost hundred years, I began to think I had a lot of learning to do in order to fit in.

"Now that I'm back, do I have to marry him still?" I asked.

"He has since married another," Nell added.

"Oh." My gaze went to the jewelry box. "Good for him, I guess."

"Would you like to dress to see your father?"

"Um, yes. Yes I would."

Nell appeared pleased. "I'll prepare your gown." She hurried out the door.

I shook my head and went to the vanity. I pulled the cell free and examined it again. Like yesterday, there was no battery and no signal – and two messages from Carter. At least he was keeping up his part of the deal and texting. I gazed at the phone, grappling with the idea that somehow, Carter was communicating with me, even though we were two centuries apart.

I wished I'd had more of a science mind. I knew nothing of physics or how any of this was possible. Not about to question it, so long as he was talking to me, I kissed the cell, my one connection to my time.

Be like Amy Pond or Clara Oswald, I told myself, recalling my favorite Doctor Who companions. They were never scared or worried when they went to strange worlds or hostile time periods.

Next to the phone was a familiar, folded coat. I touched the soft brown leather. The lawman with the beautiful eyes had given it to me. I recalled meeting him clearly, down to his reticence about telling me anything, but not what happened before that ended with me waking up in a crater.

I picked up my cell, more interested in the messages.

It should be mid September, 1842, claimed the first. *The girl you're pretending to be shares your name! Isn't that an awesome coincidence?*

The décor of the room and Nell's explanations seemed to support the bizarre words.

"Kind of a weird coincidence," I whispered to him. Starting to smile, I read the second note, hoping for information about who I was supposed to be.

Put a passcode on your screen.

"That's it?" I murmured. "Genius enough to send me back in time, male enough not to realize how big of a deal that really is. No tips on how to … wait, do they even have flushing toilets?"

I sent him a long message in response with half a dozen questions. The alleged brain chip that held historical knowledge hadn't kicked in. At least, I didn't know anything more about bathrooms than I did before.

Just as I finished, Nell returned, this time with a long dress draped carefully over her arms.

"You want me to wear *that*?" I asked in surprise and started to laugh. "It's September! I'll burn up."

"It's your father's favorite gown, Miss Josie. He bought the material from Spain, because it matches your eyes." Nell's gaze misted over.

I took two drama classes and didn't feel too silly pretending to be someone's daughter in the eighteen hundreds. It was like a really intense play. But the wardrobe …

Ugh. The gown looked heavy and uncomfortable – not the kind of clothing I was accustomed to wearing – and came in two pieces: an elaborately decorated bodice and layered, bell-shaped petticoats. It was as far from yoga pants and a tank top as anyone could ever get. My bestie back home used to say I was too nice, because, right now, I was going to wear that mess of a gown and probably end up overheating and dying of dehydration rather than refusing and upsetting a complete stranger who appeared ready to cry.

"Sounds great," I said. "So … how is Father?"

Nell set the gown down on the bed, left and returned with more items of clothing: a chemise, corset and stockings. She spoke as she moved briskly. "He is not well. His health has been declining since your disappearance, and his mind is not right. I fear for him, Miss Josie. He is too agitated by your return. You must strive not to jest the way you always do and to be dutiful."

Dutiful. Ha! "I'll be good, Ms. Nell," I replied cheerfully.

"Come!" she said and motioned me over.

Nell stripped my nightgown off with speed that left me embarrassed. Seemingly unaware of my nakedness, Nell pulled free a clean shift and tugged it over my head.

I pushed my arms through it then eyed the corset. It appeared rigid and unfriendly. I soon had a reason to despise it even more.

Nell fastened it around me then yanked the ties as far as they would go, binding and tightening it around me until I wasn't able to draw a full breath. With my waist held in and my breasts pushed up, I tossed my head back to try to breath better.

And then it hit me.

"Um, Nell?" I asked. "I need to um … go to the restroom." I was definitely not looking forward to my options in this regard.

"To make?"

"Yes. I think."

Nell left my side and went to a wardrobe. She pulled out two pieces of china: a dainty, porcelain, round bowl, and what looked like a gravy boat and set them down. She rested a cotton washcloth on top of the big one.

"Chamber pot and bordalou, as you prefer," she said.

I eyed both and began to wonder how many of my aunt's antique china pieces were really *bordalous* instead of dinnerware. "Right," I mumbled. "Love my bordalou."

Nell smiled patiently and stood aside, waiting.

"Isn't there an outhouse or something?" I asked.

"A lady does not use the same water-closet as the servants!"

Okay, whatever. "Can I have some privacy?"

Nell nodded her head once. "I'll bring you some tea."

"Thanks." I watched her leave then stared at the pot. *This is gonna be rougher than I thought.*

I snapped a photo of the two dainty urinals and sent it to Carter, pretty sure he'd get a kick out of it, then pulled up my chemise. Unable to bend over, I thanked the heavens repeatedly for the intense yoga classes I took with my aunt as I lowered myself with pure thigh power.

Ready to laugh at the idea of peeing in a bowl, I managed to do it and stand.

Only when I stepped away did I realized I had completely missed the pot.

"Shit," I muttered, face getting hot at the idea of Nell seeing what I had done.

As if on cue, the matronly nanny opened the door, carrying a tray of tea and delicate cups.

"I can explain," I started, startled. "I didn't mean to go … make on the floor."

Nell wasn't fazed. "The doctor said it would be a while until your mind returns to you."

There's no response for that. It took a lot to embarrass me, and in that moment, my face was hot.

"Let us finish. The tea will be cool enough to drink," Nell said without missing a beat.

After peeing on the floor, I wasn't about to complain about another layer of discomfort.

Nell stood on a small stool and draped the petticoats over my head. I stood with my arms in the air while the nanny tugged it down over my body. She placed the bodice on next, and another set of straps or ties was tightened. I lowered my hands. In addition to the layers, the gown had long sleeves as well.

I was burning up.

"Sit. Drink your tea while I straighten up," Nell said. "Your favorite breakfast will be cold soon."

I mumbled a *thank you* and sat. I was hardly able to move, and my breathing was becoming labored. I struggled to pour tea in the stiff get-up and sat back finally, tea cup in hand.

Tea smells the same now as it does in the future. I sipped, added sugar, and then drank it down. The familiarity of a cup of tea did more than I expected to settle the part of me that was a little shaken at the thought of being dropped into the eighteen hundreds with the mission of finding two men, one of which I was supposed to stop from doing something in a few days.

There was cut fruit, ham and boiled eggs for breakfast, along with a slice of bread with jam. I ate what I could but quickly found it hard to keep much down with my torso in a vise.

"Are there … Indians near by?" I asked when it was impossible to eat more.

"Yes. Your father's lands borders theirs."

"Great. We can go visit."

Nell paused in her chores of straightening my room. "Miss Josie, that would not be appropriate."

"Because ..." I waited and sipped my tea.

"They're savages and you are a gentlewoman."

Good lesson. "But if we're neighbors, doesn't Father talk to them?"

"Not often." Nell began brushing my hair with a thick brush. "Don't you get it in your mind to upset your father by asking him to visit the Indians. He's delicate, Miss Josie."

"I won't." I grimaced. She didn't bother to pluck out the knots in my curls but was raking through them. "What do you think happened to ... uh, me during the time I was gone?"

Nell's strokes paused for a moment before they began again. "It's not possible for an un-chaperoned, unwed girl with your beauty to survive away from her father's house for long this side of the Mississippi, especially with so many savages taking slaves and the cavalry conscripting anyone they deem lost. There's no real law out here, either," she replied. "I reckon you went east like you always said you would and got yourself knocked about bad."

"It sounds like quite an adventure."

"None of your jests Miss Josie. A woman is safe in her father's home and her husband's. Nowhere else in this godforsaken Indian Territory. This isn't Boston."

I considered the words, not certain why they confused me so much. Maybe because my life was so different. It was intriguing to witness firsthand – yet unsettling as well.

"What if John ... Father ... doesn't want me here?" I ventured. "Will my appearance upset his health?"

"Nonsense, child. You came back ... different, I'll admit, but he has never stopped waiting for you. He will love you as he always has," Nell said. "You leaving broke him. He's a different man, Miss Josie.

He won't be angry no more about your fiancé and he won't force you into a new marriage."

Seated in a stranger's house with a woman who thought me someone else brushing my hair, I felt guilty for a moment, like what I was doing – pretending to be someone I wasn't – was somehow wrong. If Carter sent me back here, he had a reason. I didn't think he'd ask me to do something that was bad, yet I couldn't help thinking the people of this house would be sad when I left.

"That's good," I said. As soon as John saw me, he'd know. A nanny might be fooled, but I didn't think a father was going to be convinced a stranger was his daughter, no matter how much I resembled the real Josie.

Nell finished brushing and twisting my hair into an elaborate bun on top of my head before she went to the wardrobe.

I glanced down at my phone and saw a message from Carter.

OMG! Of all the things you could send me pics of, you chose THAT?

It took effort not to laugh. Nell already thought there was something wrong with me for running away. I tucked the phone in a pocket in the gown and gazed around me, amazed at the relative comfort of the room compared to the near squalor of the bedrooms I saw on the tour at Tombstone. John was wealthy – a pleasant surprise I'd thank Carter for later.

My thoughts turned to my mission. How did I find the two men I sought in a world without so much as a phone book, let alone the internet? Did I go door to door until someone recognized the name? Or wait for the brain chips to activate?

Nell knelt in front of me with a pair of leather booties. I lifted my feet one by one and placed them in the boots.

"There," she said and sat back, satisfied. "Now, we must meet your father."

I rose - and almost fell. Lightheaded from the corset, headachy from unexpected brain surgery, I braced myself against the table.

"Nell, I can't breathe!" I gasped. "You gotta loosen that thing."

"You must be attired in the proper style," Nell said. "You will adjust."

This is the craziest thing I've ever heard of.

I struggled to catch my breath then straightened. It took a moment for me to find balance. "All right. I'm ready."

Nell was smiling, her eyes filled with tears. "Welcome back, Miss Josie. I've missed you dearly," she said.

Guilt stirred once more. I bit my tongue and forced a smile. I had to play along. If I hurt these people, it wasn't on purpose. I was here for a very good cause: to save a million lives.

Except I had no idea where to start or even if I landed in the right place to make a difference.

I trailed my governess out of my room. Nell was speaking quietly about the people who lived in the house, as if to remind me. I tried to listen but wasn't able to concentrate, instead taking in my surroundings with curiosity. I was in my own wing of a two-story house that appeared to be quite large.

A sweeping stairwell led to the first floor and the front door, which was flanked by two massive rooms with expensive, period furniture, including a piano and a harp.

At least my fake-daddy is rich, I thought. Portraits of stern men lined the wide corridor on the main floor, which was edged by closed doors. Judging by the paintings, my father was going to be a grave, bearded man who looked ready to order my beheading.

"Oh!" Nell exclaimed suddenly, stopping. "You cannot see your father for the first time if you aren't wearing the necklace he bought you on your last birthday." She pulled a small box from the depths of her apron and opened it.

"Wow," I breathed.

The black choker contained an emerald the size of my thumb.

Nell put it on with steady fingers, and I touched it. That would definitely pay off my student debt.

I'm going to hell for that thought. My goal had to be to leave as small of an indent on these people and this time period as possible. I definitely wasn't going to steal from them.

We stopped in a doorway to a masculine study that smelled of pipe smoke.

"He must be with the savages still," Nell said, a note of disapproval in her voice.

"The ones that found me?" I asked.

"Yes. They brought you to us last night."

"Do you know from what direction?" I asked quickly, heartbeat quickening.

"You were on their land." Nell shrugged. "Wait here. I'll fetch him."

"Shouldn't I thank them?"

Nell faced me, startled. I had the sense I had said something wrong without knowing what exactly.

"It would not be appropriate," Nell said finally. "Wait here, Miss Josie."

Bullshit. I waited for her to disappear out the door then followed, easing the heavy wooden door open and closed behind me. The scent of wood burning and horses reached me. My gaze swept over a corral with three horses, multiple barns of ranging sizes and a carriage parked nearby.

Nell hurried towards a tall, bearded man with a cane and a top hat who stood with two men wearing faded badges on their vests. Two Native Americans hung back from them.

I started towards the group, wanting to know from what direction they'd brought me and the distance, so I was able to find my way back. Whether or not it mattered, I wasn't certain. But I woke up in the past in that spot; it held some sort of significance. Maybe it was where Carter would pull me back to the future. At the very least, I wanted to grab a couple chunks of the moldavite before returning.

Pain shot through my head once more. I touched it with one hand, not wanting to stop and nurse it. Sunspots appeared, and I shook my head. The reminder of my involuntary brain surgery irked me. I hoped the chips did what Carter said they would. Not one to bear grudges, I decided the socially awkward man would benefit from a couple pieces of advice about how to kidnap and send people back in time.

My step slowed when one of the men noticed me. If his nose had been less crooked, his jaw straight and his bushy eyebrows trimmed, he might pass as rugged. But the combination, along with the amount of dirt on his exposed skin rendered him merely ugly. His eyes were brown, not the gorgeous green I had seen last night.

"Josie?" The slightly hoarse voice of the tall, bearded man drew my attention away from the scowling lawman. "It's really you!"

There was no sternness in the man's face. His age was hard to judge. His hair was pure white and the wrinkles around his eyes deep, but his eyes youthful and blue. I didn't think he was over fifty, though the hard living west of the Mississippi had aged him much faster. His face lit up like it was the best day of his life.

"Hi, Father," I said awkwardly with a glance at Nell. I had never said those words in my life.

Nell was crying and smiling.

Did I curtsey? Bow? Grovel? I resisted the urge to fidget, once again feeling like I had entered someone else's dream.

To my surprise, the elderly man swept me up in a tight hug. Combined with my corset, I was rendered momentarily unable to breathe and fought to keep from pushing him away. His slender form was gaunt, nothing but skin and bones beneath the pressed suit. He smelled of pipe smoke and sweat.

"You look like your mother." Tears shone in his eyes, and he kissed my forehead, taking my cheeks.

"Thank you," I murmured. His look was not something I would ever forget. The pure, selfless joy of a parent over his child, aimed at *me*. That had never happened. For a moment, my amusement at this world, and the sense it wasn't real, trembled.

I was pleased that Carter dropped me off somewhere safe. But I couldn't help thinking why here? Where my departure was going to break the hearts of two good people who truly believed me to be someone I wasn't? I was going to save so many lives. Maybe hurting two people shouldn't matter, but it did.

John's smile grew even wider, and part of my heart melted. He was truly happy to see me. He saw no difference between his real daughter and me, and I was suddenly envious of how much he loved his Josie. I had rarely experienced a major holiday where I didn't think about my parents and certainly missed them.

His features were so happy, his eyes shining. His joy was contagious, and I yearned for it to be real and directed at me. The kind man before me made me wish I had known my father, who died when I was two.

"It's um, good to be home," I added more softly, touched by his emotion, even if it was misdirected. "I wore your favorite dress."

"Matches your eyes."

I forced a smile, guilt drifting through me.

"I was thanking the sheriff who returned you to me," John said, moving away to face the two men near him and the Native Americans behind them.

Stoic and stone-faced, the lawmen appeared hard to read. A

Native American in his early thirties stood a short distance away, as unfriendly as the lawmen, while his teenage companion was a couple feet back holding the reins of four horses.

"Ma'am, I'd like to speak to you about your whereabouts the past year," the sheriff said.

My gaze fell to the man who had rescued me – and stuck. Tall, lean, with the striking green eyes, rugged features, high cheekbones, a strong jaw and a face almost as dark as the natives', he was closer to my age than John's. His clothing was worn, dusty and stitched in multiple places, his boots scuffed and the star-shaped sheriff's badge on his chest like something I had seen out of a western movie.

His eyes, however, were pinned to me as if he already knew my story was bogus. Carter had vaguely warned me about *the others* I might encounter without defining who they were.

The hairs on the back of my neck rose in mild alarm at the fear I had been figured out on day one. I wasn't certain what to say, not with the rugged cowboy and his green gaze distracting me. The sense I had gotten last night, that he was hiding something about how he knew to find me in the crater, returned.

It's not possible, though.

"When she is rested, Sheriff," my faux-father said. "You will not upset my daughter so soon after her return."

"Of course not, Mr. John," the sheriff said. "The Indians convey their congratulations at having your daughter returned."

"They did what the sheriff wasn't able to," John said to me. "They found you when I thought you were gone forever."

"Amazing," I agreed. "Thank you all." This I directed at the Indians hanging back behind the sheriff.

Suddenly, everyone was looking at me hard.

"Why, Josie. Wherever did you learn Indian?" John asked.

My brow furrowed.

"She did not know our tongue last night," the older Native American said with a frown.

"Not here," the sheriff replied to the restless native. "You must consult with the shaman over what you found."

"What you found?" I asked, puzzled. "Me?"

"You really understand us." The sheriff's features appeared even more severe.

Shit. It all sounds like English to me. I clamped my mouth shut, suspecting by their uneasy looks that I wasn't supposed to know Native American but kind of grateful one of the microchips in my brain was working.

"We are done here," the sheriff said. "I expect to see you in town soon to talk, ma'am."

It didn't sound like the conversation was going to be a good one. My rescuer wasn't pleased about seeing me healthy and on my feet despite pulling me out of the crater and giving me a coat. The lawmen tipped their hats to my faux-father and turned away.

"Wait!" I called, eyes on the Native American. "Can you tell me where you found me? Just the direction. That's it."

The native exchanged a look with the sheriff.

"West," he said at last.

I sensed I had managed to piss him off somehow and watched them go to their horses.

"What did you say, my daughter?" John asked.

"Just uh … thanked them," I replied. "You cannot understand them?"

He chuckled. "You always did regale me with jests." He started towards the house. "We have much to discuss, Josie!"

I watched the men who found me ride away towards the west. It was possible that the sheriff was suspicious and shuttered towards everyone. The pioneers had a rough life, from what I recalled. They had no driver's licenses or biometric identification systems here, either. It wasn't like he was able to run my fingerprints to verify I was their Josie.

Maybe this was his issue: the sudden reappearance of John's daughter was suspicious.

I hope that's it. That there were more people in the past that didn't belong, time travelers like me, was an idea that seemed likely to blow my mind.

I trailed John inside and into his study. Unable to move past his expression at seeing me, or the guilt it caused, I felt like I had to tell the kindly man that I wasn't really his daughter. His emotion was too pure, his heart too good for me to lie to him. After all, once I found Taylor Hansen and Running Bear, I was leaving. My heart was kind of squishy. I didn't like hurting people.

John was seated in the sitting area, and I made an effort to prepare what I was going to tell him.

However, my first challenge was making it to the low, low settee across from him without cutting off my air supply. I struggled to sit without pitching over or asphyxiating.

"It is very fortunate you returned this week, my daughter," John started. His voice was warm. One of the house servants lit his pipe for him. "Your timing is perfect."

I watched the servant, uncomfortable about an era that included slaves and servants. Settling on the settee, I waited, uncertain why now mattered and too curious to hijack the conversation. If he noticed the awkward way I sat, leaning to one side to breathe decently, he said nothing.

John waved the servant away, and the two of us were left in quiet. He puffed on his pipe. When he didn't expand on his declaration, I decided to speak.

"I need to tell you something," I started.

"I imagine you have much to say about where you've been," he replied, smiling. "Much I don't want to know. I am simply grateful you're back. This week is special."

"Really? Why?"

"It is the week I was to revise my will. But I've sent word that I no longer need to do so. All my property and goods will go to you, as planned, rather than your cousin, Philip."

"Oh." *What does this have to do with anything?* He was gazing at me expectantly. "But, I mean, you have many good years of health left, so I think maybe Philip might be a good choice, especially since I … um, am young." My words sounded forced and awkward to my own ears. Heat crept up my neck.

"True and you are an unmarried female. We are not in England any longer, and I fear a woman with no husband will not be taken seriously in her inheritance here," he agreed. "I've taken care of it as much as possible, though. It would behoove you to find a husband before I go, young lady, and it would make your father happy."

My mouth dropped open. Nothing came out, so I closed it, amazed I had just been told to find a man so I wasn't disinherited.

Not that it mattered, but I was beginning to understand the need for a feminist movement better than I ever had in any class I took.

None of this will be real in a couple of weeks, I reminded myself. Another thought surfaced, one I realized was probably important. Whatever I did here, the real-Josie might have to live with when she returned. So maybe being able to claim an inheritance was a good thing.

"But, on this, I will not press you this time," John continued. His look at me was tender, loving, like a doting father who truly didn't know a stranger sat before him. "If you choose to marry soon, so be it. If you do not, so be it. I am grateful to have you as my daughter."

"Thank you," I murmured. "About my return. I –"

"I am dying, Josie."

I shut up once more, staring at him. He was thin, yes, but he didn't look ill.

"The doctor said I'd be gone in a week."

As much as I didn't want to connect with people who had been dead for two hundred years, I found myself plunged into a moral dilemma. If Carter put me here for a mini-vacay, then he had to know the real Josie was going to be gone just as long. If John died during the time period …

Which was worse? Letting him believe I was his daughter for a few days? Or revealing the truth and knowing he might never know peace of mind about his daughter, if she didn't return before he passed?

Not exactly the vacation I had hoped for. My heart gave me one answer, my mind a conflicting one.

"What was it you wanted to tell me, my dear?" John asked, blue eyes settling on me.

Before I spoke, I knew my heart had won out. "I'm just glad to be home," I replied. "I am sorry I can't remember much of anything."

"The doctor said you might never. Said you likely got hurt a year ago and wandered off, never knowing who you were, until you were found by our savage neighbors."

I had never met the doctor, but I liked him as much as I did Nell. Both were trying to comfort a dying old man.

"They were kind to you?" he asked.

"Yes, very."

"I feared they would not honor our agreement." John reached forward to pinch a small amount of loose tobacco and place it in his pipe. "There have been many skirmishes of late. We are fortunate that the sheriff is here."

"He's … interesting," I murmured, not yet convinced he didn't know something he shouldn't about me. *He's not someone I'd want to cross either.* The men of this place were much harder and unfriendlier than I was accustomed to, but I guessed it was warranted in an untamed frontier.

"He's half-Indian, raised by the natives. It's why he can keep the peace here, unlike other places." John sighed. "The frontier was not so dangerous when we moved here."

I listened, unusually interested in the sheriff born of two worlds. In my time, it made him intriguing. Here, in a world where war was inevitable, I guessed it made him useful – and probably universally ostracized.

"The Indians are dangerous?" I asked.

"They are but one danger out here. Outlaws, robbers, cheats. The red men have been just to me. I have a history of dealing with them fairly, in granting their people refuge during the Great Storms that befell the plains twenty years ago. Their chief wants peace. He never forgets a kindness, and we share grazing lands for our cattle and sheep. But I fear, with the restlessness on the plains, my generation will be the last that knows peace."

I listened, too aware of how the story ended and uncertain what to say. John was right, but I hoped to change things.

He rested his head back against the chair in which he sat as if needing a breather. I pitied him. He was dressed in a black suit, his beard trimmed and his knobby fingers displaying some of his wealth in the form of gold rings laden with large gems. He was a classy man through and through, and I loved the idea he and the Native Americans next door worked together on the rugged plains.

A grandfather clock decorated with brass fixtures and inlaid with mother of pearl ticked away the seconds near the entrance of the study. Not wanting to disturb the ill old man, I rose with effort and went to the shelves of books that would be worth a small fortune in my time. Brass, wood and other antiques were used as bookends or decoration: multiple intrinsic clocks, old military weapons and swords, a shadow box with medals indicating John had served some sort of military service, an elaborate clay pipe collection displayed in velvet boxes, ivory carvings, portraits in varying sizes of men and women, and several photographs of his wife and daughter.

I studied one. John appeared very different – robust, strong, dark haired and bright eyed – though the photo wasn't that old. The girl I recognized as the real Josie appeared in her mid-teens.

Okay. I've got no brothers or sisters. His wife appeared in earlier photos of the family but none from when Josie was about ten onward, which I took to mean my pretend-mother was dead. It disappointed me more than it should have to know the real Josie didn't have a mother, either. We had something more in common than looks.

John stirred. I returned to my settee and managed to sit as he opened his eyes once more.

"Forgive me," he apologized. "I grow weaker daily."

"No worries, Father," I murmured. "Nell warned me about taxing you."

"It is a true shame. I find you again only to be leaving you alone."

I like him so much. Genuine and sweet, John cared about me – or rather, who he thought I was – the way I had always hoped my real father would have, had he survived. How awful was it not only to lose my father young but to know real-Josie's father was going to pass away before my eyes, too? He was a good man, and I had a soft spot for good people.

"Your cousin Philip will likely come tomorrow," he continued. "You must be certain to rest. It is rare when you two meet that you do not end up squabbling like the children you once were."

I smiled. "I feel well, Father. Aside from a headache, that is."

"Good. Then I need rest." He rose with effort and stood,

appearing paler than when we sat down.

What was wrong with him? In an era where the medicine was barbaric at best, I felt sadder for him. "I hope you're not in pain, Father."

"There is no pain that can compete with the joy of seeing you here, my dear." His features glowed with happiness. "You looked a little peaked."

Because I can't breathe in this thing! I offered a small smile, affected by his concern, especially when his own life was so short. Something about him touched me, as if we were meant to meet or were somehow connected. I couldn't shake the sense that he was familiar, along with Carter, even though it was impossible.

"Thank you, Father," I said. "I think I need fresh air."

"Nell will accompany you wherever you go." There was firmness in his tone. "I will not lose you again, and later today, we will take supper together, like we did every night before you left."

"It would be my pleasure."

"Very well then. Go for some air, and I will rest."

I hefted myself to my feet without losing my breath and left the study. The scent of his pipe smoke clung to me.

I made my way through the house to the stairwell and up, padding back to my room. Unable to understand why Carter put me here of all places, if the men I sought weren't close, I was trying hard to put the pieces of the puzzle together of what was going on here, like where the real Josie went and what happened if she suddenly came back.

Grateful to find Nell not present in my room, I stretched back and unfastened the ties on my bodice then dug around to get to the corset. Once I had loosened the straps, I drew my first deep breath in an hour.

"Oh, thank god!" I muttered. Part of my headache eased

immediately. My ribs felt bruised, and I stretched over my head to make sure nothing had fallen asleep.

My phone buzzed. I pulled it out.

Language skills kick in yet? Carter had written.

Pleased to hear from him, I perched on the edge of my bed to respond. *Yep. What's the other one? A history chip? Oh, BTW – what happened to the real Josie Jackson who belongs here?*

He took his time with his response. I crossed to a pitcher of water and thick glass, pouring myself a drink.

The sheep outside the window caught my eye again. They were perfectly huggable, though I didn't think I would be able to bend over to pet them let alone hug them in the silly gown. Sipping water, I sat near the window. John had sheep, cattle, horses, goats, pigs and chickens. Having lived my entire life in crowded southern California, I viewed the rolling hills and animals that belonged to him with barely contained excitement. Surely during my time here, I'd have a chance to explore the prairies, meet every animal, and learn more about this era than possible in history classes!

At the buzz of my phone, I looked down.

Great! The other is an empathic memory chip. Said the text from Carter.

Do I feel in color or something? I wrote to him, perplexed.

His response was a smiley face, followed by a more detailed explanation.

It's hard to explain, but you'll know when it kicks in. Your logic chip will process the historical records and feed that to the chip that enhances your emotional quotient. It'll help you interpret a course of action based on historically enhanced intuition.

"Sure. Why not." So he planted three chips in my brain, not two. *Not a fan of involuntary brain surgery. I know why I needed them but … yikes. Next time, tell me up front???* I responded. Rereading it, I typed him a second note about possible side effects of them doing brain surgery on me.

I'm sorry, Josie. I should've been more upfront, was his fast answer. *There might be some side effects, but they've been tested enough that I don't think any of them are negative. A couple of the chips' functions are in the developmental stage – the empathic memory chip in particular was thought to be theoretically impossible, but I did it!*

There was a part of me that wanted to ask how they had tested these brain chips enough to know there were no side effects. I hesitated to ask. Every once in a while, I sensed something … dark without understanding its source. As if knowing what I thought, Carter sent another note.

Trust me, Josie. I wouldn't put them in your head if they were dangerous to you.

Somewhat appeased, I reread his explanation about the empathic memory chip. It made no sense to me, but I guessed I'd find out when it kicked in. I messaged him once more about the real Josie.

"Miss Josie?" Nell's call was muffled by the closed door.

Shoving what she referred to as the devil's box into my pocket, I straightened my dress hastily and smoothed it out. The door opened.

"Your father said you wanted air." Nell held a parasol in one hand. She wore a dark hat and gloves. "Did you wish to go to town?"

I had completely forgotten about the town I saw last night. I bounced to my feet, ecstatic at the idea of seeing a real life Wild West town and hopeful of finding at least one of the men I sought. "Yes! What an awesome adventure!"

"You always did love town." An odd expression crossed Nell's face. It was no singular emotion but rather, a complete lack of anything. She went blank for a moment, glassy-eyed and frozen.

"You up for this?" I asked, concerned.

She shook her head. "Of course." Nell released a sigh but didn't give me one of her disapproval looks.

The odd spell passed, and I joined her at the door.

"Miss Josie, would you go to town without your bonnet?" she asked, askance.

"I guess not." With a look around, I wasn't able to determine where said bonnet was.

"I'll fetch it." She disappeared into the adjoining room. I trailed her to the doorway of a dressing room and saw a second fireplace, large basin for a bath, stands with different gowns displayed, and a wall of wardrobes.

I had an entire wall dedicated to bonnets. Impressed, I watched her carefully check several of them with a critical eye.

My phone vibrated. I turned away and glanced down, not bothering to unlock the screen for the short message.

No one knows. She never returns.

Any doubt I had about pretending to be John's daughter to make his last days peaceful fled at the note. Sorrow for the man who missed his daughter as much as I did my father dampened my excitement about going to town. I replaced the phone in my pocket, pensive.

I didn't belong here, but I felt like I owed it to the man housing me to make his life a little happier before his death. If no one knew what happened to real-Josie, then there was a good chance she died, like Nell had hinted at earlier. Wasn't it better to give John and Nell hope? To do a little more good than I originally planned?

"Here we are." Nell returned.

Blinking out of my thoughts, I forced a smile and faced her. Aware of what she and John were both missing, my heart forbade me from disappointing either of them while I was here. I'd be gone soon enough, John dead, and Nell forced to face the truth about the woman she'd cared for.

She placed the bonnet on my head and tied it beneath my chin.

"And now, adventure," I proclaimed.

"These high spirits are not appropriate, Miss Josie," Nell said, though a smile leaked through her grave expression.

"I want you to be happy, Nell," I told her. "You and Father both."

Tears filled her eyes. She turned away and strode into the hallway.

I followed – and paused. This time, it wasn't just déjà vu that hit me with unexpected force but more like a dream I couldn't quite remember. The image and sense of *knowing* were almost strong enough to be a whisper.

It came from further down my wing, specifically from the door at the end. A shallow feeling, faint whisper, dark image … Movement, firelight, two voices …

"Miss Josie, are you coming?"

Nell's yell from the bottom of the stairs cut whatever it was short. My gaze lingered on the door. Something had happened there, and it defied any logical explanation that I could know such a thing.

Empathic memory chip. Was that it and how did it work?

"Yes!" I called. Without understanding why, I hurried to join her, running away from whatever it was I almost saw at the end of the hallway.

Chapter Five

I DIDN'T CATCH MY BREATH UNTIL I LEFT THE HOUSE. THE SUN dispelled the lingering unease from upstairs, and I took a moment to admire the sleek black carriage waiting for me.

Nell had the reins, and I slid onto the bench seat beside her. She deftly drove the two-person buggy away from the house and into the prairielands. Waist high grasses bowed and rustled in an early fall breeze. They stretched as far as I could see, meeting the blue sky dotted with clouds in the distance. Hills rolled gently, sometimes hiding surprises I discovered when we crested them. Fluffy white sheep and cattle appeared over two peaks, one of which was tended by John's ranch hands.

Rather than be impatient by our relatively slow speed, I found myself immersed in admiring landscape unlike any I had ever seen.

"It's so peaceful," I murmured. "What is that?" I pointed to the six-foot stake with a red flag on its tip at the top of one hill.

"It marks the edge of the savages' land. Your grandfather owned two thousand acres in this territory, before the government decided to resettle the Indians out here. Your father marked the edges with flags," Nell replied. "The red men cross the border to reach the road, and they allow your father's herds to graze on their land in exchange. They share several large ponds."

"He gets along well with them," I commented. "Is it like this everywhere?"

"No. The cavalry responds to skirmishes between the savages and gentlefolk regularly."

"But didn't we kind of just take their land? I mean, is it a surprise they're unhappy about it?"

Nell glanced at me. "You best keep comments like that to yourself."

I flinched, a sudden headache piercing my temple. It flared then died quickly, fading to a distant ache. An odd sense filled me, and I tried to determine what it was.

Memories that weren't mine. They floated through my thoughts like fragments of a dream that persisted after I awoke. I watched them, mesmerized by the idea of seeing into someone else's mind.

Historically enhanced intuition. It was the ultimate survival tool, one that gave me insight into the thoughts of everyone around me. Instead of the internet, *this* was maybe how I found the men I sought. *Carter, you are a freakin' genius.*

As I watched Nell's memories, I frowned.

"You're dying from a tumor, aren't you?" I asked her.

Nell's sharp intake of breath was enough of a response.

"You had two children who died in their youth. Your brother has dementia but your tumor will take you before the dementia does."

"You are starting to remember," Nell said.

"No … I mean, maybe." The memories weren't mine, but they were clear, like I had read them in a book. I tried to recall anything about John but wasn't able to.

Empathic memory. Did it mean I only remembered or knew things about people near me? If so, it wasn't going to be nearly as good as the internet. I'd have to find someone who knew Taylor Hansen and Running Bear.

"Who told you of the tumor?" Nell asked quietly. "I forbade the doctor from revealing it to your father. He has been through enough."

"You love him, always have," I observed. "Why didn't you tell him?"

"Bite your tongue, lest someone hear you!"

I laughed, looking at the open prairie that ran on all sides.

"You came back changed indeed," Nell said, disapproval still in her voice. "A woman of my station cannot love a man of your father's station."

Definitely a different time. I kept the thought to myself.

"What was I like?" I asked. "Before I ... disappeared?"

"You have always been very sweet. Delicate. Your father sheltered you, and for good reason. He is the wealthiest man this side of the River, and there are many men who would prey on you or him." Her memories supported what she said. She was recalling me as a happy child with fondness.

"His money comes from England, from his family," I said, the images in my mind flowing fast.

"Yes. His father was a nobleman. His elder brother inherited the title, but Mr. John was left a great inheritance by his mother and his uncle."

"So I have always been ... comfortable," I assessed.

"Very. Spoilt, if I do say so." Nell smiled. "Your father gave you whatever you wished, except when it came to the man he wished you to marry. There are few men here worthy of the hand of the daughter of a noble line. But there was one, and you opposed the union. You have always been smart and stubborn, traits you inherited from your father."

Maybe I have more in common with the real Josie than I thought.

"You ran away on the eve before your wedding. Completely disappeared after a huge dinner your father threw. The sheriff and all your father's money were not able to find you."

At her words, the memories stopped suddenly. Like there was a wall there. I had no reason to doubt Carter's brilliant inventions, and yet, I wasn't able to explain why Nell's memories ended on the afternoon real-Josie disappeared while Nell spoke of the evening dinner. She had missing time or memories somehow.

"It sounds like I was taken," I said, frowning.

"We thought so as well. Your father could not bear the idea that someone he knew had done something so foul, so he told everyone you left him because of the marriage."

"I wish I could remember."

"Maybe it's better you don't. The doctor says he has met many people who are unable to recall tragedy, and he feels it's better for them that way."

"Hmmm. Maybe." *I want to know what happened to her.* An image popped into Nell's head. "You blamed … my cousin Philip."

The memories began to flow again, this time of the blond man with a beard and cold eyes. "Don't you repeat that to no one, Miss Josie. He has been after your father's money since before you were born," Nell said. "Your father spoilt him, too, the son he never had, but he left all his money to you." The gravity on her features faded. "But, you have returned. There is nothing Philip can do. You are better served finding a husband soon, my child, even so."

"John … Father said the same," I said, amused. "I'm pretty sure I can take care of myself."

"It is not fashionable for a woman to speak her mind as you do, and a woman's right to land is not always recognized in the uncivilized new world."

I rolled my eyes and gazed at our surroundings. We were quiet the rest of the way to town. Uncertain what to expect, I was surprised by how busy the tiny town I had seen the other night was by daylight.

"Every landowner and his son is here," Nell said, anger in her voice. "They heard you were back. Each of them greedier than the last! No daughter of John is going to sully her hands by wedding any of them."

"Whoa," I said with a laugh. "You're cute, like an angry grandma. I can take care of myself."

"That frightens me more." Nell eyed the men in town as we entered.

"My god – a real, live stagecoach!" I stared at the lumbering mode of transportation that was popular in the West. It was pulled by a team of four horses with two men seated on the driver's box. It appeared worn, the wooden carriage dusty and the spokes of large wheels flecked with mud.

"A woman of your station travels by train," Nell said with some disdain.

Not far from an inn where two stagecoaches were parked was a raised platform with a noose dangling from a center beam. I had never seen a real live gallows before. "Do they *hang* people here?"

"Yes, Miss Josie, they do for infractions of violence. We are one of the only frontier towns that's peaceful, for which we can thank the half-breed Sheriff."

The same sheriff that wanted a word with me. The sight of the noose gave me the creeps, and the warning about who issued hangings didn't help. "How often does he hang people?" I asked.

"Every Saturday at noon."

My mouth dropped open. "So often?"

"The sheriff is serious about his duty. He hangs white men, black men and red men, even a woman who killed her husband."

"Wow."

Nell nodded seriously. "Your father no longer attends the hangings, but most of the town does. The saloons offer free beer that day."

Never expected a hanging to be an excuse for a party. "So there's a trial, right? It's not just one man deciding to hang people?"

"There are always trials and appeals, unless the crime has enough witnesses or was too terrible to await a trial. The sheriff hangs every man involved in a scuffle with the Indians, red, white, slave or mixed. No trial."

Any thought I had about wanting to see the sexy sheriff was gone. Instead, my mind turned to ensuring we never crossed paths again.

"We are to find you a new bauble or jewels or finery for a dinner this evening. Your father insists," Nell said cheerfully.

From gallows to jewelry. It was all in a normal day here. I shook my head. "I didn't bring any money," I said.

"He gave me your purse. Find what you like, and we will get it. There is nothing here you cannot buy."

"How much did he send?"

"One hundred dollars." Nell whispered the amount then looked around to make sure no one else overheard.

"Is that a lot?" I asked in the same tone.

"Child, please! It is more than most of these men will make in a year!"

"Wow," I murmured. "Can my father afford this?"

"Of course. It's pocket change to him."

I should definitely thank Carter for sending me to John. If John considered a year of a man's wages pocket change, I understood why every landowner was in town to court me.

In suits, bowties and some with top hats. I studied those we drove by, curious about their dress and mannerisms. A couple of them bowed while nearly everyone stopped what they were doing to stare.

"None of them are particularly handsome," I mused. I was never much a fan of beards, and most of the men here had them.

"They are not," Nell agreed. "You can find a much wealthier man when we head to the city."

I snorted, the defensive nanny endearing. With this many people, though, how was I supposed to find the person I sought? Could my empathic memory process everyone?

"The sheriff isn't here," I murmured. "I guess he isn't interested in my hand."

Nell gave me a look of reproach. "He is not only poor, but is half *savage* and proudly claims them as kin."

"Trust me – I want nothing to do with him. But he's a lot easier on the eyes."

"Quiet now, Miss Josie. You must not entertain such thoughts about a man like that," she warned. "He is lucky the soiled doves take him, but he will never have a wife, especially not one of your station."

"Soiled doves?"

Nell raised her chin towards one side of the street. I looked and gasped. Women stood in front of a two story wooden bordello, their manner of being half-dressed leaving me no question as to the kind of establishment it was.

"It's a brothel!" I exclaimed. "A real live, Old West brothel! Outstanding! We've got to talk to them, Nell."

"Enough of your jests, Miss Josephine." The note of mild alarm was enough to tell me that my nanny was at her wit's end.

Disappointed yet fascinated by the women of the night, I didn't take my eyes off them until Nell pulled to a halt.

It was then I noticed the sheriff, leaning against the wall of his office, watching us with hard green eyes. He appeared relaxed, his wiry body robed in worn clothing with patches on his pants and shirt. He was too hard for me to pity, but I wondered if there was a part of him that was bothered by the fact he was isolated from pretty much everyone. I didn't imagine he had many friends since he was half-Indian and sent men to the gallows every week. His eyes stood out in a face rendered tanned from his time in the sun. He wore a wide-brimmed cowboy hat.

That is one sexy cowboy, I thought, unable to look away. Had I ever seen anyone else pull off the standoffish sexiness and quiet strength? I knew a conversation with him was not going to go well, but there was something compelling about his combination of outdoor ruggedness and intensity.

If he didn't go around hanging people … In the sea of men with black suits, he alone stood out. The movement of someone dressed in browns caught my attention, and my gaze went to a small group of natives gathered at the edge of town.

The Native American who was with the sheriff this morning was present, and I resisted the urge to interrogate him about where exactly he found me.

I concentrated on him but was too far to read anything about him the way I had Nell.

"Are we going there?" I asked, indicating a small market at the edge of town.

"Indian and local goods?" Nell shook her head firmly. "We only buy European goods and those brought here from Boston. It's not fitting for a woman of your station to be seen at an Indian market."

"Nell." I sighed. "Please? I really want to go see."

"See what?"

"What I missed while gone."

Nell pursed her lips together but parked the carriage close to the edge of town, in front of a tailor's shop.

I managed to get out of the carriage with some grace and brushed the wrinkles out of the dress Nell probably spent hours ironing. She handed me a pouch that jingled, an indication they thought my sense present enough to give me some money. I observed the downtown area with a smile. It smelled funky, of horses, smoke, people and waste, but I was seeing something no one in my time had.

"Josie, my cousin."

I turned and glanced at the man who was little taller than me with cold, blue eyes, a mustache and a suit that looked new. He approached, followed by two other men. He was the man from Nell's thoughts.

My empathic memory kicked in when he was within arm's reach. I saw his and Nell's and suspected the empathic memory chip was activated by proximity. The images began flowing when he was within arms reach, and I watched them. I had been fascinated by Nell's memories, but those that flowed from this man were disturbing: of the time he'd slapped real-Josie when she was thirteen and tried to rape her when she was seventeen. He viewed me with desire and contempt and John with absolute disdain.

Taken aback by the images, I realized Nell's suspicion wasn't misplaced.

"Philip," I replied.

"You look different," he said, studying me with a frown. "I was worried my ill uncle had been taken advantage of by some … harlot." His eyes went down my body as he spoke, and they rested on my breasts.

Bad man. The images in my mind seemed to confirm that. He wasn't thinking about Josie's naked body but the small frame of another woman struggling to escape him while he choked her out.

"Still beating and raping your servants?" I asked, frowning. Before Philip, it hadn't occurred to me that the empathic memories would also show me the kinds of secrets and sins that people generally didn't want known. Or maybe a man like this didn't have reason to care in an era when women didn't have many rights.

His gaze flew up to my face.

"Spending your coin at the whorehouse and on wagers," I continued. "You are no different, either, cousin."

I heard Nell mumbling under her breath while Philip stared at me. The men behind him chuckled. Finally, he smiled tightly.

"My cousin. Always one to jest," he said loudly enough for everyone near us to hear. "I missed you, Josie."

I didn't want a man like him to hug me but didn't resist, afraid of drawing too much of his attention. He smelled of whiskey and smoke and held me too tightly, yet it was the memories that made me almost ill.

"Tell me, harlot. What did you do with my cousin?" he whispered.

"Why, whatever do you mean, cousin?" I asked in a syrupy sweet voice and pulled away. "I do believe you grew a few inches while I was away."

"You will not lie to me when we are alone," he returned for my ears only.

"I've seen what you do to women you're alone with. There's no chance of that happening," I said in the same quiet voice.

We glared at each other for a long moment before he finally stepped away.

"What a grand thing for you to return when your father is so ill!" he proclaimed. Several of the men around him murmured their assent.

"Be nice to him." Nell all but dragged me back to hiss into my ear. "He is powerful, Miss Josie. In a month, he'll be the mayor."

It took effort for me not to roll my eyes. Aware the governess knew the customs of this world far better than I did, I plastered on a smile. "Will you walk with me, cousin?" I asked, holding out my arm.

He took it, and we began walking.

"My father sends his regards from England," he said as we moved slowly down the road.

I almost laughed but caught myself. His memories told a different story than his words. "Is this a test, cousin?" I asked. "Your father has been dead for fifteen years at least."

"You must have known the real Josie."

"I *am* the real Josie."

"No, *cousin*, you are not. And when your father is gone, I will insure my inheritance is ripped from you and you are cast back whence you came. Though if you choose to stay in my home, you will do so with your legs spread at my desire."

I did laugh at that. It was the wrong reaction, which didn't quite register until his face turned crimson. "My apologies, Philip. For a moment, I thought you were serious." I smiled at him. "The sheriff might be interested to know about the woman buried beneath your pig pen."

He appeared uncertain how to take my words. "That was our secret, cousin," he said with a look over his shoulder.

I really hate this guy. The images of the woman he killed, albeit accidentally, were forefront in his mind. What real-Josie was doing there, I didn't know, but she was young and too frightened of her older cousin to speak out. "And I will keep it for you, as I promised long ago."

Philip was looking at me anew.

"Let's not fight," I told him. "My father is ill, and I am not well myself, if you hadn't heard."

"I had," he confirmed. He regained his composure quickly. "I see evidence of your madness in your speech."

Dick. My gaze strayed towards the market at the edge of town.

"Not there," he said, following my look. He sneered. "Not with the *savages*." The memory in his head made me freeze in place: an Indian girl, little over ten, who worked in his household. The sight of her screaming and bloodied while he held her to the ground …

It was the worst of all the images in his head. Not that him raping his servants was acceptable, but the fact he *relished* hurting the little girl … I tried to push it away, to stop the images from coming.

A stab of pain went through my head once more in response, followed by tunnel vision and the sense of floating. It took a moment for me to ground myself and pull my mind out of the abyss to become aware of my physical body once more.

"My cousin has not yet recovered from her ordeal," I heard him saying. "Your concern is greatly appreciated."

I blinked away the sunspots to see him standing in front of me. I was slumped against Nell, seated on the raised sidewalk, surrounded by a crowd of anxious men kept at bay by Philip.

"Sorry," I managed. "Just … need a moment." *And to ask how to turn the chip off.* Knowing the dark secrets of everyone around me would quickly become a curse, especially since I wasn't here long enough to right the wrongs I uncovered.

Nell's memories were agitating me as I tried to recover. Philip and the others were too far away, but Nell was running through every time in real-Josie's life when she'd fallen, sprained something or otherwise gotten hurt. It was definitely not helpful to have the distressed images of a little girl crying in my mind right now.

"Give her some peace, gentlemen," the gruff, low voice of the sheriff directed those around me. I sensed him approach without looking up, not too excited to have drawn his attention. "Miss Josephine, you can rest in my office." It wasn't a request.

I stalled for a moment, embarrassed to swoon like I was weak and still a little freaked out by all the people he hanged. Maybe there was some damage done to me from time travel, or maybe it was the intensity of feelings and memories that weren't mine. I felt claustrophobic despite the open skies and land of the Old West.

"Let me help you." The sheriff knelt and wrapped an arm around me.

His scent snapped my attention out of my mind. Horse leathers, dust, sweat – and dark male musk tainted by a hint of sweetness.

I breathed deeply and said nothing, a little too aware of the warmth and solidity of his body as he easily stood with me tucked against him. I was no stranger to men's bodies or touch, but this was different. Better. Almost familiar, like his scent, John and Carter. Aside from the fact he was sexy as sin, his eyes were absolutely stunning.

Staring up at him, I didn't realize I had been leaning into his hard, wiry frame too long until he lifted his eyes to mine. The arresting, light green depths were as intriguing as his scent. His face was shaven, the high cheekbones, a sign of his mixed heritage casting hollows in his cheeks.

No memories. Nell stood two feet from me, her memories flowing freely, but there was nothing from the sheriff's direction.

He cleared his throat, as if uncomfortable holding me. "Can you walk, ma'am?" he asked.

His tested politeness heightened my awareness and the desire not to sit down with him and talk.

"Yes. Sorry." I stepped away. "I, uh, am feeling not completely well."

How long had I been staring up at the sheriff like a lovesick fool? *Long enough for Nell to notice.* She was frowning fiercely. Her expressions left me no doubt as to the lecture she'd give me later about how a woman of my station was supposed to behave.

I wanted so badly to roll my eyes but didn't, instead occupying myself by dusting off my dress.

"If you'll come with me, ma'am, you can rest. We can have that talk I've been wanting to have with you, too," the sheriff said.

I froze. There was a guarded note in his voice, one that told me he wasn't about to take pity on me, even if I did just almost pass out.

"I think I need to return home and rest, sheriff," I managed.

"It wasn't a choice, ma'am." He offered his arm.

Dammit. I forced a smile, though. "Then I'd be delighted." If he caught the sarcasm in my tone, he didn't react.

The amount of people around me startled me. Nell wasn't joking about everyone being there to try to win my hand, my first day back. Initially curious, I began to sense how easily I would be overwhelmed by the masses, if the floodgates opened and released a crowd's worth of empathic memories.

And their secrets … I wanted to believe not every man here was like Philip, but I didn't want to know what else people were hiding, either.

I glanced up at the sheriff when we cleared the crowds. The determination on his features was enough of a warning that he hadn't lost his resolve to interrogate me. "Maybe you can tell me how you found me last night and why you are so set on talking to me."

He glanced at me. "Because I think maybe your business is elsewhere, ma'am, not foolin' a good man like John."

"Foolin … ah." He, too, suspected I wasn't the real Josie. Unable to read his memories, I wasn't going to pass any test he gave me. Startled by the thought, it took me a moment to respond. "I don't know what you're talking about."

"We both have our secrets, ma'am." He released me and moved ahead.

Who the hell is this guy? He had no empathic memories or maybe, the chip worked selectively. Without knowing for certain how it was supposed to work, all I knew was that it was silent around him.

The sheriff strode down the walkway and leapt off rather than taking the stairs, leading me towards his office at a quick pace. Nell trailed me, the obedient servant in public, while I suspected my nanny had a few choice words to say to me once we were alone.

"Nell, will you please go in with me?" I whispered when we reached the door to his office.

"Of course, Miss. You should have a chaperone."

Feeling more confident, I walked through the open door of the sheriff's office. His partner was gone, and a second door propped open led to three cells with iron bars.

"This is like a movie!" I stood in awe of my surroundings for a moment, taking in the roughly hewn wooden desks, wanted posters and the sheriff with his wide cowboy hat and lean cowboy body. "Fantastic!"

"Ms. Nell, I'm gonna have to ask you to wait outside," the sheriff said, sitting on the edge of his desk. He removed his hat and set it beside him.

"Yes, sheriff," Nell said.

I turned to glare at my nanny, who had ducked her head and turned to leave.

"Nell!" I hissed.

"People here know I tend to put them in cells to cool off if they don't listen to me, ma'am," the sheriff said. "You can spend five minutes talkin' or overnight."

Nell fled.

Pretty sure Nell is getting revenge for me stressing her out. I said nothing but pressed my lips together.

"Have a seat, Miss Josephine," the sheriff said a little too casually.

With a deep breath, I turned and sat the best I could in the snug bodice in what I hoped was a proper sit. I had missed loosening one of the ties, though, shifted twice and soon found myself leaning again to relieve the pressure around my chest.

The sheriff was studying me. "You all right, ma'am?"

"A little tired."

He looked me over but said nothing else about my odd position.

"Let's start with what happened a year ago, when you disappeared," he said, resting his hands on the desk behind him in a stance that was deceptively relaxed. His dark hair was mussed from the hat, and the six shooters he had slung on his hips rested against the desk.

He looks like a real cowboy, I thought, momentarily mesmerized by the combination of quiet strength, handsomeness and low, quiet command. The exotic slant of his cheekbone and chiseled features were straight out of a movie.

"I don't remember," I replied.

"Convenient."

My eyes narrowed. "You aren't interested in what happened a year ago," I assessed.

My empathic memories weren't working. Nor were the historical records I was supposed to be able to access. Without either, it was going to be harder to figure out what the sheriff wanted. Philip's motivation was clear: he wanted my land, money and me lying dead in a ditch.

Such things meant nothing to this stranger, but he was after something from me.

"You're right. I'm not," he replied calmly. "I am interested in how you keep appearing every few months and leaving again. Every time a little different. A little lost."

"I don't know what you're talking about."

"We suspected the other girls were after John's wealth. They must've heard about his missing daughter and were trying to take advantage. John's mind is too far gone for him to understand this."

I listened. "So you want to interrogate me to protect John. That's very sweet of you." For some reason, that made me feel a little better about being there.

"Partly true." The enigmatic sheriff offered a half-smile. "And partially because I want to know what's really going on."

I wanted to be the real-Josie for John because he needed peace of mind before he died. With the sheriff … well, it was more of a survival instinct. The man was dangerous and too quick to sentence people to hanging.

"I appreciate you looking after my father in my absence. But I really don't know what you're talking about," I said firmly. "The doctor will verify I have no memory of the past year. My dear cousin Philip and governess will verify that I have knowledge only I can possess."

The sheriff studied me, hard gaze never leaving my face. I didn't recall ever meeting anyone quite this intense before. The silence grew tense and awkward, and I dropped my focus to his desk.

"Taylor Hansen," I read his wooden nameplate aloud. "*You're Taylor Hansen!*" Did Carter know the man I sought would find me instead of me finding him?

"Funny thing, ma'am, the other girls got that same look on their faces when they heard my name," he replied dryly.

Carter would've told me if he sent others back. I didn't believe the sheriff's tales about other girls fully. It sounded like entrapment to me, though it did make sense that conniving people would try to take advantage in an era where a woman was defined by her father and husband's money and status. Itching to text my handler, I clasped my hands in my lap to keep from snatching my phone.

"Who were these other girls?" I asked carefully. "Why do you think I'm one of them?"

"What should concern you more is what happened to them. No

one saw them leave town."

A chill went down my back. Was the good sheriff threatening me or warning me? From his expression, I wasn't certain. The tension between us was thick enough to make me uncomfortable, and he watched me like he might a bluffing poker player while I tried not to stare at one of the most attractive men I had ever met.

"If there's something I need to know, ma'am …" He trailed off.

"Not to my knowledge, Sheriff," I replied. "You found no trace of the other girls?"

"None."

"And they just appeared at random?"

"From the sky. Like you did."

I stared at him. Now *that* made me want to hide in a cell and call Carter. It was one of the rare moments in my life where I was speechless. What was worse: I suddenly recalled why I hadn't taken a third drama class in college – because I was a terrible liar and an even worse actress.

"Sheriff." Philip's intrusion couldn't have come at a better time. "What business do you have with my cousin?"

I almost sighed.

The moment he stepped foot in the office, the empathic memories began working. I tried not to react to the scenes flowing from my faux-cousin, not when I knew how closely the sheriff was watching.

Why did they work for Philip but not the man identified by Carter? Was the sheriff testing me the same way Philip had?

"My business, Philip," the sheriff responded, ignoring the wealthy man's pointed tone.

"Consider it over."

"For now," the sheriff allowed.

I rose quickly and went to the door. Dislike of my cousin was second only to fearing the sheriff knew something he shouldn't about me.

Worse, I had found one of the men Carter sought but didn't dare talk him long enough to find out what he was doing here.

"G'day, ma'am," the sheriff called after me.

I waved over my shoulder, anxious to be away. Nell waited outside the office. Snatching her arm, I tugged the woman with me back towards the carriage.

"Cousin," Philip called.

I rolled my eyes but turned.

"If he bothers you, you tell me. He has no right to be questioning a lady about her doings," Philip said firmly.

"You're absolutely right, cousin," I replied. "Thank you. I will let you know."

Philip appeared pleased by my admission. Quelling the urge to run, I smiled at him.

"If you'll excuse me, Philip, I am feeling unwell," I continued. "Nell will see me home."

"I will call on you tomorrow."

I turned away, all but dragging Nell towards the carriage.

"We need to go," I whispered.

"I told your father today was too soon for you to be out," Nell said, worry in her voice. "He said you loved to go to town and wanted you to buy something special for your return. I told him, she's not right yet, Mr. John, you can't -"

"I'm fine," I said, glancing back at my cousin. "I hate that man."

Nell followed my gaze. "You best keep that to yourself, Josie. He's powerful and wealthy. When your father is gone – God bless him – you will have to be careful of your cousin."

I guessed that a society that valued a man's opinion over a woman's was going to be difficult to navigate, if I wasn't out of there after John's death. I was going to ignore Philip as much as possible, and not pry into his mind again. Uncertain what to do about the sheriff, the only thing that came to mind was seeking guidance from Carter.

My attention was caught once more by the crowd at the edge of town. Every fiber in my body wanted me to run home before the sheriff tracked me down, and yet, I was drawn in the direction of the market.

"You're right, Nell," I said. "That man will never set foot in our house, once my father is gone."

"I reckon it'll take a shotgun to keep him out," Nell said.

"I think that can be arranged."

My nanny gave a rare smile.

"Before we leave, I'm going to see the savages," I said and started forward, determined to learn the location of where I had landed in case I needed to return to the spot.

"Miss Josie, it's –"

"Puh-lease, Nell. Everyone saw me almost pass out. They'll assume I'm confused."

Nell pursed her lips and trailed. I slowed when I reached the edge of the market, taking in the goods displayed on the back of wagons or spread out on blankets. Nell was right about there being a mix: a bearded old man with gold teeth grinned as I passed a wagon bed filled with dented bronze candelabras. Two Native American women ceased talking when I reached their display of leather decorative items. Roughly hewn furniture, lanterns, horse tack, handmade blankets … there was a little bit of everything in the nineteenth century version of a flea market.

The handmade, hammered silver jewelry with polished rocks displayed by a little Indian girl caught my eye, and I did my best to crouch without grimacing to see better.

"Did you make all this?" I asked.

The girl's eyes widened. She shook her head and pointed to a sloppily woven, leather bracelet adorned with wooden beads that lay among several others of much better skill.

I smiled and picked it up. "It's beautiful."

"I sew better than I braid. I make clothing, too." The girl smiled hesitantly.

I opened my purse and dumped coins into my palm, not recognizing any of them. Standing, I turned to Nell.

"What are these?" I asked.

Nell sorted them in my palm. "Half cent, full cent, half dimes, dimes, quarter, half dollar, dollars."

"So if I give her a quarter?" I asked, struggling to follow the different sizes.

"A quarter?" Nell appeared appalled. "Ain't worth the half-cent she'll charge!"

"I'm not following you at all," I said.

"The quarter is worth fifty of the half-cent," Nell explained.

"Ooohhh. That I understand." I plucked the quarter free and replaced the rest of my change. I held it out to the little girl, whose eyes bulged larger than the coin offered.

Satisfied with myself, I continued onward, the bracelet in my hand.

We reached the end of the small market, and my focus shifted to the horses being herded into a corral nearby by men who appeared to be authentic cowboys.

Amazing.

"Miss Josephine."

I turned at the unfamiliar voice to see the Native American who had accompanied the sheriff to John's approaching, the little girl trailing him with a look of distress on her features. He held out the quarter.

"We do not need your pity," he said firmly. His dark eyes flashed with fire, and his features were taut. He wasn't scowling, but he wasn't friendly either. He regarded me as if I were an alien.

"It was not pity," I said. "Kindness. You brought me back to my father."

"He repaid us in full."

"But I didn't, and it was my life," I said. "It's for her, to buy herself a present."

His hand dropped. He was close enough for me to start to see his memories. He was thinking of his family, including his niece, the little girl I had bought the mal-formed bracelet from.

"If I may ask, what were you doing out there last night with the sheriff in the first place?" I asked. "When you rescued me?"

The man's jaw tightened. His mind was racing, and I didn't quite get how all the images I saw were connected. Compared to Nell and Philip, his memories were disjointed. There was no flow, only flashes.

"Your uncle is ill," I said, tilting my head to the side. "He has little longer than my father, which means …" I trailed off, the images in my mind troubling me. They weren't his memories as such but encyclopedic style historical accounts of the slaughter I was there to stop. There was no obvious connection between him and the accounts, and the disjointed picture forming confused me long enough for me to realize I was being stared at by more than one person. "Are you Running Bear?"

"I am."

My mouth dropped open. Carter was brilliant. He dropped me off in a spot where the two men I sought rescued me!

"Miss Josie, we must go," Nell said.

I waved her off and continued addressing Running Bear. "We need to talk," I told him.

He stepped back. These images were memories. My eyes ... they reminded him of the daughter he had lost several years before during a cavalry raid. She also had blue eyes. The disjointedness flickered, and his thoughts unfolded in a logical flow before once again breaking into flashes.

"You know who hurt your family but told your uncle, the Chief, you didn't," I said. "Maybe because you feared he'd talk you out of what you might be planning? A raid ... or ..." I wasn't able to tell the full story or reasoning. The empathic memory was a hodgepodge of facts and patchy memories, some of which didn't match up at all, as if the recorded accounts about him were different. Almost like his family's slaughter happened. And then didn't. The history books didn't know, but his memories were clearer.

"What are you that you know things you should not?" he managed, searching my face.

"A starman," his niece said, smiling. "Like the shaman says. You came from the sky and landed in my uncle's –"

"Hush, Blue Stream," the man said harshly enough for the girl to jump. She peered up at him.

Despite his gruff rebuke, the girl held only admiration and love for her uncle, her memories of them playing earlier that day.

"What are these starmen?" I asked curiously. "You've seen people fall out of the sky before?"

"Yes, we – " the girl started.

"Stay away from my people and my land," Running Bear ordered in a voice that left me no doubt what would happen if I crossed him. He pushed the girl away, and the two of them rejoined several natives standing a few feet away.

Starman. How many people had they seen fall from the sky? I burned to ask the girl but feared her uncle after what I had seen in the empathic history. The sheriff's claim about there being more than one woman sent back to play the part of Josie returned.

I barely knew Carter. Did he purposely *not* tell me I wasn't the first? Or was this another of his failure-to-relate-to-other-humans issues?

Running Bear met my gaze once more, and I saw it. The strange spark that lit up his aura for a split second, a sign from whatever crazy stuff Carter put in my head. Why didn't Taylor glow like this, if he was part of whatever event was supposed to happen on the twenty fourth?

I ached to pursue and yet was afraid to after his warning.

"You, savages, keep your distance," Philip snapped, waving his cane at them. "You will not sully the daughter of my uncle."

The natives turned away.

"Your father is too kind to those wild men. Josie, you must need rest to have come this far. You are not in the right mind," Philip scolded me. He waved his hand at the wares of the merchants around us. "This … junk is not worth your time. Nell, I will report to my uncle you let her dirty her hands in such a place."

"My apologies, Mr. Philip," Nell said.

"I know what will please your father to see you buy. I have arranged it already. Return home, and I'll ensure it arrives."

I almost revolted at the condescending tone. Nell shook her head, and I relented, following my alleged cousin like a good little puppy back towards the carriage. Unhappy, the ride home seemed much longer than it had going to town. My mind never strayed from the native that wanted nothing to do with me and the sheriff who knew I didn't belong.

Only when I was in my room was I able to text Carter again.

Am I a starman? And does the person I'm looking for glow? And why did the sheriff say there were three other girls who were here before me?

I shoved it away just as Nell walked in. "Miss Josie, we must get you ready for dinner." She had a different gown draped over her arms.

Not one to complain, I nonetheless groaned internally. I had been sweating and uncomfortable all day.

"Your father is excited," she added with a smile. "You've made him so happy, Miss Josie."

At the mention of the kindly man, I guiltily dispelled my internal grumbling about the clothing. It wasn't right to stress the dying man out, not when I was the reason he was happy for the first time in a year. Still somewhat conflicted about whether or not I should tell him the truth, I stood and let Nell strap me back into the corset and a new gown before we headed downstairs to the formal dining room.

Chapter Six

LATE THAT NIGHT, I AWOKE IN AN OUTRIGHT PANIC. SITTING UP, I stared at the crackling flames of the hearth, unable to register why I was shaking and felt the need to run. Fear flew through me, its source unknown. There had been a dark dream ... two voices, a fireplace, blood ...

Pain stabbed me through the temple. I gripped my head in my hands and dabbed at the warmth trickling from my nose. The sight of my blood grounded me, and I forced my stiff body to relax. It was around one in the morning, according to the collection of clocks around my room.

What is it with clocks? They're everywhere. John had a strange obsession with time.

The curiosity as to why John liked them faded. Climbing out of bed, I crossed to the washbasin and dipped a washcloth, holding it to my nostril.

Wind whistled and howled by my window and slapped the shutters against the siding somewhere in the house. The sky was mostly clear, the moon bright, and the prairie's grasses nearly flat from the force of the gusts. Assuming the wind woke me, I sat down next to the window, admiring the view, until my nose stopped bleeding. I wasn't a stranger to sinus infections, and I hoped I wasn't getting one here. It wasn't like I could run out to Walgreens for Sudafed if I did.

An image I didn't recognize was in my head, not mine yet not belonging to anyone else, since I was alone. It was of a cave and …

An aerial view of John's property with a route highlighted to an unknown destination. Intrigued, I sat up. The map flashed like any other image and then faded. Not wanting to lose it, I sprang to my feet and snatched my phone from under my pillow, writing down what I could recall in a blank text.

The map was meant to be followed. I understood this as well as I knew it was not of my imagining but something placed there by whatever it was Carter did to me. I lit a lantern by following the sequence of steps Nell had gone through and walked into the adjoining dressing room to find something more comfortable than a gown to wear.

Josie had no pants. It took ten minutes of searching to find something I'd consider wearing on an adventure like I planned. There were too many elaborate gowns … and simpler gowns soft enough to tell me they were quite old. I pulled on one of those that fit more of a Regency England time period than the Old West. They had likely belonged to Josie's grandmother or mother.

Far more comfortable in it than what Nell dressed me in, I pulled on my boots and a long riding habit of wool. Proud I'd been able to figure out how to dress myself with the overbearing clothes, I tucked my phone in a pocket and crossed to the door.

I thought for sure several times that I'd wake the entire house with all the creaking the floors did. No one stirred, though, and I made it down the groaning stairs to the bottom floor and the wide front doors. Fumbling with the locks, I was nearly blown over by the harsh wind outside and barely caught the door before it smacked the wall.

My hair tossed around me. Closing the door, I wrestled my tresses into a sloppy braid that managed to subdue most of it and ran to the barn. The wind was a combination of warm and cool as autumn blew across the plains to replace summer.

Entering the cozy, quiet barn, I sucked in a deep breath of the familiar scent of horses and hay. It took only a moment to realize that John had horses of incredible quality, along with polished, soft saddles and bridles that would cost a lot in my time.

I selected a horse and prepared him for a ride, silently thanking my aunt for pushing me into dressage when I was five.

Moments later, I was outside in the brusque wind, headed at a quick walk on horseback towards the road leading to town. When I was far enough away from the main house not to be overheard, I pushed the horse into a canter.

It was much harder to follow the map when on the road than it seemed in my head. At some point, I was supposed to leave the road and head west, towards the territory of the Native Americans. But that point … well, I failed to recall the terrain features, except that it was somewhere around a huge tree, and there weren't many of them.

I rode over two hills before spotting the tree – and another flag marking the edge of John's property. Hesitating only a moment, I switched directions and nudged the horse off the road, trying to follow the map in my head.

The hills continued in this direction, though I began to see shallow box canyons, a river in the distance, and wider valleys. The grasslands bowed to the wind, the rustling sound loud, while the horse snorted every once in a while and picked his way through the grasses.

Pulling out the notes I made, I checked our course to see what else I needed to look for.

"*Canyon with a cave in its wall.*" I read my notes aloud. "Great work, Josie. This is why you never got more than a B in college. You suck at notes." I allowed the horse to walk in the direction it chose and closed my eyes, trying to recall the map without luck.

Gotta tell Carter the chips need to be more interactive. When they chose to work, they were fantastic. But I had no control over them, and that was annoying.

From what I remembered, the cave hadn't been too far. I opened my eyes and stood up in the stirrups to get a better look around. Another canyon was to the east of me. The river disappeared into it, indicating it was larger than I could tell from here.

I guided the horse in that direction. A trail appeared not far from where we were, and I realized the Native Americans had established paths through the grasslands. The horse followed the narrow trail towards the canyon, and we reached the edge before I pulled it to a halt.

The deep canyon seemed to come out of nowhere. Invisible from afar, it resembled something we saw in Northern Arizona in the Grand Canyon National Park, though far more isolated. The river was at the bottom, some two hundred feet below. Between us was a rocky, grassy slope – and a shelf-like trail carved by years of use that ran from the top where I was to the river.

Cave. Unable to understand its importance, I sensed … darkness from the direction of the cave in the wall below me. It had to be the empathic memory chip; there was a faint whisper, and another instinct of *knowing* that wasn't inherently mine.

Doubting the path was wide enough for the horse, I left it at the top and went to the narrow path running along the canyon wall. I started down it, startled by the relative stillness and quietness of the air without the heavy wind. With one hand on the wall and another righting my scattered braid, I made my way carefully towards the cave in the side of the canyon wall. If not for the full moon, I wouldn't be able to see where I went.

The whisper intensified, and half-formed visions bombarded my thoughts. I stopped several steps before the cave.

None of these images were good. Even if I couldn't quite grasp them and didn't understand their sources, I could tell something bad happened here. It was like the introduction to a horror movie: slashes of red and black, shadowy movements, the unexplained kaleidoscope of places and inanimate objects, and the general sense of foreboding that made the hair at the back of my neck stand up and my heart race.

A fire flickered to life, casting light and shadows outside the cave, and I sucked in a sharp breath. My intuition was urging me to flee. The map brought me here for a reason, though. I needed to find this cave or maybe, the person inside it.

Be like Amy Pond, I told myself again. She had never backed down from an adventure on Doctor Who. Carter was sort of like the Doctor. At least, I didn't think he sent me here for me to die before I had a chance to change history the way he wanted. I purposely didn't think about what I had learned, that there might've been other girls sent back before me.

I drew a deep breath and moved towards the cave, pausing in the open entrance.

It was larger than I expected, extending a good thirty feet into the canyon wall, and stocked with barrels and crates along the back wall.

A Native American man sat on a wooden box towards the back, staring at me with a mix of puzzlement and intensity. A glow flared around him briefly, the way it had at the market.

"Running Bear?" I called uncertainly.

He rose, tense, with one hand clenching a bloody knife and another a rabbit he was skinning.

The flickers of memories were faint, jumbled with the insistent whisperings and dream-like images emanating from everywhere in the cave. The chips were confused again, unable to read him clearly but reading the *cave* itself.

Not Running Bear. The man was an identical twin. The scar running down one side of his face marked the difference between the two men, along with the odd intensity and cold eyes. Running Bear hadn't been happy to see me at any time our paths crossed, but this man was … hostile.

The historical chip was telling me about the massacre that he would commit, the same tale it told me about Running Bear. I realized with some dread that it wasn't able to tell the difference between the two men. In fact, there was nothing anywhere in my mind that mentioned there being *twins,* as if the knowledge was either never recorded or lost somewhere in history.

But the visions of blood and shadows, of anger and hatred, belonged to this man. *This* was the man I could see starting a massacre.

There's something very wrong with him. My empathic memories were scrambled and overwhelmed by the cave, for there was more than one source to the whispers, and they were spread around the cave, as if …

Dead. There were people buried in this cave, people whose lives had ended violently, right here, by the man whose mind was too tangled for me to read. Why hadn't Carter told me I could read objects and places in addition to people?

"Who are you?" I whispered.

"Fighting Badger." He was studying me. "How did you find me?"

"I, uh …" There was no explaining microchips and a mental map. My eyes went to the floor of the cave, to the places where the dead lay. I had the sense of disconnecting with the world around me, of watching rather than existing.

How was it possible for me to sense something like that? Had Carter put something else in my head that let me read objects and places, or was this empathic memory chip much more powerful than he let on? Was this what he implied about the chip when he said it was experimental?

How was I able to read *dead* people?

"You are a spirit," Fighting Badger voiced quietly.

I shook my head, struggling to focus with the whispers and images. A small part of me was warning me to run, telling me I should fear this man and place, that they were both evil in a way I didn't know existed before tonight.

"You must be." He followed my gaze to a random spot in the cave, where the whispering was loudest at the moment. "Only a spirit can hear others."

"You can hear them, too?" I asked, surprised.

"They are loud tonight." Fighting Badger tossed his rabbit and knife down then wiped his hands on his pants. There was an emptiness to his eyes. Though I wasn't a superstitious or religious person, or someone who really thought twice about souls and the afterlife, I experienced the strange sense that this man had no soul.

"They are." I swallowed hard and shifted feet. He was built like someone who tracked, hunted and killed his own food, the opposite of the comparatively pampered life I lived, which meant I wasn't going to get far if I made a run for it. "You are not a ghost and you can hear them."

"I hear them because they are mine. I did not free their spirits. They stay with me. They are mine."

He's a fucking serial killer. One who collected souls instead of other souvenirs of his victims.

"Come, ghost. You must sit with me."

"I'm not one of your spirits," I objected.

"I know." Fighting Badger sat down near the fire and motioned for me to do the same.

I glanced towards the path that led back to my horse.

"I will hunt you, spirit or woman," he told me calmly.

"Okay," I whispered. Not wanting to step on the dead, I made my way through the unmarked graves to the fire and sat across from him.

My best friend always said I had a knack for making friends of the least friendly people possible. I doubted she had a serial killer in mind when she said it, but I was about to test her theory. If I survived, she was right.

"You are Talks to Spirits."

"No, actually, my name is …"

His sharp look made me clamp my mouth closed. My chest was tight, and I had the urge to cry, since I wasn't able to run. Recalling my mission in the past, the hope of saving a million people over the next two centuries, I took a deep breath and offered a small smile. "Very well. I am Talks to Spirits."

"Did the wind bring you?" he asked.

"Sort of. I had a … dream about this place and so I came."

He was gazing at me intently. I hoped he wasn't debating how to kill me, but his mind was too twisted and dark for me to make sense of. How would it be to live with a mind like his? Some memories I was able to make out, like the fact he hadn't spoken to anyone in a month or left his cave except to hunt.

"You're alone here," I assessed. "You have been for a while."

"My spirit speaks to you?"

"A little, yes."

"What does it say?" He leaned forward. "I cannot understand it. My spirit and mind are strangers to me."

And there it was – full-formed pity for a serial killer who

comprehended how screwed up he really was without knowing why. How was I born with a heart bigger than my common sense?

"It says you're lonely," I murmured. "That you keep the spirits with you for this reason."

He lowered his eyes to the fire. He had no other real emotions I was able to read, nothing but the darkness clouding his mind.

"You came from the sky, like the others," he said.

"What others?"

"There are six of you. My brother is one, and so are you. The others I do not know."

Brother? Interest replaced part of my fear. Was he talking about Running Bear or did he have more brothers?

"The spirits are never happy." He glanced to my left, where a whisper originated. Not the loudest of the memories from the dead, it was the closest to me.

I had a microchip in my brain. What was his excuse for hearing the whispers?

"Maybe they want to be free," I said.

He glared at me.

"I mean, I know why you keep them, but maybe if they were free, they'd leave you alone."

"They're *mine*."

I jumped at his sharp growl. He was tense again, agitated, the shadows in his mind churning.

"I understand." I raised my hands in a sign of surrender. "Don't be upset. I don't think there are many of us who can hear them." I began to realize that I'd never be able to tell anyone about my empathic memories with the exception of Carter. Hearing Fighting Badger talk about the whispers that didn't exist outside of us made me realize how crazy it sounded.

"No. Only us." He shook out his shoulders. "Where did you come from that you can hear them?"

"It's a really long, complicated story."

"Very well." He tossed me a canteen and then settled a pot over the fire. "I will make us dinner while you tell me this story."

Dinner? I almost laughed. But didn't. "It's kind of crazy," I said. "I don't think you want to hear it."

"Crazy," he repeated. "Perhaps we share a spirit." A ghost of a smile crossed his features.

Not a chance. I definitely wasn't his kind of crazy.

"Speak!" he ordered.

I jumped once more. Seeing his mind, knowing about his solitude and *fearing* him as I never had anyone else, I made a swift decision to tell him the truth. Because no one would believe him if he shared it, and I didn't want to end up buried in his cave.

"I'm from the future," I started.

He glanced up from gutting the rabbit without otherwise reacting.

Slowly, I began to speak, as much out of fear as nervousness and the slim hope that if I made it until dawn, maybe someone would send a search party out for me. I told him everything from when my parents died to what I did in college and how I met Carter and my mission here in his time. My life was relatively mundane until Carter.

Fighting Badger listened while prepping a stew. He settled back to let the food cook and watched me as I spoke.

"… and that's it," I finished. "Sound crazy?"

"No."

Why was I relieved by his response? "You can't tell anyone what I told you, though. It has to be our secret."

He nodded. "Running Bear would not start a war," he added. "He is very kind."

"Would you?" I asked.

Fighting Badger appeared pensive. "This is my home. The spirits could not go with me if I left them. I would have to collect more."

"Oh, Jesus no!" I exclaimed before I could stop myself. "But I think you're right. You should stay here and not start a war."

Rather than appear angered, he was amused by my outburst. "You are the first who has spoken to me without believing me crazy."

"I do think you're crazy," I replied. "But not because you can hear the spirits."

He seemed to find that funny. I didn't know why. I wanted to tell him he was a psycho lunatic, and yet, I found myself connecting with him over a skill neither of us was able to share with anyone else. That I had something in common with a serial killer was one of the greatest surprises of my life.

"My father cast me out when I was ten," he said. Twisting, he pointed to the corner of the cave. "I put him there, far from the fire, so he could not get warm."

Oh, god. The longer I stayed, the harder it became not to freak out. But I listened to his words instead of my clamoring instincts. "Why did he cast you out?" I asked.

"I am different. I collected the spirits of animals when I was too small to collect those of men."

"These spirits … they're your friends?"

He nodded. "I taught myself to make a fire," he said and motioned to the blaze. "Running Bear taught me to hunt."

These images were clearer, childhood memories of a man who idolized his twin for taking care of him. I was able to see that Running Bear – and to my surprise, Sheriff Taylor – were both present in his mind. They visited him frequently and brought him toys and treats, like he was …

Still a child. Understanding rendered me nauseated. A lonely child, exiled at a young age, already on the precipice of madness.

They didn't have the resources in this time to deal with him. I didn't want to sympathize with a serial killer but it was difficult not to sympathize with the lost child he'd been.

"You love them both," I murmured. "Don't you?"

"Yes. My brothers care for me."

The sheriff – who had hanged half the town, if Nell was to be believed – couldn't know what Fighting Badger did to his *friends*.

"You won't kill me, will you?" I managed in a tight voice.

"If you will be my friend, I will not."

"I will be," I said quickly. "I'll bring you grilled corn and wooden toys next time I come, like your brothers do."

He appeared pleased by this response. He was a young predator, quick to change his mind about whether his visitors were dinner or entertainment.

"I will not start a war," he decided. "I cannot leave my spirits, and I promised my brothers not to take more."

Sheriff Taylor knew. My stomach was churning, along with my thoughts.

"Eat." Fighting Badger ladled stew into a tin cup and passed it to me. The steaming soup smelled good, despite the feast I'd eaten for supper. He poured himself some soup and sipped it.

I followed his lead and was pleasantly surprised by the flavor. "This is really good," I told him.

"One of the spirits told me how to make it."

"How are you able to hear them?" I asked, puzzled.

"Maybe I have magic in my head like you do."

"Maybe. Can you hear the spirits of those who are alive?"

He shook his head. "My father said I was destined to become a shaman but that my connection to the spirits was so strong, I went mad. They decided to teach my brother in the ways of a shaman instead of me."

"That makes sense." For a moment, I let myself overlook the fact he'd killed somewhere in the neighborhood of ten people and buried them in his home because he was lonely. "If I had heard the spirits when I was young, I would be crazy, too."

We ate our stew in silence. Soon after, a chill touched the back of my neck, and I twisted to see the sky outside was growing lighter. My nerves were close to shot, and I was starting to feel overwhelmed by the whispers and knowledge that I was surrounded by death.

"I have to go, Fighting Badger," I whispered, praying he let me leave.

"Not until it is full light. You will get lost."

I almost wept at the words. He really wasn't going to add me to his collection. Facing him again, I stretched my legs and wrapped my coat around me more tightly to keep the chill of dawn from reaching me. It didn't make sense that the twin most likely to do something on the day Carter had identified had no intention of leaving his cave. With dread in my stomach, I realized I'd have to make good on my promise to return, at least once.

"Can I come see you on September twenty fourth?" I asked.

"When is this?"

"Nine days from now."

He considered. "It is a long time," he said. "You will come sooner."

"How about I come back in five days and then again in nine? That time I told you about, when something bad happens, is in nine days. I want to come by and make sure you are safe that day."

He nodded. "That will do."

"What do you want me to bring you from town?" I asked. "Grilled corn?"

His eyes lit up. "Yes. And some for the spirits."

"I can do that."

"I will make us stew."

"You do make a good stew," I agreed.

"Fighting Badger? Josie?" someone asked from the entrance.

I twisted, startled to see the sheriff framed against the lightening sky. Relief trickled through me, followed by unease. He was alarmed, tense, his gaze on Fighting Badger.

"What're you doing here, Josie?" he asked in a hushed voice.

"Talks to Spirits," Fighting Badger corrected him.

"That's right," I seconded, not wanting the serial killer at the back of the cave to get upset. "I have a new name."

"All right, Talks to Spirits." The sheriff nudged his hat back, intent gaze on me. "What're you doing here?"

"The spirits brought her," Fighting Badger answered for me. "Did you bring me anything, brother?"

Brother?

"I did." The sheriff pulled a roll of leather from where it was tucked between his belt and pants. "This one is cherry flavored." He entered the cave and passed Fighting Badger the item. "I need to take Talks to Spirits home."

"Home? She's from …"

I held my finger up over my lips. "Our secret, Fighting Badger, remember? Friends keep secrets?"

He nodded. "Take her home, brother."

The sheriff all but hauled me to my feet and swiftly marched us out of there. The morning was cool and cloudy, the scent of rain in the air. He said nothing until we reached the top of the canyon. Then he spun on me and took my arms, glaring down at me.

"Do you have any idea how stupid that was?" he demanded.

My eyes blurred, and I nodded.

"Fighting Badger has … a problem. He's isolated for a reason. No one who goes to his cave comes out alive."

"I did." I swallowed hard and struggled to regain my composure. "We have something … in common." Wired and scared after the long night, I wasn't able to stop the tears. I covered my face with my hands, relieved to be free yet horrified by the experience.

The sheriff released me. "Miss Josie, please don't cry. I didn't mean to scare you. You don't have any idea what I'm talking about."

"But I do." I wiped my face and met his mint green gaze. "I know you hide him, I know he kills people and collects their spirits. I know one of his brothers fell from the sky the same way I did."

"How can you know this?" His look sharpened.

"Because I do. And right now, I need a hug."

His expression went from searing to uncertain. "From me?"

"Do you see anyone else out here?" If I wasn't so freaked out, I'd have laughed. As it was, I closed the distance between us and wrapped my arms around his lean frame. His scent, familiar in its own odd way, and the heat of his body brought me back from the scared place in my mind. I didn't try to stop the tears; they weren't going to leave me alone until I released them.

The sheriff hugged me against his hard form. "There's something special about you if you're still alive," he murmured against my temple.

You have no idea. The shakes and tears stopped soon after they started. "Good thing you're always around to rescue me," I joked weakly and lifted my head to see his face.

"I think you rescued yourself this time, Miss Josie." He offered a small smile. There was warmth in his gorgeous eyes for the first time since I met him. "You need to stop wandering off." Almost absently, he brushed tears from my cheeks with his thumb.

"I can take care of myself." Though I secretly did enjoy the feel of his strong embrace.

"You survived my brother." His grip tightened around me. "Josie, you need to be careful here."

"What do you mean?"

"I think you know."

Pressed against him, with the sense of familiarity hanging in the air between us, it was almost impossible for someone like me to lie. "Have we met before?" I asked instead. "Why do you seem to know me?"

"We haven't."

I waited for him to say more and strained to read him the way I could everyone else. The chip wasn't able to process anything about him. The silence stretched as we gazed at one another, a familiar tension stirring. This one I recognized – attraction, if not interest – but didn't want to.

This man was little better than Fighting Badger. The sheriff killed someone every Saturday at noon to the tune of a block party I wasn't about to attend.

"I better get home," I murmured.

He released me. "I apologize if my brother scared you, ma'am."

"Brother. Can you explain that?"

"I was adopted at an early age by the mother of Running Bear and Fighting Badger."

"So you fell from the sky."

The sheriff tensed. "That reminds me. We never finished our conversation about where you went for the year you were missing."

"We probably never will." I flashed him a smile. "Unless you want people in general knowing about your brother and his friends."

"Are you threatening me, ma'am?"

"Why yes, Sheriff, I think I am."

He studied me, amusement in his bright gaze. "I'll keep that in mind the next time you need rescuing."

"I told you. I can take care of myself." *For the most part, anyway.*

I strode to my horse.

"Maybe you can right now, Miss Josie. But one day, someone like you is going to find her way into a problem she can't get out of. I'm likely the person who can help you."

I paused. Sometimes, I got the feeling we were talking around something we both know but were unwilling to bring out into daylight, like time traveling or psychopathic family members. I didn't quite know how to respond. Carter had said the sheriff was dangerous without specifying why or how. Whenever we met, I had the urge to leave too quickly to uncover whatever it was Carter wanted.

In hindsight, I should've asked Cater many more questions about this two-week *vacation*.

"Are you saying you'll hang me out to dry?" I asked and mounted the horse.

"I'm saying, there's a give and take to the world, ma'am. If you need my help again, it won't be free."

"Then I'll make sure not to need your help again." A little tired and rattled from the night, I was anxious to put as much distance as possible between me and the cave with the crazy man. "Have a good day, Sheriff."

His arms were crossed. Unruffled, he was nonetheless unhappy. I didn't want anything to do with him, but I was also relieved that his quiet strength stood between the madman below and me.

I wheeled the horse and bolted back the way I came from, determined to make it home before Nell awoke and had a meltdown. The night didn't seem so scary in the full light of morning, though I wasn't able to purge the shadowy images I had seen in Fighting Badger's mind.

I had never met someone like him, and it disturbed me on too many levels for me to define. Pity, fear, shock ... I intended to keep my promise to return and visit him, because a small part of me wanted to think there was some good in every person I met, including Fighting Badger.

Even Philip, the cousin who was headed to my house to visit today. I didn't know who was worse: a man with the mind of a ten-year-old who killed people so he had friends or a rapist aware of what he did.

At least I have Nell and John. They were good people, through and through.

Chapter Seven

THE HOUSE WAS BEGINNING TO WAKE UP WHEN I SNEAKED BACK in. I barely made it to my room, pushed off my boots and riding habit and checked my phone for messages when Nell knocked on the door.

"Just a minute!" I yelled. Without changing out of the clothes I'd left in, I scrambled to jump under the covers of my bed.

Nell opened the door and glanced around. Ever the astute nanny, she noticed the boots in a place other than where she left them and raised an eyebrow at me.

My mind raced. "Okay. You caught me," I said. "I was, uh, trying to dress myself." Tucking the phone under my pillow, I flung off the blankets and stood.

"I see." Nell frowned. "It's clear you need my help." Without another word, she opened the door to the dressing room. "Would you care for a bath, Miss Josie?"

I snorted. I was beat and tired from the long night. "That sounds divine."

"Very well. I will prepare it for you. Breakfast will be in the parlor with your father and cousin. The storm didn't scare him off, unfortunately."

Storm? I went to the window. In a matter of ten minutes, the brisk wind had pushed in a line of clouds that were devouring the sky. "Great. So he'll be here all day," I muttered.

I retrieved my phone. The sound of running bath water came from the dressing room, and I put my back towards the direction where Nell was to check my messages. Carter had sent back long responses, though his first was the one with all the emojis.

TWINS?! That's not a part of my planning or research everywhere! Do you know how rare it is for ...

"Yadda, yadda." I scanned his rant about Native Americans and twin stats to find something interesting.

Starmen sounds like a video game. If your emo-radar went off and people glowed then yes, you found the right guys who are the catalysts, those who change history. You need to get close to the twins and Taylor to find out what their plans are.

"Shit." I chewed on my lower lip. I texted him back. *Slight problem. Two of them hate me and one might be a serial killer.*

In all his texts, Carter said nothing about the three girls. Which meant it was probably important if he was avoiding it. I asked him again about them, and his answer made me shiver.

There may have been others before you. Not a yes or no, but a definite sign he'd deceived me. *Serial killer?! Okay, I definitely need to do some research.*

"Why did you lie to me, Carter?" I whispered. I didn't ask him, troubled. This seemed like more than the usual oversight or side effect of his odd personality. The dark sense stirred again, one I took to originate from the empathic memory chip.

One that told me Carter was hiding much more than this.

"Miss Josephine!" The sound of Nell shuffling around in the anteroom made me think the bath I had heard about was ready.

I took my phone, going to the doorway. To my delight, the water was clear and steaming. I pulled off the clothes I'd put on last night to hop into the water. *Oh, god this feels like heaven!* I hissed at the heat and buried the phone beneath my shift on the nearby chair, aware of how Nell viewed the devil's box.

My mind was tired – but wired with energy. I wanted to know more about those who came before me, about Running Bear and Fighting Badger and how the sheriff was connected to everything.

"You awoke early," Nell said.

"Yes. Nell, can we visit the Indians today?" I asked.

"Of course not."

"That's what I thought." Puzzled how I was going to find Running Bear, who bore a potentially dangerous grudge, let alone talk him and his brother out of slaughtering people, I leaned back. The one idea that surfaced: telling their chief, who seemed to want peace, if John was to be believed. But I couldn't do that, either, with Nell dogging my every step. "How is Father this morning?"

"Well. Happy." Nell's expression softened.

"Good." I smiled. "What are we doing today? Another trip to town?"

"Heavens no. Even if the storm wasn't coming, your father had five marriage proposals on his desk this morning," Nell said.

"No one asked me."

"Why would they?" Nell raised an eyebrow. "It's your father's responsibility to choose a good husband for you."

That's just so wrong. "Do the Indians or half-Indians have arranged marriages?"

"Josie, dear, please. You should not be thinking of them or talking about them." As if to emphasize her point, Nell grabbed a brush with thick bristles and began scrubbing my back.

"Ow," I muttered. "That looks like it should be used on a horse."

"You are one odd girl."

I rolled my eyes and bore through the bath, robbed of any chance to enjoy it by Nell's ministrations.

An hour later, I was dressed and waiting for Nell to tell me what was on our schedule. When my nanny didn't immediately return, my gaze fell to the sheep, visible out the open windows. Most had been herded into a corral or the smallest of the many barns by farm hands. The sky was gray but not yet raining, the wind loud and brisk.

I always wanted animals. John had tons of horses and sheep. Curious to explore my temporary home and avoid Philip as long as possible, I left my room without waiting for Nell and strode out of the house. Several farm hands were out, preparing the property for the storm. Shutters were closed, buggies rolled into the massive carriage house, canvas tarps thrown over hay and other items that might fly away, and the wells covered. Most of the animals present were huddled together or being led into barns.

I watched the efficient, quick preparations that told me they were used to storms here and entered the horse barn. All the stalls were filled, and half the barn was roped off to form a makeshift corral for additional horses.

The horse I borrowed was eating and came to the stall door when I approached. I reached out to rub his forehead. "Thanks for not telling anyone about our escape last night," I murmured.

Smiling, I stroked the smooth hair of its jaw and soft skin of its muzzle. It blew out its nostrils in response, ears flickering.

Anxious to visit the sheep before Nell found me, I left the barn and walked around it to reach the large pen with goats and sheep, pausing to observe what looked like an old well. The waist-high stone circle was boarded up and sat among piles of loose straw that had been recently tarped down.

An odd memory flickered, less of a vision and more of an instinct, the strange sense of knowing that plagued me at Fighting Badger's cave. There was history to the old well, and not a good one, if my enhanced memory was to be believed.

I forgot to ask Carter how I can read dead people and places, I thought absently.

I leaned over the stone, trying to see through the cracks between boards into the depths of the well. Wind pushed me aside and I gripped the boards, testing them. Some appeared old and cracked, the nails holding them in place rusted. Others, however, looked newer, if weathered. I rested a hand on the newer ones, trying to capture the whisper I heard from the well.

There was more than one, I realized with some puzzlement. Unlike Fighting Badger's cave, where the whispers came from different places, these were all centered at the bottom of the well.

One ... two ... three. Three distinct, if fuzzy, images.

"You found Fighting Badger. Running Bear told me not an hour ago that you knew about my uncle's illness. How is this possible, Josie Jackson?"

I whirled. The man I least expected to see stood near a stack of hay. The sheriff was edgy, his intense gaze on me. It was a difference from earlier, when he'd almost been friendly while comforting me.

"My cousin Philip is here." I warned him with a quick glance towards the barn and the house beyond. "I get the feeling you two don't get along."

The sheriff shrugged. Undeterred, he moved towards me, bringing with him the intensity of a man not about to leave until he had his answers. Any ground I thought I'd made with him was gone.

"Who is your uncle, and why do you think I know anything about him?" I asked, confused. I eased away to put the well between us, once more racking my brain for any memories, images or feelings that could be attributed to him.

All I heard was the whispering from the well.

"Running Bear told me what you told him," the sheriff said with tried patience. "His uncle is my uncle."

"Ah. Right," I said. I hadn't thought once about what to say if someone called me on my strange knowledge. "Well … was I right?"

"You know you were."

"Oh." I looked away. "I overheard my father mention it."

"No one knew. Even his children." The sheriff was circling the well again. "And *you* are a terrible liar."

Dammit. I started to retreat. His pace quickened, and he reached across the well, snatching my arm. Holding me in place, he circled the well. His grip was tight without being painful, but it was the fire burning in his green eyes that unnerved me.

"You're scaring me a little right now," I murmured.

"What exactly are you doing here, Josie?" With his lean body and his unexpected, visible anger, I didn't want to push him.

How was I supposed to take that question? Was he asking why I was behind the barn – or why I was sent back in time? Because I had the sense again he knew exactly who I was, as impossible as it seemed.

"If you're threatening my family, there is no limit to what I will do to you." He regarded like he was considering dropping me into the depths of the well.

Like the others.

The faint memories of this place were getting stronger.

That can't be good. What if Carter cranked up the juice too much on the chip in my brain, and I started communicating regularly with inanimate objects as well as people?

Sheriff Hansen moved closer again. Not liking the expression on his face, I hedged.

"Look, I can explain everything," I said, wetting my lips

nervously. "I wasn't threatening your family. I didn't even know they were your family until you told me!"

"Then speak," he ordered.

"I, um … first, can I ask you what happened the night you found me?"

The muscles in his jaw ticked. *Definitely not the right time.*

"The truth is I can't tell you how I got here or how I know about your uncle. I'm a … uh, victim of circumstances." I focused hard on him to avoid the strange whispering from the well. As before, the sheriff's mind was silent, unwilling to share its secrets with me the way others did. "I don't know anything about you."

My gaze went up to his face again. He was even tenser.

Thunder rumbled in the distance, and the next gust of wind carried sprinkles.

I didn't know what to say in the thick silence. The whispering behind me was really distracting, the man before me probably debating whether or not he'd kill me.

"Do you hear that?" I asked, irritated. I tried to twist in his grip, but he held me in place, moving closer to keep me from moving. The back of my legs hit the stone wall.

"Hear *what?*"

An image flashed, and I froze.

A flash of blonde hair in the moonlight blinding her as she fell into darkness … the form of someone standing over the well, peering into it.

"Breathe." The sheriff's voice reached me.

I was on my knees, clutching at his clothing. One of his arms was around me, holding me against his strong chest. I met his gaze. His steady look soothed me while his full lips and rugged features made desire warm my lower belly.

"I'm okay," I whispered, a little overwhelmed by the spell, coupled with his presence. Blood trickled down my face. Dabbing at it, I sat back to take my weight out of his arms. Helping me one moment, about to kill me the next, I didn't quite understand where I stood with this man.

"This is what happens when a madman puts things in your brain," the sheriff said softly. "You're in over your head, Josie. Whether or not you know it, you need my help."

Did I hear that right? Speechless, I gazed at him.

He said nothing more, simply steadied me with his wide hands on my body.

"Who are you?" I managed at last.

"I could ask you the same," he replied.

"Josephine!" Nell's alarmed cry came from the front of the barn.

"Look, the others eventually sought me out. They knew what you haven't figured out yet, that they were in trouble. When you're ready to talk, come find me, but don't wait too long. You don't *have* too long," the sheriff told me.

All kinds of spidey senses went off in my mind, none of them good.

"The night you found me. You were expecting me, weren't you," I said.

His jaw clenched. For a long moment, his cold stare was his only response. "You are involved in something you cannot possibly hope to escape alive. If any part of you thinks I'm telling the truth, come talk to me."

I shivered. *What the hell is going on?*

"Nell!" he called, standing. "She's here."

I shook my head to clear it and pushed myself to my feet. The sheriff stood back. Nell appeared around the corner and dashed to me.

"My god!" she exclaimed. "Miss Josie, don't you never, ever run off like this again! If I had to tell your father –" She flung her arms around me, almost hysterical.

I listened to her babble, eyes on the silent man watching me. The well was still whispering. There was one way to know what its secret was, but I didn't look forward to digging around for a dead girl.

What to do about the sheriff …

This is what happens when a madman puts things in your brain. How did he know what Carter did to me? More importantly, was my nosebleed a sign of something more than an oncoming sinus infection?

"Miss Josie!"

"I am well," I told her, forcing my attention back to my babysitter. "I got dizzy."

"Dizzy? Again?"

"I'm just tired."

"You need to see the doctor," Nell declared. "Your father and Philip await you for breakfast. After, I'll send for Doctor Green."

"Ugh. Philip," I said with a tired smile. I looked around, not certain if I wanted to invite the sheriff or not. His touch had sent a thrill through me, but he scared me a little. "No doctor, Nell." *He can't help me anyway, if something is wrong with the brain chips.*

"Quiet, child. You need help." Turning to the sheriff, Nell asked politely, "Will you join us, Sheriff Hansen?"

Please say no, I willed him. I didn't feel ready for the talk he wanted to have. I trusted Carter, despite the occasional misgivings I had about him. I didn't know what to think about the sheriff, except that I needed time and space to clear my head.

"Much obliged but no. Give Mr. John my regards," he said. "Tell him we found those missing sheep of his."

"He'll be pleased to hear it."

The sheriff tipped his hat and started the other way around the barn, as if he, too, needed to put distance between us.

I walked with Nell around the barn and entered the house. She accompanied me to the dining parlor, where a small breakfast feast waited.

"You stay here," she said brusquely. "Your father and Philip must be smoking cigars."

I sat and waited until I heard Nell's footsteps fade before I pulled my cell free.

What if someone figures out I'm not supposed to be here? Like Taylor Hansen?

I waited, listening for the sound of anyone coming.

That's not the kind of change history needs. Carter's response made me roll my eyes. His second message was even less encouraging. *I can't confirm it, but I think he's one of those people I warned you about, who doesn't want history changed. They can be motivated enemies. If you could figure it out, it'd help me decide how to manage him.*

Manage him. It didn't sound like a good thing. I sighed. I wasn't manipulative and had never been a good liar. How, then, did I figure out what I needed from Taylor and determine which twin I needed to be wary of?

I texted Carter again. *I'm having nosebleeds. Is that a side effect?*

Voices came from down the hallway. I watched the text bubble pop up that said Carter was writing a response and urged him silently to hurry.

It is. Not a good one. Anything about the chip's abilities that seems unusual?

"Aside from reading people's memories?" I almost laughed. After a quick hesitation, I answered him. *I can read living people, dead people and places. Is any of that abnormal?*

Not wanting to miss his response, I slid out of the second entrance of the room into the servants' hallway that led to the kitchens.

Yeah, it is. Let me do some research, came his response.

"Research. It's the answer for everything." I nibbled on my lower lip, pensive, and tucked the phone away.

So the sheriff had been correct. The nosebleed wasn't normal.

Did I venture out and talk to him or wait for Carter to do his research? My goal was to save lives, and I wasn't expecting anyone else in this time period to know I was from the future. Carter hard warned me about the sheriff, and now, the sheriff had warned me about Carter.

I was almost too tired to process what all that meant.

If nosebleeds were an issue, could the man in this time help me more than Carter?

And what – or who – was in the well? My stomach churned at the idea of discovering the truth, but I didn't think I could remain here without knowing for sure.

Hearing Philip and John, I darted back into the dining room and sat down at my setting. The men entered, and John's face lit up the way it had yesterday.

I love that. I knew I didn't deserve it, because I wasn't his real daughter, but I let myself wallow in the happiness of knowing I was the center of his attention.

For now. I had a list of things to do after this breakfast and the storm cleared.

Chapter Eight

SEATED AT HIS DESK, TAYLOR LISTENED TO THE STORM BEATING doors, windows and loose planks of wood against the building. He gazed at the ceiling, thoughts burdened by the news he'd learned recently. Fighting Badger had come to him and Running Bear about Josie's visit, but this was not his greatest concern.

His greatest concern sat in front of his desk, newly arrived during the daytime storms and rescued from his steaming crater, the same way Taylor had plucked Josie out of hers.

"I'm retired not dead, Lance," he said at last. "Why did they think you needed to be here?"

"Ripple effect. They're seeing changes that shouldn't be taking place and tracked it to here and now. Lots of activity for such a sleepy little place," Lance replied. With a sharp blue gaze and inability to sit still that reminded Taylor of an undisciplined recruit, the man before him was athletic and wary.

"I got it handled," Taylor said.

"They don't think you do. Besides, you *are* retired. This isn't for you to handle."

Taylor was quiet, aware that whatever he said had to be voiced diplomatically. Pissing off an aggressive man like Lance would only make it harder for him to assess what needed to be done. Lance would shoot first and leave without asking questions. It was the opposite of Taylor's style in handling time travelers like Josie. "I know the place and people. Why not work with me?"

It was Lance's turn to grow pensive.

"I have to live here when you're done. I chose this place for my retirement," Taylor pointed out. "I'd rather not make a mess like you're known for."

Lance flashed a smile. "I'm effective."

"You're sloppy."

"I get the job done. I protect history." Lance shrugged. "Does it matter if it's messy or pretty, if I'm taking care of my business?"

"It matters to me," Taylor said firmly.

"All right, Sheriff." Lance snorted. "We'll work together, unless you get soft and can't pull the trigger."

"Violence isn't the only answer."

"Whatever. What are we dealing with?" Lance shifted forward and rested his elbows on the desktop.

I really hate new agents. Every crop of new time agents was a little more arrogant, a little less respectful of the worlds, times and people they were charged with protecting. "Carter."

Lance's smile faded.

"As usual, there's no way to tell what he wants. He sent back someone too clueless to interrogate."

"The traveler has to know something."

"Carter's smart, Lance. There's a reason he's our number one most wanted." Taylor tapped one of the posters on his wall in emphasis. "The traveler knows only what he told her, like every other traveler he's sent back to different eras. I've interviewed hundreds of them, all with the same story about Carter."

Lance tapped his fingers on the desk. "Her. You've got a soft spot for women, if what I heard is true."

"Old-fashioned respect. I came from an era like this one. My mama beat it into me."

"Well then, I'll pull the trigger for you, old man." Lance smiled.

Taylor gave him a warning look. "Not how I do business, and you won't either, since you're on my territory."

"I'll be good, Sheriff." Lance nudged back the brim of his hat and sat back. "You know, I thought Carter was a myth."

"He's very real. Very active." *And getting more dangerous with the technology that lets Josie speak to spirits the way Fighting Badger does.* Taylor hadn't yet decided how to handle that issue, because it meant Carter had embedded sophisticated technology in her head that his people knew nothing about.

What was stranger: Carter obsessed over advanced technology for the brain but hadn't yet learned how to return his travelers to the future or the times they came from. It had taken Taylor little more than two seconds to assess Josie didn't know she was permanently stuck here, unless his people decided to return her to her time.

"All right. You call the shots. What're we doing?" Lance asked.

"Right now, nothing. Watching."

Lance grimaced. "I'm a man of action not *waiting*."

"Then this will be a lesson for you. Patience."

The shutters slammed against the side of his office loud enough for Lance to jump. Taylor sat still, unconcerned, while the newer agent shifted in his seat.

"We can wait for a few days," Lance allowed. "But if I don't have progress or something to tell them soon, they're threatening to send The Mongol."

Taylor's hands clenched into fists. An agent taken from the Genghis Khan era, The Mongol was wild, unpredictable and strong, a man of unparalleled violence and strength. Their paths had crossed only once, for The Mongol was normally reserved for situations where absolute brute force – and usually a massacre of some size – was all that would save history from the actions of men like Carter.

Josie didn't stand a chance against Lance. She wasn't even a speed bump for The Mongol.

But worse than this was the sense that The Mongol wasn't coming for one life. He never did. He was coming to reset history, to core the source of the ripples they were seeing in the future, and Taylor had an idea of what that meant.

"Then we'll have something to tell them," he said softly.

Chapter Nine

It stormed for three days straight. The worst part wasn't Philip, who pretended to be a half-decent human being in front of John. The worst part was not being able to leave the house. Three days of food, backgammon, cards, war stories by Philip and John, nightmares like that from the first night and vague answers from Carter about what was wrong with my head.

Because there was something. He finally told me that much.

Three days of building anxiety about the well, the sheriff, the days ticking by where I couldn't change history. I was used to the southern California lifestyle. It rarely rained like this and never for more than half a day. I was active all the time, bike riding, walking, yoga in the backyard with my aunt. I found myself doing yoga twice a day in my room during the rainout to keep from going stir crazy.

On the fourth day, the rain stopped at some point before I awoke, and the sun peeked through gray clouds to find its way past my drapes into my room. The familiar patter of rain on the roof was gone, and I rose quickly, excited at the prospect of leaving the house.

Throwing open the drapes, I studied the world outside, forbidding the clouds from opening up again. *Wait until Philip is gone,* I ordered them. The property was muddy. If Nell wanted to go anywhere, it'd be by horseback this day and not the carriage whose wheels would sink into the mud.

"Miss Josie!" Nell's call came from down the hallway. "Come quickly!"

I was halfway to the door before I remembered going out in my nightgown was viewed as scandalous around here. I pulled on a housecoat and my boots and left the cozy bedroom I was starting to like.

The memory, the one from down the hallway that slid into my dreams at night, was more insistent today. Pausing, my gaze flickered to the last door. I'd intended to check it out during our time held hostage by the rain, but Nell managed to keep me busy. When not with Philip and John, I was with John, reading in his study or learning to repair buttons and mend my clothes – a task I did with absolutely no joy or skill whatsoever. My fingertips were sore from how many times I poked them accidentally.

But truth be told, I had time to visit and hadn't wanted to, afraid of what I'd find in the room down the hallway. Afraid it'd make me think ill of John, the man whose love for his daughter only grew brighter and happier the more time we spent together. He was the sunshine of this place. After meeting Philip and Fighting Badger and beginning to doubt Carter, I wanted there to be a ray of sunshine, and I needed it to be the man who could've been my own father in a different place and time.

"Miss Josie!"

"Coming!" Turning away from door down the hallway, I hurried through my wing into the gentlemen's wing, where Philip and John stayed.

Nell was in front of one room and motioned for me to hurry.

I did so, breathless by the time I reached the room that was

John's. I entered the antechamber and trailed Nell into the bedroom, where John lay in bed.

He was pale and wore a dressing gown beneath heavy blankets. The room was hot, the fireplace blazing.

He managed a faint smile. "My Josie," he said, holding out a knobby hand.

"What's wrong? Are you ill?" I asked. I went to his bedside and sank down in a chair, taking his warm hand.

"My body. It is weak," John said. "My heart is happier than ever."

"I sent for the doctor," Nell said. "Your father awoke very unwell, Miss Josie."

Shit. My initial thought, that I'd never leave the house and accomplish my mission, was replaced by deep guilt at the idea of begrudging the man smiling at me the way he was.

"Nell, you are to contact my friends and all my neighbors, including the savages," John called. His and Nell's memories were both of the day real-Josie's mother died in this very bed.

"Is it necessary?" I asked, confused. *Not John.* He was a good man, one I didn't want to see pass away.

Nell said nothing and nodded grimly.

Concerned, I stayed at John's side, listening to his wheezy breathing. The moral dilemma raised its head once more. I didn't really know what to do. It seemed like he deserved the truth about his daughter, but being so weak, I wasn't certain he could take it.

"I am glad I was able to see you again," he said, smiling.

"Don't talk like that, Father," I chided him. "You will be on your tomorrow and the next day … every day," I told him cheerfully.

"I hope so, my daughter. I wish to see you married."

Ugh! How did any self-respecting woman survive this kind of life? "Then you better stay strong and healthy, because it'll be a while."

He chuckled. "So stubborn. Like your mother."

"Nell says I'm stubborn like my father."

"Rightly so," he agreed.

I watched his memories. They shifted to happier times, of the woman he wed thirty years before. His love for her was as strong as his was for me. *I wish I'd known her. I wish he'd been my father.* They weren't the right thoughts for me to be thinking, not when I knew very well I was sent back in time for an important reason.

Yet sitting by John, I couldn't help thinking *this* was where I needed to be at the moment instead of racing around the countryside to find Running Bear.

"Uncle!" Philip's voice drew my attention. He rushed into the room, to John's other side. "What is it? Are you dying?"

"Show some respect, Philip. He's not dying," I snapped.

"Peace, children," John said. "I am dying, but it will not be today. When I am gone, you must care for my Josie, Philip."

"Of course, Uncle."

"Find her a suitable husband."

"I give you my word, John, that I will not allow her to marry any man who would shame the family. I will keep my eyes on her every action."

His statement sent a chill through me.

"Don't you worry about me," I urged and squeezed John's hand. "Worry about staying strong."

"Yes, my sweet Josie." John's eyes closed. His breathing remained steady, if shallow.

Unwilling to deal with Philip, I stayed at the side of my adopted father. Philip left a few minutes after John fell asleep. I studied John's haggard face, surprised by the intensity of the pang of longing that went through me.

What would it have been like to have a father as good as real-Josie's?

I frowned and ran my thumb over the loose, wrinkly skin of his hand. Checking my phone, I sent Carter a quick note to let him know I hadn't had any nosebleeds yet today. His response was fast.

Good. I almost have a solution.

Impressed by the genius, my doubt about him – triggered by my last interaction with the sheriff – was once more called into question. I hated overthinking anything. I would rather trust my intuition and my faith in humanity, but it was really hard to determine what was going on here. After the three days trapped in the house, I was restless for answers, to find what was in the bottom of the well, to talk to the Native American twins and uncover what the catalyzing event was that I was here to prevent.

Hell, I'd talk to Fighting Badger again, if it meant I learned something new.

But mostly, the same instinct that didn't want me doubting Carter also wanted me to talk to the sheriff, the sole person here who seemed to know something I really needed to. *If only he didn't hang people at the drop of a hat …*

"Miss Josie," a man said, entering.

I looked up. He was middle-aged, slender, and dressed in black, carrying a black bag. He rested the bag on the bed beside John and touched John's face.

"Doctor Green," I said, glancing at Nell. "What is wrong with my father?"

"His health has been declining for months now."

"But why?"

"His heart is bad."

His heart is so good. I almost said something but stopped.

The doctor checked John's heartbeat. Philip paced in the doorway, and Nell wrung her hands nearby.

"He's resting peacefully," the doctor said finally. "He will need more sleep. He should not leave his bed, unless necessary. Philip, may I speak to you?"

I watched the two men step into the hallway. The doctor spoke for a few minutes. Philip nodded grimly and motioned for the doctor to follow him out.

"He's not going to make it long, is he?" I whispered, eyes returning to John.

"He may just be tired. He was more active the past several days, since you arrived, than he had been in months," Nell said. "He wanted to go to town today."

There was a note of denial in Nell's tone, one that made me pity her. I was sad, but she was on the verge of being devastated. I wiped my face, compassion for the elderly man and his suffering while also wishing I had had more time to get to know him.

Two-week vacation, I reminded myself. *When I get home, they'll all have been gone for a very long time.* It was an awful idea that the people around me were already dead.

"Cousin," Philip called from the doorway. "A word."

I hated the way he spoke to me but joined him in the hallway.

"The doctor believes your father doesn't have more than a day, maybe two, before his heart gives out." Philips words made my breath catch. "I am gathering what family can make it here within a day. If there are any acquaintances you wish me to contact?" By his doubtful look, he didn't think I knew anyone.

"What of the Indian Chief?" I asked. "They have been neighbors for years and share land."

"A practice I will put an end to when John passes."

"Not if the lands all go to me."

"Cousin," Philip smiled. "Your claim to his property will not stand in court. You have no husband and no real claim, unless you can prove you are his daughter. You disappeared a year ago. The courts will believe a father first, a faithful cousin second."

Anger trickled through me. He was sure of himself, already discrediting my ability to hold onto John's lands. They weren't mine, but the thought of a man like Philip taking over anything of gentle John's made me mad.

It was getting harder to remember that I was here for one reason only: to keep Running Bear or his twin from starting a war. I didn't need the drama of John and real Josephine's life.

But I couldn't help liking John a lot and hating Philip, either.

"We will discuss this when my father is gone. Until then, you will respect my wishes," I told him. "The Indian Chief will be invited here." *If I can't get answers, I'll bring the answers to me.*

Philip's assured smile faded.

I turned my back on him and returned to John's side.

He slept the entire day. I sat beside him, texting Carter when possible, and holding John's hand when Nell or Philip or a servant or other visitor was present. I barely noticed the passage of the day, until someone came in to light the candles and lanterns around the room.

Nell brought me a small dinner. When finished, I rose and went to the fire, body stiff from sitting still all day. I watched the flames, allowing my mind to roam restlessly. No matter what, I had to get some fresh air in the morning, or I'd go crazy. John was too sick for me to go far.

The well – and the woman I saw falling into it – drifted through my thoughts.

It wasn't the real Josie I saw in the distant memory, but it was someone, possibly one of the girls the sheriff had mentioned. I had been about to pry the wood off the top when he appeared. Nell was likely to be too worried about John to hover around me if I stepped out to the barn for some air.

"Josie, you should rest. Tomorrow, the house will be full. You will have to entertain, and I don't know if you're well enough yet," Nell told me primly. "To bed, child."

I didn't roll my eyes like I wanted to and forced a smile. I had too many questions about what was going on around me, and I wasn't able to stop thinking about the well. And … I was more worried about John than I thought I should be.

I went to my room, grateful that Nell didn't follow. Upon entering, I stretched back to untie the girdle and took a deep breath.

The comfortable room was warmed by the fire with light from lanterns giving it a cozy glow. I found myself smiling, liking the bedroom that technically belonged to a stranger.

I went to the jewelry armoire to replace the necklace Nell insisted I wear this day. I went through the drawers, surprised by the amount of jewelry. It was expensive, too, with each necklace, ring and bracelet laden with precious or semi-precious stones. They were all well cared for and polished without even a fingerprint or smudge showing.

I admired them, unable to fathom why a girl who lived with a father like John and jewels this spectacular would ever consider running away, unless the man John wanted her to marry was a real monster.

With a grunt directed towards the bulky clothing, I knelt to reach the drawer at the bottom of the armoire. It was jammed, and for a moment, I wondered if it was just for show. With a hearty jerk, I dislodged it.

It was shallow and empty, except for a cell phone charm that read *Happy Graduation!* in one corner.

I stared at it. "What on earth?" I squeezed my eyes closed then opened them. The flashy, twenty-first century charm clashed with the world I was slowly adapting to.

Unease went through me. I plucked it up and saw it was

connected by a thin wire to something beneath the bottom of the drawer. I pulled it, and the false bottom popped up.

"Three cell phones."

Just like the sheriff said. Three other girls sent to live with John, maybe even for the same reason I was there: to change history. I had wanted to write them off as posers after John's money, until Carter confirmed others might have preceded me. My faith in him was shaken once more, and I hesitated to touch the cells. The whispers were back but too faded for images to form.

There was something wrong about these phones, an instinct, a knowing, a flare of intuition that told me something bad happened to those who owned them.

None of them left. Sheriff Hansen had said.

Three phones. Three whispers at the well ...

Both located on John's property.

No. The man on his deathbed had nothing to do with this. I couldn't even entertain the possibility.

Coldness filled my chest, freezing it. I cocked my head to the side, struggling to decipher what the empathic memories were attempting to convey. The only thing I saw was the same images from down the hallway: shadows, blood, voices, a fire. The energy or memories around the phones were too weak to show me anything.

I touched one phone. The cool metal beneath my fingertips made my dread grow stronger.

"Flip phone," I almost giggled, a little hysterically. The bulkiest cell phone was clearly from the late nineties, while another looked like it was closer to five years old. The third was newer, maybe two years old. The women they belonged to had been taken from different years but sent to this one.

I touched the start button at the bottom of the youngest phone, not expecting its screen to light up.

It did. Like mine, there was no explaining how, given the lack of battery power and signal. There were fragments of a few messages on the front screen from the same contact I had: Carter.

Where are you?????? Read the most recent one. The others sent slivers of panic through me.

No matter what - don't let him know why you're there.

I can't let this happen again. You WILL NOT go to …

I swiped my finger across the screen, alarmed at the idea there was some kind of danger here – one that Carter knew about and was refusing to share with me. To my frustration, the screen was locked by a passcode.

I set it down and reached for the next one. There were two messages on the screen from Carter.

How does he know who you are?

Get out. NOW.

I tried to unlock it but found it passcode protected, too. I picked up the oldest cell phone, certain there was no passcode on it. Its screen was tiny, dim, and cracked beyond repair, a reminder of how far cell phone technology had come in the past twenty years. There was no keypad, just numbers with letters, and a quick examination showed no camera, either.

A crack of lightning startled me. My eyes went to the window. I hadn't been outside all day and was surprised to see the sky still covered with dark clouds after the three days of rain. Lightning rippled through them in the distance, followed by a low grumble of thunder.

Not another storm! A gust of wind tossed the drapes into the air. I rose and crossed to the window, closing it. I watched the sky for a moment, eyes falling to the barn, and I wasn't able to stop the thoughts that formed.

Three phones. Three other women from my time had been in this room. Three voices in the well.

What was going on? I didn't want the truth to be what I was inching towards, that someone in this house had a hand in getting rid of my predecessors.

I returned to the armoire and took a picture of the three phones then carefully replaced them beneath the false bottom. Satisfied it look the same way it had when I found it, I closed the drawer and sat back on my knees.

"Who put you all here?" The questions swirling through my mind took a moment to crystalize. My heart was beating fast.

What danger lurked in the house or nearby town?

I can't let this happen again, Carter had said.

Fear blazed to life within me. Of all the mysteries, this was the one that scared me the most. I could see Philip being in on this but no one else.

I sent Carter the picture I had just taken and a text.

I think you're keeping something important from me. If I'm in danger, I need to know, Carter.

Why not at least warn me?

Thunder drew my gaze towards the barn. I went to the window once more and gazed out.

The whispering I had heard around the phones was too faint, but that around the well was louder. If I couldn't read one, I should be able to read the other. Gripping and releasing my cell phone, I couldn't help thinking I needed to know what – or who – was in the well. I dared not risk waiting until the second storm was over.

The stable hands finished rounding up the horses and secured the barn before trotting towards the servants' wing of the house.

I tucked my phone in a pocket and moved away from the window. Going to my door, I opened it, expecting to find Nell loitering the way she always seemed to be. No one was in the hallway, though I heard the movement of someone in one of the rooms whose door was cracked open.

I crept towards the stairs, cringing when the floorboards creaked beneath my light step. I hurried down the grand staircase, eyes darting around to make sure no one saw me.

The house was brightly lit and quiet. Voices of the visitors from town came from the parlor, and I assumed Nell was with John. The shutters had been drawn on the windows on the main floor, and I hurried to the front door, pulling it open. Stepping out, I closed the door quickly and breathed a sigh of relief that I had made it this far. The wind was strong, though it contained no telltale droplets of moisture that would precede another hard rain.

I took it as a good sign and raced from the house to the barn, pressing myself to the side not visible from the house. I tucked errant hairs caught up in the wind behind my ears. The charged wind was exhilarating, warm and cool swirling around me in a dangerous dance.

Lightning like that from the night I arrived made me look upward, and an instinct wriggled. If I had arrived in a lightning storm, was there some way for me to leave during one, too? Was Carter's weird magic or technology tied to the charge of electricity from lightning?

Why am I thinking about it now? It wasn't the day I was supposed to change things, and yet, with John almost gone and the mystery of the three other girls twisting my insides, I couldn't help wishing I could hop in a car and just go home if things got too bad here.

My phone vibrated in my pocket. I hurried to the back of the barn, where the loose hay had been covered with heavy canvas to keep it from blowing away. Leaning against the back of the barn, I pulled out the cell to read Carter's message.

You're the fifth girl we've sent back to this time. Four of you were supposed to take on the role of John's daughter. The other three identified Taylor and disappeared soon after he realized who they were. It was the first straight answer he'd given me about the others.

"Five girls?" I gasped. There was too much behind his simple explanation for me to know where to start asking questions.

I had found three cell phones. Did that mean another woman was still here somewhere? Or had she been sent from a time with no cell phones?

"Four girls meant to take the place of John's daughter," I repeated, confusion turning to anger.

Do you mean John knows I'm not his daughter?

I pressed send, panic mixing with my anger. I shoved the phone in my pocket, gaze going to the well. Unable to suppress the need to know what happened, I crossed to it and gripped a wood board, yanking at it. A splinter pierced one finger, but the board gave.

The whispering was back. Tossed around by the wind but eerily present, trying to tell me a story I wasn't able to understand.

I leaned over and peered into the well. It was too dark to see anything. I withdrew my cell again and flipped the camera to flash then lowered my arms as far as I could into the well.

I snapped a few pictures. The brilliant flash was almost as bright as the lightning and I winced, hoping not to draw attention from the house.

A crack of thunder almost made me drop my phone. I yanked it back and hastily retreated to the barn wall to get out of the wind.

Carter had responded.

It's possible. He's in the late stages of senility, so he may not understand that. But I don't know what happened to the other girls; I just knew we had to risk sending you back to save lives. Remember - if you don't succeed, a million people die.

His response managed to calm and confound me. Whatever his

reasoning, he was at least being more honest this time, though why he wasn't straight up with me before, I didn't know. I decided to ask a question I should have when this adventure started.

How do I get out of here? I texted next. *Is it through the storm, like I came here?*

I sent the message and then flipped to my photo reel. It contained only the pictures I had taken since arriving. None of those I had of my life were present, and for a moment, I felt a deep sense of loss.

What if I was stuck in the past without anything to remind me of my world?

I blinked away the thoughts. I wasn't about to give up on Carter, my purpose or my belief that there were good people like John and Nell in the world. I forced myself to focus on the pics I had just snapped.

Focusing on them, I stifled a cry. The camera had picked up what I wasn't able to see – but which I could hear through the whispers.

I had found three of the four women Carter sent back.

Chapter Ten

THREE HEADS WERE AT THE BOTTOM OF THE WELL. ONE BONY skull stared up at me, its long blond hair all that identified it as a woman. Another head with long, blonde hair was face down with its skeletal remains covered by a faded blue gown while the third head was off to one side, alone, with no body or clothing or anything identifying about it except for her hair.

Blonde hair. Like mine. Three girls sent back to pretend to be the daughter of a kind but senile man named John. It made sense that they'd all look similar, which meant every girl who came before me ended up murdered at the bottom of the well.

But why and by whom?

"Sheriff?" I whispered hoarsely. He knew or suspected me of being just like the other three. He'd flat out admitted that none of the other girls made it out of the town alive, and he'd been prowling around the well earlier that day.

Had he somehow figured out they were in the past to stop him from the massacre that was coming?

If so, who had put the phones in the armoire? Why did he offer to help me and rescue me the way he had?

I stared at the images, nauseated. The dry well had been filled with dirt to a point, but the fall was still far enough to kill someone if they went in headfirst.

Or were thrown in after being killed elsewhere.

My shock began to wear off, and I sent the image to Carter with a note. *Not totally sure, but I think these are the other three women you sent.*

He had already texted a response to me about leaving.

"*You leave when you succeed in changing history. The plains have a lot of lightening storms this time of year with enough power to send you back,*" I read aloud. "What if someone figures me out and throws me into a well, Carter?" Once again, I was stuck on the idea that there was more than bad communication here, that the darkness I sensed came from my intuition warning me not to trust Carter fully.

My hands shook. There were tears on my cheeks and the image of the girls in the well remained on my screen. I could hardly believe it was real, that I lived a hundred feet away from a well filled with the remains of the women who might've been there for the same reason I was. At least I figured out my danger, though I had no idea which direction it'd come from. Philip was first on my list, followed by the sheriff.

Fighting Badger … but he collected bodies in his cave. He didn't throw them in wells.

A message popped up on my screen.

My god. You need to work fast. We sent you all back to John, because he is in the right location, senile and would accept you without question. I don't know how someone figured out what we were doing. If you can get DNA, we'll confirm if those three are your predecessors. Any idea where the fourth is? She wasn't like you all.

"Really, Carter? DNA?" I replied.

How did he not think that sending back four girls to the same old man wouldn't raise suspicion? That cousin Philip and nanny Nell weren't going to notice when someone unrelated to the family like the sheriff had figured it out?

Um, I'm not crawling down there for DNA samples. I replied. *There's a lightening storm tonight. If I can talk Running Bear out of starting a war, can you bring me home tonight?*

I pushed myself away from the wall. I trotted around the side of the barn, no longer caring how nice John was or how bad the storm was going to get. The Native Americans had said their lands were towards the west, along with the location where I had arrived. I was going to tell their chief about the rampage and then go back to the moldavite and wait for Carter to get me.

Entering the warm barn, I saddled the horse I had borrowed a few days ago and led him out of the barn, mounting after I closed the door. The gown in all its layers was uncomfortable and bulky but thick enough to protect me from the wind.

I oriented myself then urged the horse to go west, towards the road that ran towards town, between John's lands and that of the natives. It was the same direction as Fighting Badger's cave. Though I didn't recall anything in his mind about his village being close, the frequency of his brothers' visits made me think that this general direction was a smart place to start.

I can't do this anymore. It took effort to suppress my growing panic.

The charged wind was growing stiffer, the rumbling thunder closer. I glanced up nervously. If my choice was to brave a storm and be home in my time by morning or stay inside where it was safe until someone threw me in a well, I would brave the storm without question.

But John ... I ached knowing he was dying. Confusion and fear sent my thoughts spiraling down scary paths, and I pushed them away. John was one man. I cared for him, but I needed to fix things. I wasn't going to be the fourth body in the bottom of a well!

I reached the road to town and slowed the horse to a trot, once again orienting myself. It was next to impossible to tell cardinal directions during a storm, but I recalled my trip to Fighting Badger's and kept an eye out for the tree.

I rode along until I found what I sought: the tree followed soon by the red flag atop a hill. It was slanted at an angle, pushed over by the wind.

Veering off the road into the grasslands, I gave the horse its head so it was able to find the best path. Lightning arced across the sky nearby, and I jumped in place, once again suspecting I was either screwed or *screwed* if I didn't finish the mission Carter sent me back to complete.

The horse's pace slowed. I tugged my phone out of my pocket to check for messages.

You can't fix history in one night.

"But we can in a matter of days?" I asked aloud, perplexed. "No more secrets, Carter. Four other girls!" I wasn't able to fathom what he was thinking sending me back after the other girls disappeared. Did he even know what happened before I showed him the picture from the well? And why didn't he come back, if people kept disappearing?

Unless they can only send us one way. The errant thought made me feel sick to my stomach. It was a better explanation for why Carter himself hadn't come back to change history or why he didn't know what happened to the girls.

No. I can't believe that about him. Though I really, really wished I'd had an empathic memory chip when we first met. Had the other girls had this skill? If so, how did they not figure out their danger until it was too late?

Carter had called some of what they did to me experimental. I shivered, horror sinking into me as I realized the enormity of what I'd learned this night.

I couldn't trust Carter. Or the people around me, aside from John and Nell. Whoever had killed the other girls was probably coming after me next, and I had no idea who that was. I had managed to contain the unease about being sent back in time, gloss over what Carter had done because he was my only link to the future. But maybe, he knew about the others, and maybe he lied to me because he was waiting for the same thing to happen to me.

My chest seized so tightly, I hunched over the horse's withers and neck, struggling to breathe.

Three bodies. I had found three bodies and learned that someone was hunting down and killing off misplaced time travelers like me. Carter knew.

I just have to change history, I told myself over and over. *Carter won't screw you over.* I wanted to believe it so much. I felt connected to Carter from the moment we met, and it wasn't a *bad* feeling.

I sat up and released a measured breath. "I can do this. I am Clara Oswald from Doctor Who. I can fix things and go home to my school loans, mochas and yoga class."

My heart hurt when I thought of John, a man who only wanted his daughter back and had been duped so far by four women. I wished I were able to interpret my enhanced instincts better to determine what happened to the girls at the bottom of the well. Did someone else pity the old man and was killing off imposter daughters to protect him? Or did someone know the other girls and I were from a different time?

I began to calm. It seemed much more logical that someone like Philip – who wanted John's money – was behind all this than some time-traveling-murderer Carter failed to mention when he sent me back. I had a strong weapon I would be able to use to protect myself in the form of the empathic memories. I was able to read Philip's memories and would know when I was in danger. I would see him coming.

But the sheriff ... I couldn't read him. How awful would it be to be sent back in time to die alone? Had he tortured the others to learn their secrets? And who put their cell phones in the armoire?

My imagination grew darker, and I suppressed it. I couldn't believe everyone around me was bad. Some of this had to be explainable ...

Maybe. Without real answers, I was going to drive myself crazy.

Thunder and lightning made the horse toss its head and whinny nervously. A spatter of rain hit me, and I realized we'd need to reach the Native Americans' village soon if I didn't want to end up drenched.

I pushed the horse into a smooth canter, squinting to see anything in the darkness that might indicate I was headed in the right direction. Thus far, no lanterns, fires or other light sources pierced the dark night.

Better to die out here than in a well. I swallowed back tears, beyond confused about what to think or do with what I had learned. The only thing that made sense was the reasoning behind my journey: to change history.

Lightning stabbed the ground too close for comfort. The horse reared, and I hung on for dear life. It dropped to the ground and bucked, unhappy about the storm.

I rubbed its neck to try to calm it then raised up as far as I was able to go to see our surroundings.

There was no sign I was headed anywhere but into the middle of the grasslands.

The horse nickered in greeting, and I sat, glancing in the

direction of its head. I looked back, startled to see the forms of two men melting out of the grassy surroundings. One moved forward to hold the horse's head.

"You are lost," he said.

A flash of lightning revealed a native with a silver stripe in his hair. He was comforting my horse.

"I'm not lost," I replied. "I'm here to see your Chief."

One of his eyebrows went up, and he glanced at the man beside him.

"You come alone, in a storm, to trespass on lands that are not yours." This voice I knew as well, the low growl of Running Bear. I cringed inside, wishing we had a better relationship, especially since I was going to rat him and his brother out.

"It's important," I said. "Can I talk to him?"

A memory floated past me followed by another encyclopedic account of the natives. The images in my mind were a mini-history lesson about the Choctaw, a matrilineal culture. When his uncle died, the next man to marry his aunt, who bore the noble blood, would become chief. He was with one of the men who was next in line and debating how to handle my request.

Interesting. On one side of the road, I can't own land because I'm a woman. On the other, only women can own land.

There was a silence, and I suspected I had caught the warriors off guard.

"Or I can stay here and get hit by lightning," I added. "My father might not be happy about that, though."

"Are you a fool or crazy?" Running Bear asked finally.

"Right now, both. It's been an awful day."

The man with the silver stripe chuckled. "Take her, Running Bear. From what you have said, this girl is a lost sheep like those her father lets graze on our lands. I am almost curious what she will ask of us."

"She cannot be trusted, no matter how much you pity this lost sheep," Running Bear warned. He approached and gripped the reins of my horse, yanking them from my hands.

"Tell me what happens," the man with the silver stripe said, amused.

I focused on the empathic memories to distract myself from the lightning striking too close for comfort.

Running Bear, too, was curious but wary where his companion had been relatively unconcerned about the foolish white girl with the blue eyes. His thoughts went to his cousin, the sheriff, and I leaned forward, interested to get a glimpse into the life of the man I suspected was hiding a great deal without any idea of what that could be.

Running Bear was thinking of how the two of them grew up, one outside the family and one inside, but with similar interests. As I watched, I saw the other three women. All blondes with strikingly similar features to mine, intelligence in their gazes and …

Fear. They'd all been afraid of something in this time period. In each of the scenes, the sheriff was with them, in town, and they were scared. The images were too hazy and unclear for me to tell for certain what was going on.

Could he have killed them? I shifted uncomfortably on the horse, beginning to think it was a bad idea to accompany the sheriff's brother anywhere, let alone on a stormy night when no one knew to look for me. There was too much I didn't know about the sheriff to want to trust him and yet, the same sense I had about Carter upon meeting him, that we were friends in another life or linked somehow, I experienced with the sheriff as well.

"I met your brother," I said.

"He told me he renamed you." Running Bear's voice was tight.

"What's wrong with him?" I asked.

"Can you tell me?"

"Not really."

"He said you could see his mind."

"Yeah." I frowned, disturbed when I considered what I had seen. "He's done horrible things. I can't stop thinking about him."

"He talks to spirits, too."

I glanced towards him. It wasn't possible to see his expression from this angle. Did he think I was crazy, too? "You and the sheriff are kind to take care of him."

"He is my brother."

Lightning shattered the sky above, and I jerked.

"It's like the lightning from the night I came, isn't it?" I asked uneasily.

"Yes. It will strike the trees before us," Running Bear told me over his shoulder. "The wind is what you should fear."

I saw his memories. He'd witnessed the meteor blaze across the sky, a different sort of brilliant fire than the lightning that night and followed it with the other members of his hunting party. He didn't see what happened when it hit, but when they reached the crater, he saw me, curled up in the middle, shaking.

"Oh," I whispered, distressed by the image. "That night … you found me in the crater."

"You were fortunate to survive the lightning."

I said nothing, aware the explanation that I had traveled from the future would only make him warier.

"Why do you wish to see my uncle?" he asked with a note that told me I better answer carefully.

"My father is ill. The doctor doesn't believe he'll survive the week," I replied. "Father asked that your uncle comes to visit him before he's gone. I thought *I* should invite him personally instead of sending Philip."

"Philip is not like your father."

"No," I agreed.

"This could not wait for tomorrow? Or the skies to clear?"

I shifted on the horseback.

"You came for a different reason," he assessed.

"Something bad is going to happen," I said vaguely. "I want to warn your chief."

"What?" The edge in his voice grew sharper.

Shit. I happened to be with a man who believed me to be dangerous rather than foolish. I sorted through his memories, realizing he still thought I was threatening his chief.

"I mean no harm," I said quickly. "The threat doesn't come from me, and it's not directed at your family."

Lightning cracked once more overhead. This time, it was accompanied by a gust of wind and a sudden sheet of cold rain. I closed my eyes to the onslaught, irked by how fast the raindrops soaked my thick dress.

"What danger comes?" he asked.

Even with the wind wailing in my ears, I was able to determine just how serious he was about me answering the question. His thoughts weren't on taking me to his village but holding me hostage until I broke down and told him. And there was something else. Someone else …

A cave in a canyon, too dark to see into, one he was trying hard not to think about.

"No!" I cried. "You are *not* taking me to your brother!"

"Give me a reason not to, Talks to Spirits."

My heart was pounding louder than the grumbling thunder. "Okay. I'll tell you. You're going to think I'm crazy, though."

"We have passed that point."

I rolled my eyes. "When your chief passes in four days, you or your brother will begin to commit violence and raids. This leads to the eventual deaths of almost a million people over the next hundred years." My brow furrowed. The image was of him being there and then not. The technology in my head was once more unable to tell any difference between him and his brother.

He was silent and I sensed, shocked.

"Whatever happens that day, it is the beginning of a war, one that ends with all the Indian tribes being nearly destroyed."

"It is not possible for anyone to know this."

"But I do." I told him firmly. "So, I want to talk to your uncle and tell him. He is like my father and believes in peace. Maybe he will be able to stop this before it starts."

His memories were sorrowful and angry, on his murdered family once more. He had issues for sure, but I wasn't able to tell if they were enough to motivate him to act or if the threat really came from his brother. The images in my head were inconsistent once again.

"Do you really think killing innocent people makes what you went through right?" I asked, testing him.

He was silent for a long moment, guiding the horse. I held my breath and worked on stopping my shivering.

"You were right. You are a fool and you are crazy. No one, even my uncle, will listen to your words," he said finally. "Fighting Badger told me what you told him. I thought him speaking out of madness, but it is *you* who speaks out of madness."

Ugh. I hate being compared to a psychopath. I didn't have much of a defense. Speaking to spirits, coming from the future … I sounded worse than his brother.

"It is a shame."

"What is?" I asked.

"My brother likes you. You made him feel less alone. When you were with him, he said he did not have to struggle against who he was. He did not want to hurt you the way he does everyone else. But you … you are too mad even for him, Talks to Spirits."

I hated that I pitied Fighting Badger. Knowing what he'd done, I still didn't want him to be in the pain he was in. The idea that I helped, even though he terrified me, soothed the part of me that was still ruffled from the visit.

"Are you taking me to him?" I asked, unable to tell what direction we went in the storm.

"No."

"Then where are we going?"

"Somewhere safe for you and my people."

I swallowed hard. His memories were in turmoil, as if he, too, was worried. His mind had flickered to the death of family but remained on his brother. No matter what Carter wanted me to believe, Running Bear wasn't the man who caused the violence I saw.

"You think your brother capable of starting this war, don't you?" I asked, holding onto the sliver of hope that the future was going to be easy to change, if not through their chief, then maybe with Running Bear's help.

"I don't know."

He led me through the prairielands as the storm's intensity built. His thoughts were too jumbled for me to determine his intentions; they flew too quickly for me to pay attention when I was worried about the encroaching lightning.

We walked for a solid hour in the rain. He showed no sign of cold or slowing, while I shivered and hunched next to the horse's neck for warmth. Only when I was too soaked and cold to feel my nose and cheeks did I notice we were approaching a cabin at the base of a hill. The faint, yellow glow of fire and lanterns almost made me groan. As we neared, I made out the shape of a large barn and fence posts of a corral. The property was far smaller than John's.

Running Bear led me to the cabin and draped the horse's reins around the post of the porch. He stood back and motioned me to dismount.

Through the window, I saw a fire blazing in the hearth. Needing no additional encouragement, I slid off the horse and made my way on wobbly feet to the front door.

The door opened before I was able to knock, and I froze. *Oh, god. Not you!*

Chapter Eleven

SHERIFF HANSEN STOOD IN THE DOORWAY, SHOTGUN RESTING against one shoulder. He was shirtless and dressed in pants that hung low on his hips, as if he'd been sleeping when he heard us approach. I stared at his lean chest and his chiseled abs, his wiry form molded from physical labor.

Wow. He was even better looking without clothes.

And then it clicked whom I was staring at. "Sorry. Wrong number," I said and backed away, not about to get stuck with the man who was a suspect in the deaths of the girls who came before me.

Running Bear blocked my path.

"Hold on," the sheriff said and reached out, taking my arm. "What are you doing out in this storm?" His green eyes swept over my features and down my soaked clothing.

"Nothing. Lost. But I figured it out," I stammered, eyes on the way his shoulder muscles moved.

"Let her tell you why she wanted to see our uncle," Running Bear said with a trace of amusement.

I gave a noisy sigh.

"C'mon. You're soaked." The sheriff pulled me into the cabin.

"You need shelter, brother?" he asked the native standing on the porch.

A clap of thunder rendered his response inaudible to me, though the sheriff seemed to hear it. He chuckled and closed the door behind me.

Not my best day ever. I moved away from him towards the fire. Too aware of his uncanny knowledge of me and the shotgun he held, I spoke before filtering my words. "You won't kill me, right?" Not that it made a difference. I was too cold to run if he said yes. My teeth chattered, and I inched closer to the fire.

"Hadn't planned on it," he replied, setting the shotgun by the door. "Running Bear find you or you find him?"

"A little of both."

"He's always draggin' stragglers here." He studied me for a moment before shaking his head. "I guess this gives us a chance to have that talk we need to have." He snatched a loose cotton shirt from the back of a chair and tugged it on, hiding the expanse of skin and lean muscle.

I knelt beside the fire, unable to feel my fingers or toes. I was in no shape to run, not with half my body frozen and the dress weighing me down. I debated silently what to say. Without turning my back to him, I got as close as possible to the fire and didn't start to relax until the heat had sunk into my skin.

"You want a change of clothes?" the sheriff asked.

There it was again. Near-concern. It contrasted greatly with his determination to talk to me and the threats of throwing me in prison until I did. "You keep gowns here?" I replied skeptically.

Amusement flickered across his chiseled features. "No, but you can wear my clothes while we dry yours."

After a brief hesitation, I nodded. He rose and disappeared into one doorway, through which I saw a single lantern burning, returning a moment later with folded clothing.

I took it and went into the room. It was a bedroom, tiny enough that my knees bumped the bed when I closed the door to change. The bedding was rumpled, a simple dresser along one wall, and a washbasin and pitcher on a table in a corner. His clothing was soft and well worn, patched and stitched several times with skill that defied mine after three days of Nell trying to teach me.

There was no sign of wealth in his humble home, and I tugged on the clothes with a silent vow to return the worn trousers and baggy shirt, because he didn't seem to have much of anything.

Unless he murders me. Then all bets are off. I sighed. He was quiet and intense – but not dangerous, especially since I knew the secret he and Running Bear hid in a cave. Yet I wasn't able to figure out what he wanted, how he seemed to know what he shouldn't, why Running Bear had memories of the sheriff with each of the three women Carter sent back.

My movements slowed as I dwelled on the images from Running Bear's mind. I was overthinking again, starting to stress about the unknown. It did me no good to dwell on it but was really hard to let go of.

I gathered my dress and returned to the main room of the small abode.

"Hang it there." He pointed to a rope strung across the cabin on one side.

I did so and faced him. My feet were cold, a chill working its way around my ankles.

His gaze lingered on me. I didn't know how to read the look and wished I had been able to access his empathic memories.

"What're you doing out in this storm, Miss Josie?" he asked with tested politeness that told me he already suspected something.

"My father is dying, and I came to –"

"You can't lie to me."

I resisted the urge to roll my eyes and returned to the hearth. He followed me with his gaze, and I found myself wishing he'd take off his shirt again. After a long moment of flustered, flurried thought, I sighed. "Are you gonna hang me?"

"Hang you?" he echoed. "You have a strange notion about me, Miss Josie." His brow furrowed, as if he was trying to figure me out. "Though I reckon you're safe so long as you keep my secret about Fighting Badger."

"Great."

"Are you going to avoid telling me the truth all night?"

I regarded him longer than I probably should have. There was something captivating about his native skin and brilliant eyes, the planed features and intelligence behind his questions that left me feeling both skewered and safe. "I found the other three girls," I said softly and watched for his reaction.

"Found?" he leaned forward, elbows on his knees. "What do you mean, *found*? Where are they?"

"They're kinda dead."

He frowned.

"Well, not kinda. They *are* dead." The words were hard to say. For once, I wished to experience the sense of being disconnected, so I could talk about them without my throat tightening and my stomach churning. With the sheriff, I never felt that disconnect. If anything, he grounded me.

"How do you know?" His intensity and curiosity were too strong for him to be faking.

"Their bodies are in the well behind the horse barn," I replied.

"And you found them how?"

"I'm not called Talks to Spirits for nothing," I joked weakly.

He tilted his head, unconvinced. It sounded ridiculous to my ears, too, but it was true, a matter of technology rather than the supernatural.

"Someone killed them," I added. "I've been trying to figure out if I'm next."

"So you ran away tonight."

"Not … well …" I debated telling him more. "Who are you, Taylor?"

"Just the local law."

"Bullshit!"

He smiled faintly. "Miss Josie, now may not be the right time for that."

"How so? You've been trying to corner me since I got here to talk. Why not now?"

"I didn't murder the others, but there's a chance I might kill *you*, if what you're doing here is … dangerous."

That's not good. We were talking around something again with neither of us wanting to be the first to crack. "It sounds weird, but … I don't think you'll hurt me. I don't know why." I sensed something … not a memory, not a whisper but an instinct, one I barely picked up. It was … warm. Cheerful. "You won't." I shivered. My wet hair was soaking through the shirt I borrowed from him.

"How sure are you?" he asked. He passed me a blanket, and I wrapped myself in it with a grateful sigh.

"*This* sure." I nodded to the blanket. "You talk mean, but your actions are very different."

"It's the Choctaw side of me."

Another charged silence fell. We gazed at one another.

"So if neither of us wants to talk about who we are and why we're here, then what do we talk about?" I asked.

"Fighting Badger told us why you claim to be here."

Never trust a psychopath. "It was a … dream," I lied.

"Tell me about this dream." He was amused again, calling my bluff.

I hesitated, debating internally. I needed help to figure out my purpose and yet, the sheriff had too many secrets for me to feel comfortable telling him everything. That said, he was also in a position to influence the twins that were confusing my brain chips.

"I had a … dream," I started. "Your twin brothers start a war that ends in the deaths of a million people. I meant to go to the chief of your tribe, so I could warn him about this dream." The explanation sounded lame to my ears, but he was listening closely.

"You want to warn my uncle that my brothers are going to start a war?" he repeated.

"Yes."

"Why would they do that?"

"I'm not sure. Something happens in a few days."

The *ah-ha* look on his face made me think I said too much. He sat back. "And you thought the chief could ensure it doesn't happen."

I shrugged. "I thought maybe he could convince them not to do something stupid before he dies."

The sheriff raised an eyebrow.

"I mean … not that he *will* die in four days, just that …" I was digging a hole, unable to stop beneath the gorgeous gaze focused on me. "Did I mention you've got a great body?" *Good deflection, Josie.*

"You're a might bit touched," he said and shook his head.

"But you do."

The sheriff ran a hand through his hair and hesitated, as if uncertain how to react.

Intrigued by the brief extinguishing of his quiet confidence, I began to suspect something else about him that never before crossed my mind. His discomfort touching me, his attempt to keep distance between us … "Do you go out with women much?" I asked.

"No. Why?"

"You like me."

His eyebrows shot up.

I laughed. "You do, don't you?"

"If this is your attempt to derail this discussion, Miss Josie, I – "

"Admit it and I'll tell you something you want to know!" I teased, sensing a new way to keep him disarmed around me.

The sheriff glared at me. "I find you a might bit attractive, yes."

"Okay." I didn't know why it was a triumph, but any give from the sexy, hardened cowboy before me was a victory. "My dream is real. Something bad is going to happen."

He waited.

"Fighting Badger is right. I can talk to spirits the way he can," I added, good humor fading as I thought of the disturbed man in the cave. "I can read him. I'm … torn between pity and horror. His mind is nothing but shadows and turmoil and pain unlike anything I've ever seen before. But he hurts people …"

"Then he is not mad. Or maybe, both of you are," the sheriff murmured. I heard his concern and troubled affection for the man. His look of consternation shifted to me. "You rode out in a lightning storm because of this … dream."

"And finding the bodies of the girls who came before me." This time when I shivered, coldness had nothing to do with it. "You know, before I came here, I …" I stopped, hearing my words.

He was listening too intently.

"Never mind," I whispered.

"Keep talking, Miss Josie. We're finally getting somewhere."

It was my turn to be in the hot seat. Racking my mind for a way to keep from being cornered by the persistent man, I retorted, "Take off your shirt, and I might!"

"That wouldn't be appropriate, Miss Josie."

I almost laughed at the Nell-like response, entertained by the repressed sexuality of a man who would have no trouble lining up baby-mamas and one-night stands in my time. "I'm afraid we're at an impasse." Victorious once more, I shifted to face the fire, content that our conversation was over.

"Nell said you were different," he said. "The doctor told me John isn't well off."

"No, he's not," I replied, mood dampening. "Philip can't wait for him to be gone." I nibbled my lower lip, once more finding it hard to look the other way. This reality was temporary and the real-Josie probably dead already. Why anything here should matter … why anything *did* matter …

"You care for John."

"Of course I do. He's a good man," I replied. "Very kind and sweet. Just wants to spend the last days of his life with the daughter he loves." The guilt was back, stronger when I realized John was likely to die soon without ever knowing the true fate of his beloved daughter.

"Yet you left him on his deathbed in the middle of the night and in a storm. What are you not telling me?"

I'm scared. I didn't want to admit it to him or myself. He was calm, even-tempered and attractive – a combination I found a little too appealing right now. I had the urge to trust him once more, the same way I did Carter. *Look where that got me.*

At first, the task to change history seemed straightforward. Now, I debated how I was supposed to change the actions of the men around me without revealing what I was, without becoming emotionally entangled about anyone like John, and without being killed off by whoever was hunting down time travelers.

"It's complicated. You wouldn't understand," I said.

"Try me."

I glanced at him, once more ensnared by his green gaze and quiet strength. The longer I was around him, the less I wanted to maintain the barrier between me and everyone else and the easier it became to talk to him.

"Tell me about the girls who came before me," I said, wanting to understand what exactly happened to them.

"They were all named Josie, all looked like you and all disappeared soon after I met them."

"Why *you*?" I asked with some frustration.

"They came to me for help."

"Help?" I echoed. "I don't understand that." What did they know that I didn't? "Swear you didn't have anything to do with their disappearance?"

"If you'll trust the word of a half-breed."

There was no self-pity or self-doubt about him, but I almost felt bad for someone who belonged to neither of the worlds he was charged with protecting.

"I'd trust you over Philip," I replied. "I just can't figure out the connection between the other Josies and you."

"You know what I see?" he asked, frustration in his voice. He sat forward, almost near enough for his leg to brush my shoulder. "I see four women who were too much alike not to know each other. Three of them disappeared within two days of visiting me, without telling me who they were afraid of or why all of you seem to be out to find me. I'll ask you, Josie. Why are *you* scared? Because it's probably the same reason they were."

I shivered, his words sinking in with more clarity and impact than I wanted.

Two days. What put the other girls at the bottom of the well? Their inability to conform to a society they weren't familiar with? Someone becoming suspicious of them? Talking to the sheriff?

The others Carter swore were trying to outmaneuver him in a chess game I wasn't able to see?

My eyes fell to the sheriff's full lips. He was sexy – and impossible to read the way I did everyone else.

"You wanna tell me what's going on before you disappear too?" he added.

I looked away.

"I didn't think so." Quiet anger radiated off him. He rose and paced in the walk space between the sitting area and the door leading to his bedroom, hands on hips.

"I'm sorry. I can't," I said.

"Even if it means you end up dead like the others?"

Ouch. I flinched.

"Look, Josie, I don't know how else to tell you this, but you being here … it's not for the purpose you think it is. It has nothing to do with Running Bear or his brother."

"How do you know that?"

He was quiet, pensive gaze out the window. "Because I do." The sheriff ran his hands through his hair. "Maybe you need help, Josie, and don't want to admit it. I reckon if the other girls ended up dead, *someone* in that house is after you. I doubt it's your cousin Philip."

"He was my first thought, too." Alarm fluttered through me. The fact the sheriff was coming to the same conclusion I did, that it wasn't a coincidence the girls were in the bottom of the well near John's house, scared me.

His words had a ring of truth to them I didn't want to hear. How was I supposed to know who the threat was or whether or not I was truly in danger?

The images in my mind of the phones and skeletons made me want to crawl under the bed and never leave. Who had done it, if not Philip or the sheriff?

Carter had given me one warning about a man who didn't want history changed. Was it possible he was resorting to killing to prevent it? If so, who was he? A townsperson who saw the much-celebrated daughter of John return four times?

"This just gets worse," I murmured.

The sheriff's suspicion hadn't softened with our talk. If anything, I guessed he was thinking even worse of me, considering I had all but admitted to not being John's real daughter.

"What happened to the real Josephine?" he asked quietly.

Holy shit. Does this guy have empathic memory? "I *am* the real Josephine."

The thick silence was tense. I didn't look at him, instead focused on the dancing flames of the fire in front of me.

"I don't want to see you hurt, Miss Josie," he added. "Despite your … peculiarities."

I smiled. "Thanks. I can handle it." *Whatever it is.*

"I don't think you can. I don't think you'll see the danger coming."

That terrifies me. I had come to the same conclusion, and I hated, *hated* thinking such dark thoughts.

"I can help you," he continued.

Studying him, I had the sense he didn't mean in the way a sheriff protected the people of his town, that he was talking around something again. I just didn't know what that entailed, why it was suddenly harder to breathe, why I suspected I was scratching the surface of something I didn't think I could handle. "I'm ready for bed," I said instead.

"You can sleep in my room."

"Thanks." I rose and went the long way around the seating area to the door of his bedroom. A part of me wanted to ask what he meant about helping me, but I stopped myself.

Carter told me not to reveal anything about who I was. Lying was hard, trusting him harder, but I had faith in both for now.

I went into the room, at once noticing the chill without the fire. The sound of rain was loud on the tin roof, the lightning gone. Wrapped in the blanket, I crawled into the covers of his narrow bed and breathed deeply. His scent was much stronger on the worn sheets and blanket of his bed.

Dimming the lantern, I closed my eyes, comforted by his homey scent. The discussion with him replayed through my thoughts, and I listened for a long moment to see if his possessions would speak to me the way my surroundings sometimes did.

There were no empathic memories here at all, as if he didn't exist or leave traces of himself the way others did. I relaxed and rested my head on his pillow, wriggling beneath the blanket to grab my cell. I typed a message to Carter then replaced the phone in the pocket of my borrowed trousers. Either the chip was faulty or there was something unusual about Taylor.

I didn't realize how busy my mind had become with the empathic memories until it was silent for the first time in several days. Instead of comforting me, all I could think about was the skeletons at the bottom of John's well.

Sleep didn't come, and every time I closed my eyes, I saw *them* and experienced a flare of new fear. After an hour or so struggling to block the thoughts and fall asleep, I sat up restlessly. It was too dark for me to fumble with the lantern.

Wrapping the blanket around me, I left the bedroom, relaxing once I entered the warmth and light of the main room. The sheriff was stretched out next to the fire on his stomach, still wearing his shirt, as if he feared me walking in on me.

"Can't sleep?" he asked, hearing the creak of the floorboards beneath my feet.

"No." I crossed to the fire and lay down beside him.

He sat, his dark hair tousled. "I'll go to the barn."

I laughed. "Are you afraid I'll bite you?"

"No, Josie. An un-chaperoned, unmarried woman –"

"Lay down and shut up, Sheriff," I ordered lightly. "I found three bodies today. You can protect me from anyone who wants to make it a fourth."

He hesitated, studying me briefly before he returned to his belly. I rolled onto my side, back to him, and gazed at the dancing shadows thrown off by the hearth.

"You don't scare easily," he observed.

"Not usually, no. I don't feel like being alone tonight," I replied. "Sometimes I think your brother is lucky in his cave. He knows there are shadows and darkness around him, inside him. I stumble upon them and see secrets no one should ever know. I want to believe good trumps evil but have started to doubt something I viewed as irrefutable before."

"Good and evil are relative."

"Like hanging men every Saturday?"

"To keep a peace that doesn't want to be kept. There are times when it takes evil to keep evil in check."

"I don't want that," I whispered. "It's not who I am, not something I understand."

"You have a good heart, Josie. You charm everyone you come across, even Fighting Badger."

"Because I *want* to attract crazy murderers!"

"I reckon it's because you want to find the good in people."

I sighed. "You think that's stupid?"

"I think it's admirable and a tad foolish."

The foolish part I understood. I didn't know how to take *admirable*. It reinforced the idea he liked me and was in denial of the fact. I'd had one-night stands and boyfriends nowhere near as sexy as he was; it was a shame he was so … honorable towards women. "I don't know if or how you're supposed to help me, but I'm glad I'm here tonight," I told him.

"Maybe to keep you out of the well."

"Now *that* is inappropriate, Sheriff Hansen. How can you joke about what happened?"

"My apologies, ma'am," he replied solemnly. "But if you are in trouble, I want to be the first you come to."

Who else would I go to? "Will it cost me a favor?"

"We'll see, ma'am."

I smiled to myself. "Goodnight, Sheriff."

"You can call me Taylor," he replied. "Goodnight, Miss Josie."

With the steady tap of rain on the tin roof, and the sexy sheriff inches from me, I fell asleep faster than I expected and slept well. For the first time since arriving in this time period, no dark dreams disturbed my sleep.

"Josephine!"

I was burning up and having trouble breathing. Assuming I was stuck under the covers, I pried myself loose from the cocoon of my blanket. The air outside my blankets was just as hot, and I sucked in a deep breath – then began coughing.

I opened my eyes and batted away at the smoke hanging over me. Fire lit up one wall of the cabin, and I stared, slowly registering that the cabin was on fire.

"Josephine!"

Covering my mouth with one hand, I squinted in the direction of Taylor's shout. It came from the bedroom. Fire was between me and the front door.

Dashing to my feet, I shoved his door open and scrambled over the bed to the narrow space between bed and window. Fumbling with the window, I managed to shove it open and leaned out, sucking in deep breaths of rainy night air.

"Taylor!" I called, disoriented.

He appeared around the side of the cabin, bucket of water in hand. Dropping it, he hurried towards me and took my arms, hauling me out of the window.

I coughed, the cold night shocking my overheated body. Taylor locked an arm around me, whisking me away from the burning cabin. I felt his heartbeat through his soaked shirt; it raced, and his wiry frame was tense, edgy.

When we stood a safe distance from the cabin, he stopped and watched. I tugged at his grip until I was able to twist and see the fire. The entire cabin was in flames despite the steady downpour of rain. My feet sank into the cold mud and I grimaced, pulling them free. I found footing by standing on the sheriff's boots and leaned against his warm frame.

"What happened?" I breathed.

"Are you hurt?" he asked.

I shook my head.

"I'd say you're bad luck," he said.

I shivered, silently agreeing.

"Might help knowing who's after you," he added.

"I'm sorry about your house, but I really don't know," I responded.

"Someone didn't want you here tonight."

We were quiet, watching the cabin collapse in on itself. I felt even worse knowing he was losing everything he owned because of me. From the patchwork on his clothing and the sparse belongings I'd seen, I doubted he had a stash of money anywhere and knew there was no such thing as house insurance in this day and age.

I glanced up at him, my gaze lingering on his chiseled face. He was grim but not openly angry, and my confusion deepened. Nothing seemed to surprise him, not me falling out of the sky or even his house burning down.

"You're giving me that look again," he said without taking his eyes off his home.

One of my feet slipped off his boot, and he tightened his grip around me. I remained where I was, in no way uncomfortable being pressed against his warm, solid body. There was no denying he was sexy in a rugged, roughened way of an outlaw. It was as much his lean frame and bright eyes as his quiet confidence and strength, the direct gaze that stopped me in my tracks and saw through my flimsy attempts to lie or deceive him.

Is he trembling in his boots being so close to a woman? The thought, and the sudden urge to laugh, were ill timed.

"I'm sorry you lost your stuff," I murmured.

"We're safe. The rest don't matter." His grip tightened around me.

I relaxed against him. He didn't seem to be in the mood for talking or letting me go. I could almost see why the other girls sought him out. Protective and strong, he was sharp, focused – and determined to figure out what was going on. A familiar flutter of attraction warmed my blood. In a way, it was a relief to be around someone whose history and memories I wasn't able to access. He was too distracted to be aware of how he held me, as if we were already intimately acquainted and not strangers.

"Let's get you home," he said with reluctance. "Nothing we can do for it now." He released me and moved away. "Wait there. I'll get a horse."

I inched closer to the fire to keep warm. Who had set it and why?

I clenched my phone, wanting to ask Carter more about Taylor and why my chip didn't work around him. I expected my flaky handler didn't know much more than I did about the man.

"Are you well, Talks to Spirits?"

I whirled. Fighting Badger was outlined against the fire. He remained a safe distance away and was armed with a bow and knives at his hips. It was far too muddy for me to get far running and besides, where would I go? My mouth went dry at the sight of him.

"I tracked him here," Fighting Badger said quietly. "I will find him and make him pay."

"Who?" I squeaked.

"The man who did this." He motioned towards the fire. "He came from town."

It registered that Fighting Badger, the psychopath who killed for friendship, was telling me he hadn't set the fire.

"My brother will take care of you." He turned away.

"Wait. Did you see his face?" I asked.

"No. He moved with stealth. Trained hunter." He tilted his head and regarded me curiously before he moved closer. "Can *you* see him?" He tapped his head.

Needing to know who it was, I approached until his memories reached me. I hugged myself, terrified by the images in my head. Fighting Badger's churning shadows morphed to show me the distant shape of a man he had tracked. Fighting Badger had been scouting the area around the sheriff's cabin, spotted the man heading from the direction of town, and pursued cautiously.

By the time he crested the hill beside which the sheriff's home sat, the cabin was already ablaze. Shadows interlaced with the memories, but I was able to make out something else. The sheriff had hinted Fighting Badger was able to relate to me, but he didn't mention the madman was *tracking* me. I saw peeks of my day at the house and my escape last night in his mind.

"You told your brother I was on your land," I said, looking up at him. "Why are you following me?"

The shadows from the fire rendered his features sinister, his eyes holes in his face. "The spirits warned me when you came. They said there was danger."

How is this possible? I didn't know what to say or how to process the idea a serial killer wanted to *protect* me. Our shared gift was a light in his otherwise dark mind. I could see in his thoughts how deeply it touched him after a lifetime of exile.

I didn't think I'd ever been so scared in my life as I was, standing in the rain beside him.

"Did you see him?" he asked with some impatience.

"Not clearly," I murmured. "He went that way." I pointed past the barn into the rainy darkness. "One man on foot and …" Was there a second man? I focused on the image. It was even blurrier than the rest of his memories but I thought I saw two.

"I will find him." The cold, soulless glint in his eyes made me instantly regret telling him where the man had gone. Fighting Badger started away but not before I got a glimpse of what he planned to do.

"He's not for your collection!" I called anxiously, horrified by the idea of putting out a hit on the unknown man.

"I do not want him for my friend."

Oh, Jesus. How do I talk sense to a man like this? "Please, Fighting Badger! I need to know why he wants to hurt me, and if he hurt the others that came before me!"

"I will ask him before he dies." The native melted into the night.

Holy shit. I stood, staring after him. As with the first time we met, my pulse raced hard enough that I felt ill, and I had trouble breathing. No singular event or person in my life – aside from the death of my parents that I only vaguely recalled – had ever impacted me the way dealing with him did. The urge to weep was almost overpowering. It came as much from the knowledge of what he'd done as acknowledgment that such darkness existed in the world. I was unaware of how obliviously naïve I had been.

Someone else was there. The memories were too fleeting, too far for me to pin down, but I sensed the second shadow I'd seen in Fighting Badger's mind. Twisting to face the direction of the hill, I knew without understanding how that whoever it was, was *there.* Watching.

"You all right?" Taylor asked, studying me as he returned with two horses.

Quivering on the inside, I nonetheless managed to smile. "Yes. A little shaken." I took the reins of one horse and turned away from the hill.

"Let's get you home."

My eyes strayed once more in the direction that Fighting Badger had gone. For the first time since arriving, I almost didn't care why I was here. I wanted to leave. Now.

"Can we swing by where you found me?" I asked with a glance at the sky. The drizzle continued, though the lightning had subsided.

"Not tonight."

I pulled myself up on the warm horse. "Just for a minute?"

Taylor glanced at me. Something passed through his gaze. He was hiding something. For all I knew, his mind was as twisted as Fighting Badger's.

"No," he replied. "We need to get you home." Wheeling his horse, he started away.

I didn't object. I had left John's house in a panic to change history and go home. There was no longer lightning to take me back to the future, and I had done nothing to alter the course of history. If anything, I learned that I just might need someone like Fighting

Badger to protect me.

Unsettled, I followed Taylor obediently into the darkness and cold rain, unable to piece together exactly who was after me.

Chapter Twelve

SIMILAR TO MY FIRST NIGHT, I MADE IT TO MY ROOM MOMENTS before Nell knocked. The sheriff had gone to find the lead stable hand to discuss caring for his horses while I fled to my room.

For some reason, I felt safer knowing he was here. He said he was going to ask to stay in the barn until he had somewhere else to live.

Moving close to the fire, I released a deep breath. My head ached and my nose was stuffed. I checked for blood quickly, grateful not to see any. It was a cold and not an issue with the implants in my brain. About to read my messages from Carter, I froze when the floorboards outside the door creaked.

Nell slammed the door open as she balanced a tray of breakfast in her hands.

"My god!" I exclaimed, heart jolting. "You scared me, Nell."

"No more than you scared your father!"

"What?" I hugged a blanket around me. "I think I'm getting sick."

"It would serve you right, Miss Josie." Despite the heated words, Nell cast me a worried look. She set the food and pot of tea on the table near the fire. "Drink some herbs. I expected you'd be ill today after you were out in the rain last night."

"Oh. You knew?"

"I did not, but your father saw you leave last night and the sheriff return with you this morning. He's displeased."

"I didn't worsen his condition, did I?" I asked.

"You did. He has not left his bed once this morning."

Dammit, Josie. I hadn't noticed anyone watching me leave and prayed no one saw me sneak in. That John was awake and witnessed both stung. The good man didn't deserve such worry, especially on his deathbed.

Nell was lecturing me in the tone I had quickly learned required no response. I had learned to tune out in the short time we'd been stuck together, but the last few words caught my attention.

"Sorry, what?" I asked.

Nell shot me a look. "Your father has decided that you will marry before he dies."

"Oh, shit."

"You should be worried. Your cousin Philip is the ideal husband."

I froze. John was sick, and Philip was a rapist if not a murderer. How long would it take for me to change history and leave?

John doesn't have long. "I think I should talk to my father," I whispered. "Can his mind be changed?"

"If anyone can change it, you can," Nell replied. "He is very worried about you, Miss Josie."

"Okay. Let's get me dressed."

Nell didn't argue. The lines around the woman's eyes were tight, an indication of her stress. I pitied her as much as I did John, wishing my appearance didn't cause anyone else such strain. Whatever happened, I couldn't get married off before I changed history. It was probably not the change history needed, and I definitely didn't know how I was going to survive this world without making a mess by refusing to adhere to the customs of this era. Women weren't taken seriously, and Philip was likely to kill me if I got in his way of taking over John's land and wealth, which I would, because he was a dick and John's servants didn't deserve to suffer the way Philip's did.

Half an hour later, I walked into John's bedchamber. He appeared worse this day than the last, and guilt made my stomach twist. He was paler, fragile. The sight of his state wore down more of the barrier I was trying to keep between me and this place, to remain focused on what I thought really mattered. It was impossible not to pity him, especially knowing that he'd never see his real daughter again.

"Father?" I ventured and went to the bed, sitting beside him. "Are you awake?" I took his gnarled hand.

His eyes opened, and his features broke into a smile that brightened everything about his sickly appearance. "Hello, daughter," he said softly. Even his voice was weaker this day. If he were angry, he didn't show it. His blue eyes glowed with warmth and happiness, the way they did every time he saw me since I arrived.

Why did I want to cry for a man I didn't know?

I cleared my throat. "Hello, Father. How are you today?"

"I fear I do not have much longer."

"Nonsense," I said and forced a smile. "You're getting stronger by the day."

"I wish it were so, my beautiful Josephine." He was thinking of his late wife, recalling the day his daughter was born and the happy childhood years before his wife died. The memories flowed through my mind as well, and tears stung my eyes.

I'm such a horrible person lying to him. But the more I saw of his mind, combined with the knowledge he was likely senile, the less I wanted him to know the truth. There was a selfish element to it, too. The little girl in me who had never known the love of a father wanted to bask in his adoration for once in her life.

"About last night," I started. "I am so sorry to have worried you." I sought out some sort of excuse that sounded reasonable to someone in this time of history about why an *un-chaperoned, unwed* woman left her home in the middle of a rainstorm at night.

"Since you returned, all I have thought about is what happened if I lost you again," he admitted. "My heart cannot take such worry."

"I'm here, Father. I'm not going anywhere."

"I know. I fear the doctor is right, though, my Josephine. Your mind is not well."

I looked down at my hand. The flare of surprise his words elicited was quickly replaced by understanding. Whoever the real Josephine was, she was an absolute bitch to leave a father who cared so much for her. She had no idea what she was missing, but I did.

"Josie, I wish to see you wed and comfortable, before I pass away."

I cringed at the words. "I understand, Father," I managed in a calm voice. "But can we not wait a little longer? You won't die on me anytime soon. I can feel it."

He smiled. "Nonetheless, you must have someone to take care of you. I have prepared ..." he stretched for a piece of paper on the nightstand and sagged.

Alarmed by his frailty, I reached for it and handed it to him.

"Thank you," he murmured. "There are names there of suitable husbands. Read them and tell me who you choose."

The man loved his daughter enough to give her a choice. I swallowed the lump in my throat, understanding how unusual it was for a wealthy father to grant his daughter a choice in this era. I read through the names. Philip and the names of seven others were listed in shaky handwriting that was at times, illegible.

"I can't remember some of these men," I whispered.

"They are all respectable men."

This is insane. Then again, *I* wasn't getting married. A woman who no longer existed was. There was no need for me to choose carefully for the real-Josie, but I had the sneaking suspicion I needed to plan for *my* safety, in case I ended up here longer than I planned or John died before the twenty fourth. Whoever hurt the other Josies could always come for me.

"The sheriff isn't on here," I noted. "Is he not respectable?"

"He is, for a half-breed, but he is also very poor."

I bit back my initial response, aware of how fragile John was. If I was going to be stuck with a stranger, I'd rather it be one I knew could probably protect me and accepted the reality that I was different. "He has a way of finding me when I am lost," I said carefully.

John gave a wheezing chuckle. "Perhaps you are right, daughter. Perhaps I should wed you to a master tracker." He laughed again before subsiding into a bout of coughing. Blood dabbed the corner of his lips, and he rested back on his pillows.

I shifted closer to rub his back and gave him a glass of water. "I should not make you laugh, Father," I murmured. "I'm so sorry."

"Nonsense. I have always loved to laugh at your jokes."

I gave a tight smile and watched him sip water from the glass. His hand shook with the effort to hold it.

With a sinking feeling, I began to think he wasn't going to last another four days, to the event I needed to stop. I didn't want to feel … *this*. Whatever this was. Sorrow, guilt, yearning … emotions that I expected to feel if John was really my father and not someone who had already been dead for a very long time before I was born.

"You are serious about me wedding soon?" I asked uneasily.

"Tomorrow morning."

"That's very … soon. I mean … you may live for a month or two more, and I don't know most of these men."

"I have chosen men who will treat you well," he said.

Except Philip. I said nothing, guessing the familial relationship was what made the cruel cousin a contender. I read through the names I could decipher once more. The image of the three skeletons in the well reminded me of how important this truly was.

If I chose wrong, I could be number four.

"Am I interrupting?" Taylor's gravelly voice drew my attention. He stood in the doorway of John's bedroom, freshly shaven and dressed as if he was prepared to leave.

"The man who finds my lost sheep." John struggled to sit up. "Come, Sheriff."

"I had hoped to speak to you in private, Mr. Jackson," Taylor replied.

My stomach twisted. What was the sheriff going to tell John? About my *dream*? That I wasn't his real daughter? The dying man didn't need that kind of stress. I didn't think Taylor would betray me like that, but I also didn't know a lot about what motivated him.

"Father needs his rest right now," I said before the weak man could respond. "I don't think you should tax him, Taylor."

"I don't intend to, ma'am," he replied coolly. "I need five minutes of his time and will be leaving."

I started to object when John squeezed my hand. "Go on, dear. Have some breakfast, and we'll talk about the list later."

With some reluctance, I decided not to argue. I kissed him on the forehead and left the bed, pausing beside the sheriff.

"Don't stress him out," I whispered.

"Your secrets are safe with me, ma'am," he replied without looking at me.

"Thanks." *I think.* I left.

The doors closed behind me. After a moment, I retreated to my bedroom for the tea still waiting for me. Spreading the paper out on the table, I began to suspect I was in a great deal of trouble, if I had to pick out a husband to wed tomorrow morning. I pulled out my cell.

Why do some people have empathic memories and others don't? I texted to Carter and put the phone away.

"Lucas Stephens, Philip Jackson, Julius … Terr … Trev …" I drifted off, unable to read John's scribbles. The names contained no empathic memories that I was able to see, no indication of who the men were or how John viewed them.

"Julius Terrence," Nell said, entering from the direction of the bathroom. "What're you doing, child?"

"Picking a husband." I waved the paper with a nervous laugh. "Do you know any of these men?"

Nell approached and peered over my shoulder. "Oh, goodness. Lucas Stephens is older than your father! Not Julius, or James …" Nell leaned over to squint. "I can't read the next name. Travis Horton is seventeen, third son of a wealthy man two townships over." She stood and shook her head. "I know little about most of them, except for Philip of course."

"He's off the list for sure," I replied. "So only rich men are on this list, right?" I twisted to watch Nell make the bed.

"I expect so. You are the daughter of a wealthy man, the granddaughter of an English noble. You should marry your equal."

"What if I didn't? Do I get arrested?"

"Where do you get these notions?" Nell shot me a look. "Or are you jesting?"

"Jesting," I murmured and returned to my tea. The warm liquid was pungent and tasted bitter. "This tastes terrible, Nell." I added more sugar.

"It's meant to treat that chill you caught gallivanting around the countryside like a savage in the middle of a storm. What got into your head, Miss Josie?"

"I don't know. Father being ill is really upsetting me."

"Ah. That I understand." Concern was in Nell's voice.

"You know it might be the last day he's alive. You should tell him how you feel," I suggested.

"Bite your tongue, Josie!"

I snorted and sipped my tea. I wanted to hunt down the sheriff before he left and demand to know what he was telling John.

"Well the sheriff is gone." Nell was at the window, watching.

"Good." *I think.* I didn't know how to view the man who stirred my blood and somehow figured out I didn't belong. "I want to see Father again."

"I reckon you do." By my hushed sorrow, Nell didn't expect John to live long, either.

I took my tea with me and returned to John's room. "Father?" I called, knocking lightly. I pushed the door open to see the doctor with him.

"Come, daughter," John said with another of his bright smiles.

I almost sighed, reassured the sheriff hadn't tried to warn John about me. Smiling, I started to the bed and glanced at the doctor. The grim expression on his face made me miss a step.

My smile slipped. I forced it back into place and focused on the dying man whose whole life was better because I was around.

"Miss Josie, I'd like a word after I take my tea," the doctor told me.

"Of course," I replied.

He rose and left us alone.

I took John's hand again, uncertain why my heart was hurting worse than my head and my stomach in knots. John wasn't really my father.

But his joyful smile …

God this is hard. The day I went for another drink with Carter, we were going to have a very long talk.

"If the sheriff disturbed you, I will hunt him down," I said firmly.

"He did not." John chuckled.

"Oh, I forgot my list," I said. "I'm still deciding. I think I'm leaning towards Travis." *A seventeen-year-old kid will be easier to handle than a man like Philip.* "I'll let you know soon, Father."

"No need."

I perked up. "Because you changed your mind about marrying me off?" I asked hopefully.

"Because I chose for you, my Josephine."

Shit, shit, shit. I curbed the curse words and instead drew a breath. It was hard to pretend to be upbeat about something that sounded downright horrible to me. "Who did you choose, Father? *Please don't say Philip!*

"A man not on the list."

I waited anxiously.

"Sheriff Taylor."

"Really? Why?" I replied. "I thought he was poor?" The dread in my stomach turned to fluttering butterflies, and my heart skipped a beat. The sheriff was definitely the sexiest man I had met here, one who was always around when I needed rescuing. But there was something going on with him, a reason why five women had traveled from the future to find him and three had disappeared shortly after succeeding. I didn't think he hurt them, but I think he knew a lot more than he was telling me.

"We were discussing the tension between settlers and the savages," his father said. "I have always been an advocate for us all living in harmony. Philip does not share my views, like many others of stature who have nothing to gain from peace. The sheriff maintains strong ties to both communities."

I listened. Before, Taylor hadn't been an option because of who he was. Now, he was John's choice for the same reason. "Did he say something to you to make you change your mind?" I asked, puzzled as to what the sheriff might've said in so short a time. Of all my options, I liked the one of the sheriff best.

But something wasn't right about John's decision, unless it was a sign of his senility.

"Not at all. We did not discuss you."

"Oh. So he doesn't know?"

"Not yet. It was my concern for you keeping my lands after I die. The natives are growing restless. You'll be safe, if he's your husband."

John was a smart man. "What if he doesn't agree?"

"The wealthiest man this side of the River is leaving him everything by way of my daughter. Who would not agree?" John asked with a smile. "It's a favor to a dying man."

"He seems really difficult. Maybe he'll still refuse," I pressed. "I don't want him to break your heart, Father." *And I don't fully trust him.*

"I will write him a letter beseeching him to humor a dying old man and his addled daughter."

My mouth dropped open then snapped shut. He loved me and had just called my crazy in the same breath. He was far too kind and weak for me to chastise the way Nell did me. Thank god this wasn't my time, that I was just a visitor. "Very well, Father," I murmured. "I can take the letter to him and … beseech him as well." *Or shred it.*

"Very good. Fetch me my quill and paper."

Spotting them on a small desk against one wall, I obeyed and brought them back to the bed on a tray.

"Go, daughter. This requires some time."

I left him alone and returned to my room.

I paced for close to an hour, drank tea, ate more treats brought by Nell, took a bath … anything to help me figure out my next step. Carter responded to my text around midmorning, and I tugged the phone free.

You should see empathic memories for everyone. If the chip is malfunctioning, there should be other signs. How often is it skipping? Any more nosebleeds or headaches?

I sent a response and tugged on my boots. Nell waited for me outside my room, armed with a letter and my cloak.

"I'll take that," I said and snatched the note intended for Taylor.

"No, you will not." Nell grabbed it back and placed it into an inner pocket of her cloak.

I grumbled under my breath and eyed the hiding place. I had until we reached town to figure out how to grab it and rip it to pieces. Not in a talking mood, we rode to town in silence beneath grey skies left over from the storm the night before.

"We need to pick up a package," Nell said as she pulled the carriage in front of the mercantile store.

"I can deliver the letter to the sheriff," I offered.

"That letter went to town two hours ago, Miss Josie."

"What?" I stared at her. "What's in your pocket?"

"A letter to your father's attorney instructing him to add the sheriff to his will." Nell was frowning as she climbed out of the wagon.

I leapt out, not caring what the onlookers thought of my less than womanly behavior. I hurried around the carriage to Nell. Before I could speak, Nell did.

"I don't know what you said to convince your father of this, but marrying beneath you is a mistake, Miss Josie."

"I didn't do this!" I exclaimed. "I told him I'd take Trevor!"

"The boy? He's little better."

I can't win with this woman. I gave a sigh of frustration and crowded Nell as we walked up the stairs towards the store. "How do we stop this?"

"You do not. You do as your father says."

"But I don't want to marry him."

Nell gave me a disapproving look.

Sensing I wasn't going to win any argument with my nanny, I glanced in the direction of the sheriff's office. The door was open. "Nell, I'm going to have a word with him," I said firmly.

"What would you say to your betrothed?"

"I'm going to tell him not to marry me or at least to wait a little longer, so I can prepare myself mentally. How can Father just toss me off on some man like he's selling a cow or something?"

"Watch your tone, Miss Josie." Nell glanced at passersby who were looking at me curiously.

"I don't want to watch my tone."

"Then go take it out on your soon to be husband."

I all but ran to the sheriff's office and entered without knocking. For once, the woman didn't follow, and I assumed it was because my babysitter was fed up with me.

He was seated at his desk, long legs stretched out and his boots crossed on the corner of the desk. Loud snoring came from one of the three jail cells. I glimpsed a man passed out on the floor. Facing Taylor, I hesitated, not quite sure how to say what I wanted to without sounding mean after he took me in last night.

"If you agree, I want to wait," I told him firmly. "I don't care what my father said or how much you may want his money. We need to … court first." *At least until my mission is done and I leave.*

Taylor's bright green gaze settled on me, his expression one of guarded curiosity. "What're you talking about, ma'am?"

"Ma'am? Really?" I asked. "We spent the night together, Taylor."

Red crept up his neck.

"I'm talking about my father's letter. He sent it to town two hours ago."

There was genuine puzzlement on his features. He leaned back in his desk. "I've been out of my office for a few hours."

"So you didn't get a letter?"

He stood and went to the door and the small box outside. Unlocking it, he pulled out several letters, and I recognized the paper John had used among them. I reached for it.

Taylor shifted his back to me in a swift block.

"Don't read it yet! We have to talk about this!" I pushed at him. I grabbed at the letter once more.

A thick cuff went around my wrist.

The sheriff tossed his mail then took my arm and tugged me towards the cells. I pulled at him, but he resolutely bullied me to the cell before sliding the handcuffs through the bars and cuffing my free wrist.

"Stay put, ma'am," he ordered and moved away.

"I'll give you a million dollars not to read that letter," I said with a groan and pulled at my hands.

"Even if such an amount existed, I'd rather read this, more so because you don't want me to." He sat down at his desk and propped up his boots on his desk before picking up the note from John.

I waited, hopeful that he found this as weird as I did. If we could work out a deal where he delayed the wedding for a few more days …

He read the letter, and I almost laughed. He went from relaxed to tense. His legs dropped and he hunched over his desk, eyes pinned to the words. Suspicion was replaced by surprise and then consternation. The silence grew tense and thick, and I waited apprehensively for his reaction. The irrational part of me feared rejection while the logical side of me prayed for it.

"My father is not in the right mind," I said finally.

"This cannot be real."

"You're right. It's not. It's a horrible joke."

He glanced at me and rose, the letter in his hand. Clearly not buying my attempt to brush it off, he froze in place for another long minute.

"You can say no. Or you can say yes to my father and delay it for a while." I added.

"Considering someone burnt my house down, a place to sleep sounds mighty nice right now."

I rolled my eyes. "You have a barn."

"That burnt down after."

"You can stay in ours."

"Much obliged, ma'am." By the look he leveled on me, he blamed me for the fire. "I take it you're opposed." He lifted the letter.

"Not *opposed*," I said, recalling his naked torso from last night, along with the fact I was leaving soon. Then again, assuming he wasn't here to stop me, he could be the right person to help me influence Running Bear and Fighting Badger, and if John passed soon … "I don't know. Maybe it is a good idea. You're not an asshole like Philip. Just not … now. The timing is bad."

"Your father says within the day." He waved the letter. He didn't appear to know how to take the request.

"True, but that doesn't work for me."

"Because of your *dream*." He gave me the knowing look Nell did whenever I said something my nanny found ridiculous. "You do need someone to look out for you."

Other than Fighting Badger? "I think I'm doing fine on my own."

He studied me, pensive.

"Are you really considering it?" I asked curiously.

"My job is to keep the peace between the settlers and savages. This would give me more influence with both than I have now, not to mention a home, a little bit of respect from the townsfolk." He shrugged. "What's not to consider?"

"Oh." So it had nothing to do with *me*. I didn't know why I was disappointed. "You'd have to deal with me all day, every day, and I tend to run away from home often."

He appeared amused. "I think I can handle you, ma'am." He lifted his chin towards the handcuffs. "Besides, you may be returning to wherever you came from soon, or disappearing like the others."

I froze. By his face, he didn't mean I'd end up in the well, but I wasn't able to stop the chill that went through me.

As if realizing what he'd said, he sighed. "My apologies, Josie. I didn't mean ... well, not dead. I meant ..." It was the first time I'd ever seen him flummoxed.

"It's okay," I murmured. "I understood." My phone buzzed. I tugged at the cuffs. "Philip won't be happy."

"Him I look forward to handling," came the hard response. Taylor picked up his hat. "Stay here, ma'am. I'm going to verify this is genuine." With a glint of humor in his gorgeous eyes, he left.

I faced the cell I was chained to, mind racing. I picked up the memories of the snoring man but nothing from Taylor. The handcuffs were much thicker than the ones from my time, and I gave up pulling at them quickly.

I had no alternative but to stay where I was and wait.

Chapter Thirteen

THE SHERIFF RETURNED LESS THAN AN HOUR LATER, ACCOMPANIED by Nell and an elderly stranger with a beard that reached mid-chest.

Taylor released me. Nell gave him a long, indecipherable look, while I debated what to say since we weren't alone to discuss this mess.

"Miss Jackson," the bearded man held out his hand. "I'm Judge Cromwell. I am finalizing your wedding papers." He unfolded a set of documents with different sized papers. "If you can make your mark here." He pointed. "It's acknowledgment that you are aware of the changes to your status and your inheritance."

I hesitated too long, wanting to stall, to talk to the sheriff outside before I committed to anything.

"Ah. I had thought you knew how to write," the judge said. "Understandable that you do not. Your husband-to-be can –"

Taylor started forward.

"Oh, I can write," I said. *Not that this will matter in a week,* I reminded myself.

The chant was becoming harder for me to believe when I had no control over this world. I took the fountain pen from the judge and signed my name. John's signature, along with Taylor's scrawled name, were already present. "Is that it?"

"It is. I'll file these immediately. Congratulations to both of you."

He was the only one smiling. Oblivious to the moods of those around him, he replaced his hat on top of his head and left.

"We need to talk," I said to Taylor.

"At a later time, Miss Josie," he replied politely.

"Come, Miss Josie. We need to return to your father," Nell said. "But not before I have a word with the sheriff."

I wanted to object but sighed and left instead. The sheriff appeared as happy as Nell about the situation. My desperation to change history and leave was growing. I pulled out my phone and shielded it from public view behind a hand fan to read Carter's latest message.

It only malfunctions with one person? He had written. *In that case, it's not the chip. Whoever this person is, he doesn't – or shouldn't – exist. Who is it? I can do some research.*

I paused mid-step and reread the message. Turning to face the sheriff's office, I frowned and studied him. He was in the doorway, quietly talking to Nell.

He definitely existed. I had felt the solid heat of his frame against mine last night. He had a full history with the townspeople and Native Americans. Everyone knew him and that he'd been raised here.

And fell from the sky.

I had no idea what to think. Turning my focus back to the cell, I texted then hastily stashed it in a pocket before Nell saw it.

"I respect your father, but I do not like this arrangement," Nell said as she approached.

"You're not the one who has to get married," I returned.

"I'd rather see you wed Philip, a man of good stature and some respectability."

I rolled my eyes. I'd take the sheriff over Philip any day. In fact, I'd take the sheriff over every other man on the list. He was sexy, enigmatic and not above riding out in a rainstorm to find me. He might make good boyfriend material, assuming his secrets weren't as daunting as Fighting Badger's.

Unable to figure out the man, I dwelt on how the hell I was going to change history when I was dogged every step by Nell. I had spoken to Running Bear without any satisfaction he had the motivation to do something Saturday that changed history. In four days, the event happened, and I had to identify what it was beforehand as well as which twin to stop.

With the sheriff close ... There was a better chance of doing what I needed to and convincing him to help, assuming he wasn't a bad guy in disguise like Carter seemed to think he was. If John insisted on me marrying – however barbaric I considered forcing a woman into a relationship – I could think of many worse fates than to be stuck with Taylor Hansen.

We returned to the carriage and left town. The package Nell had gone to pick up sat at my feet wrapped in brown paper and twine. It was squishable and felt like clothing. I nudged it a couple of times.

"Miss Josie, we must discuss a wife's duty on her wedding night." Nell was hushed despite the fact we were completely alone on the road leading from town back to John's. "Since your mother is long passed, the duty falls to me."

I almost laughed. Nell was dead serious, so I stifled my humor and the urge to tell my nanny that I was already well aware of what happened between a man and woman in private.

I let Nell talk until the large ranch house came into sight before it hit me. "Wait. You're saying I have to sleep with the sheriff?"

"When you are wed, it's a wifely duty."

I started to smile, stopped, and shook my head. "Bizarre." Like I imagined every woman in college who enjoyed the party scene, I had had sex with multiple boyfriends over the years and even three one-night stands. Sex with Taylor wasn't out of the question, and the thought made my insides warm.

And … it might make him more amenable to helping me. Not to mention, I'd probably enjoy teasing him. Asking him to take off his shirt had made him blush; what would me showing up naked in his room on our wedding night do?

Laughing out loud at the image in my head, I realized Nell was staring at me.

"Have you not been listening?" she asked.

"Sorry. I have. It just hit me you were telling me this for a particular reason."

Nell pursed her lips. "I don't care for this either."

"Yeah. I mean, he's a total stranger and according to your tradition, I have to not only marry him but sleep with him."

Nell eyed me.

"It doesn't strike you as a strange custom?" I prodded.

"Not at all. The bloodline and inheritance must be passed to someone. Legitimate children are the best way to ensure a family's legacy."

"So you don't think love should trump a legacy?"

"Maybe among those with nothing to pass down."

I laughed at the inadvertently saucy response. I looked around at the hills of blonde grasses, not quite processing how serious my situation was. I was itching to text Carter again.

"Oh." Nell's gasp was followed by her wrenching the horses to a halt before we reached the barn.

I caught myself against the front of the wagon. Nell bolted out of the carriage and up the stairs to join a frowning servant I had seen around the house. She was waving frantically at me.

"Miss Josie, come now!" Nell shouted over her shoulder and hurried inside.

Not John. A similar sense of urgency hit me, and I dropped any attempt to be graceful and sprinted, passing Nell before she reached the top of the stairs. My pace slowed when I slid to a halt in front of John's door.

The doctor was present, hands clasped and expression grave. John's rattling breathing reached me at the door. He appeared even frailer than earlier, his pallor that of the near dead.

"Father," I said, entering.

His eyes fluttered open. They were glazed, unfocused. White film covered them. "J… Josie?" He reached out towards the sound of my voice.

I dropped onto the bed beside him. "I'm here, Father."

He offered a faint smile and closed his eyes.

"Miss Josephine, he will not survive the night," Doctor Green said quietly.

"He has to," I replied. "He has to see me get married. Right, Father?"

John tried to chuckle.

Nell entered, wringing her hands.

I shifted to breathe better after my sprint only to realize my chest was in a vise brought on by emotion. It wasn't the corset choking me this time.

"Nell … we must see my … Josie wed tonight," John wheezed.

"Father, don't worry about that right now," I urged. "Your health is far more important."

"He's right," the doctor said. "If you are to keep your inheritance, a husband will need to be in place before John's death."

"I don't care about my inheritance!" I snapped, amazed they thought of money at a time like this. "I care about my father surviving the night. What sense does it make to have a wedding when he needs me by his side?"

John squeezed my hand. "It will give me great pleasure to know you are cared for before I go, my Josephine."

His words deflated my resistance. *Only a few more days,* I reminded myself. This wasn't my mission. Whether or not John died made no difference in what I was dropped into the past to do.

But sitting next to him, running my fingers over the bulging blue veins and knobby knuckles of his hand, listening to him wheeze …

He was too real. In my time, John had been dead for almost two hundred years. The disconnect between a name I might've seen on a tombstone and the man it belonged to dying before my eyes made me dizzy once more, as if fighting my presence in the past shorted out my brain.

"Miss Josie!" Nell took my shoulders. The doctor was bent over in front of me, peering into my face. I blinked him into focus.

I straightened. I was sagging on the bed, close to passing out once more. "I'm okay," I said. "Just a little distressed."

"I'll send for the sheriff," Nell said and scurried away.

"I'm already here." The man I wasn't sure whether or not I wanted to see stepped into the room, hat in his hands. "I had hoped to have a moment with …" His eyes went to John.

The dying man was sleeping, his breathing harsh and shallow.

"Did you follow us here?" I asked with a quick glance at John. If my pretend-father saw him, he'd insist on an immediate wedding, which was the last thing I wanted.

"No, ma'am. I left after speaking to the judge again. Do you have a minute?"

I left John's side and went to the door, joining Taylor in the hallway. "You should probably not be here," I told him, distracted by the fear John might awaken and reach out for me again.

"Didn't he want me here for the wedding?"

I gave an exasperated sigh. "If you aren't here, there can't be one!"

The sheriff smiled faintly. "Ma'am, I came to tell him I changed my mind about marrying you."

"You did?" I focused on him, surprised. "Why?"

"Why? This isn't ... right."

"You're the first man with any sense around here." His expression mirrored what I felt. I smiled in puzzled curiosity. "Then why did you agree at first?"

"How better to help you, if I'm with you every day?"

My phone buzzed with Carter's response. I didn't understand why Taylor thought he was supposed to help me or why the other girls before me had sought him out – and then ended up at the bottom of a well. I knew nothing about the man before me. His simple past, that he was raised by the natives, explained nothing about who he was or how he was always around when I needed rescuing.

"Miss Josie! Your father! Is he dead?"

Omigod, asshole. I faced Philip, who dashed up the last two steps of the stairwell down the hall. "He's not dead!" I exclaimed. "Give him some peace, Philip!"

"He wished you wed before he died, and the house servant told me he was nearly gone. I see no other suitors around, cousin," Philip snapped in response without even glancing at the sheriff. He offered a smug smile and strode into John's room.

"How do you do that?" I asked Taylor, watching the jackass of a cousin go to John's bed.

"Do what, ma'am?"

"You're always in the right place and right time." My own words rang in my head, and another possibility trickled into my thoughts. Was the sheriff like me? A time traveler? Someone with special knowledge or a crazy chip in his head that told him things he shouldn't know? The sense was back. Something about him was almost familiar or …

… empathic memory. It had been teasing me, never fully forming but present nonetheless, like a dream that escaped as one woke from a deep sleep. Failing to capture it, I sighed.

If Taylor was anything, he wasn't easy to read. Either he played his part here with zealous devotion or I was grasping at straws. It almost made sense he was a time traveler, but I didn't know why he was sent.

"I'm fetching the preacher!" Nell whipped by us.

"Preacher? Why for?" Philip demanded, trailing her.

I grimaced and resisted the urge to smack him. His pinched features were the last thing I wanted in my life at the moment. His thoughts were not good; he already had a plan to marry me and lock me away permanently in a basement while he enjoyed John's money.

Unable to tolerate the way he thought of John, I spoke without thinking. "Do you not love your uncle for being kind, cousin, instead of for his money?"

"You watch your mouth, *cousin*. When your father is gone, I will teach you some respect the only way a woman understands it." He hissed for my ears only. His attention slid to the sheriff for the first time. "Sheriff? What are you doing here? This is a family affair. No one has broken the law."

"My apologies for bothering you all," Taylor said and slid his hat off. "I'll leave you to family business."

Whatever I thought about Taylor, I'd take a chance with him over Philip any day. "He's here because we're engaged," I grabbed Taylor's hand as he headed towards the stairs.

"Betrothed?" Philip looked at me blankly. "You? To *him*?"

"Father wished it."

Philip turned red and marched into the bedroom.

"You're marrying me," I told Taylor.

He gazed down at me, taking in my features. My heart flip-flopped once more at the direct look. "It's what you want?"

"John chose you. So … I'm just a woman. What choice do I have?" I asked.

"I don't believe that for one minute." He folded his arms across his lean chest. "I warned you, ma'am. There'd come a time when you needed a favor from me."

I stared at him. "How … I mean, *did* you know this was going to happen?"

"That ain't possible, Miss Josie."

Yet the glimmer in his eyes told me it was. "Fine. What do you want?"

"The truth for one."

"Ugh."

"For two …" he glanced around. "I'd like to retire here with you."

"Wait. You *want* to be with me?" I asked, startled.

"What's not to want?"

The option of being stuck here had never crossed my mind. With his quiet strength, chiseled body and face, ability to see through a lie and protective instinct, he was the perfect package, a man who would keep my secrets and support me without question. I had felt relatively safe with him since we met, with the exception of the details surrounding the night he found me.

Was I attracted? Definitely. Did I think I might be able to trust him? Probably. But if he thought I'd stay here with him forever, he was flat out wrong.

He doesn't have to know that. Except I was a horrible liar. "Look, Taylor …" Meeting his gaze, I paused, grappling with how to say what I wanted to. "We're connected somehow already. I've always felt this. I don't know how or why. I think you could be someone I trust, but … retire? Here?"

This time, I was the one talking around the truth.

"Assume by some miracle, you end up staying here," Taylor said, amusement glittering in his eyes. "You could be worse off."

"Yeah. I didn't mean …" I flushed at his intent consideration. My gaze strayed to the bedroom, where Philip had succeeded in waking John and appeared to be speaking urgently to him.

"I can't let him have you," Taylor added more softly, following my gaze. "You do need someone looking out for you, whatever you decide."

It's not the time for a rant about feminism. I nodded instead of speaking. "Who better than the sheriff?" I agreed.

"You'll tell me the truth."

I opened my mouth to speak.

"Not now." He held up his hand. "Later. The kind of secret that stays between a man and wife."

The sense this might mean more to him than me tickled my mind. I had been drawn to him since we met. No part of me, however, considered staying here permanently an option.

I wasn't leaving the house with John in the throes of death, and I wasn't going to remain here without being married off to someone. Whether it was the abusive Philip or mysterious Taylor, I had to choose a husband for the next four days. Carter was going to pull me out when I finished my mission. In the meantime, the sheriff could help me stay alive.

If I had to be stuck with someone, Taylor was my obvious choice.

"Okay," I said finally. "Truth."

Taylor's gaze lifted. He moved past me into the bedroom and approached Philip. I watched in surprise as he took the arm of the man clearly protesting John's choice of son-in-law and escorted him outside the room, down the stairs and to the main floor.

John appeared restless.

I entered once more and sat by his side. "I'm here, Father," I said.

He sighed, a flicker of his previous joy in his eyes.

The sight of it destroyed me. I didn't deserve the look or emotion. Tears I didn't think I should feel pricked my eyes. I had never known my own father and was losing the father of real-Josie, a man I shouldn't have ever met. One whose love for his daughter was completely selfless, unconditional and pure.

Sitting next to him, I felt dirty. I had never loved anyone the way he did me or rather, who he thought I was. He deserved to know about his daughter, but I couldn't say the words. I didn't *want* to say the words and forever lose the way his loving look made me feel.

I focused on his face.

The doctor stepped away into the hallway, speaking to Nell and the preacher beside her. I sneaked my phone out of my pocket to check Carter's message. For once, he had responded with a thorough message.

Taylor was identified by the first woman sent back to that time period and the rest of you were given his name to figure out who he is. You were the first to have the memory chip installed. If the chip can't read him, it's because he shouldn't be there – at all. He doesn't exist anywhere in time or history. Even the knowledge you shared of him being a sheriff is nowhere in the history books. Basically, he is operating in time without leaving any trace.

I read it, struggling to understand what Carter was really saying. It wasn't possible for someone simply not to exist when he clearly did. I texted a quick note back, *What the hell does that mean?* hit send, and pocketed the cell once more.

"Josie?"

"I'm here," I said and took John's hand again. "Right beside you. The uh … preacher is here, too."

"Tell … Carter … thank you."

My breath stuck in my throat. "W … what?"

John smiled once more and squeezed my hand.

"Miss Josie, we are to do the ceremony at once," Nell said and took my arm.

"No, wait!" I tugged away.

"He has not more than an hour!" Nell hissed in my ear. "Do not disappoint him now, Miss Josie! I forbid it!"

How can John know Carter? I let my governess pull me away, silently willing John to stay alive long enough for me to ask him about Carter.

The preacher, Taylor, doctor, another well-dressed man I took to be the attorney, Judge Cromwell, and even a fiercely frowning Philip stood in the bedroom. The preacher's bible was open and Taylor was before him, too calm for me to read. I joined them and took my place beside Taylor, the sense of disconnect returning.

"Talk about a shotgun wedding," I muttered.

"*You* dragged *me* into this," Taylor whispered.

"Hush, Miss Josie, Sheriff!" my nanny hissed.

"Go sit by my father," I ordered her. "He shouldn't be alone right now."

Nell obeyed.

Taylor glanced at me with a look that expressed his bafflement at the impromptu wedding. The preacher began reading hastily with occasional glances towards the bed, as if to ensure John was still alive. I half-listened, too stunned by the evening to digest what was going on. I itched to ask John about Carter.

"… ring," the preacher said expectantly.

Taylor cleared his throat and shifted.

"This was her mother's. It is meant to be hers." Philip held out a massive ruby and gold ring to Taylor.

"Repeat after me, Sheriff," the preacher directed. "With this ring, I thee wed …"

Taylor mumbled the words. He took my hand and slid the ring onto my ring finger then met my gaze. In that moment, it was the two of us in the middle of the sacred rite I was nowhere near prepared for. The calm around him indicative of a man with no history and no existence buffered me against the onslaught of memories from those standing too close. Taylor took my hands, and I saw a flicker of uncertainty in his gaze, a sign he, too, wasn't quite ready for this occasion.

I experienced the disconnect once more, the sense I was watching myself go through the bizarre ceremony rather than living it. At one point, I murmured an *I, do,* and then Taylor leaned forward to give me an awkward, quick peck on the lips.

Then it was over. Everyone but Philip appeared happy, and I forced a smile as they congratulated me. My gaze went to John. He was awake. Nell had propped him up with pillows to see. While the film over his eyes kept him from witnessing it, he still smiled broadly.

The flock of people moved from me to John's bedside, and the preacher immediately began last rites.

I listened to the solemn words spoken softly. The heads of everyone there were bowed while I stood back, struggling to remain afloat, unattached, when I felt like I was getting ready to drown in their world. The harder I tried to pull away from feeling anything, the more difficult it became. I stood perfectly still, afraid of moving for fear of jarring loose the emotions building inside me.

Why did I feel so sad about John? It was more than my soft heart at work. The longing was back, the fervent yet wasted wish to know my own father, combined with the sorrow I still experienced whenever I thought about my parents dying in a plane crash.

Someone took my hand, and I blinked, looking up to see Taylor gazing down at me. He squeezed my hand, attention returning to the bed where John lay. I continued to gaze at him in consternation, not understanding when my purpose here became so complicated.

The rattling of John's breathing slowed and then stopped. His pallor changed quickly from one of life to death, and his features relaxed as he slid into permanent sleep.

Nell stifled a sob, while the others prayed in silence.

I watched, frozen in the place between places, a stranger to this world and the sole person the dead man loved. I owed him more without understanding what exactly my obligation was to a man I had only known for several days.

"Miss Josie, if you would like to say your farewell." The preacher rose and stepped away to make room for me.

I went mechanically, not sure how my body worked when my mind had stopped. Seeing John like this left me cored and empty, no matter how much I told myself he wasn't my real father.

I bent over the frail old man and planted a kiss on his forehead.

"Goodbye, Father. I wish I had known you better." *Or at all.*

Straightening, I began to think again, to comprehend why the death of a stranger was traumatizing. In saying farewell to him, I was also telling my own father, another man I had never known, goodbye. I was two when he passed, too young to understand what I did now of life and death.

"A night of sadness and also of joy," the preacher said.

"The undertaker will be here shortly to prepare the body for burial," the doctor said. "Miss Josephine, my deepest condolences and most heart felt congratulations."

I acknowledged him with a nod, unable to look away from John.

"Come, Miss Josie. Sheriff, Jeremiah will show you to your chamber."

I didn't resist when Nell took my arms and steered me away. She held my hand all the way back to my room. I entered and sat heavily, gaze on the dancing fire.

Nell didn't speak this night like she normally did. She brushed my hair and laid out my sleeping gown, along with an overcoat this night and slippers. I changed and pushed the slippers aside to lie down on my bed.

"Miss Josie, your husband awaits," Nell called from the bathroom. "Don't you go lying down yet."

"He can wait until I feel like dealing with him," I said, a bit miffed at having the silence disrupted when I was trying to sort out my emotions.

"Miss Josie! He's the master of the house now!"

Sex was the last thing on my mind. I couldn't purge my thoughts of the vision of John lying on the bed.

Tell Carter thank you. What was the connection between them?

"I'm not going." I said and lay down anyway.

"Miss Josie!"

"No, Nell!"

Nell appeared too surprised to react. If I didn't feel numb, I would've laughed at her expression.

There was a tap at my door. Nell shook her head and went to answer it.

I rolled onto my stomach, not caring who it was. If Philip wanted to beat me senseless this night the way he did his servants, I didn't think I'd feel a thing.

The door closed. "Just tell him I don't feel right tonight, Nell," I said before my nanny could speak.

"I don't reckon you do." Taylor's low voice startled me.

I sat up. Nell was gone. He was dressed the way he had been the night before, in loose pants and cotton shirt and barefoot.

"I'm not expecting … " He motioned to the bed and cleared his throat. "To tell you the truth, I'm a little afraid of Nell."

With a startled laugh, I looked quickly to the door to make sure Nell hadn't remained behind.

"I thought we could talk. That's it," Taylor said.

I glimpsed the sinewy muscles stretched across his wide torso visible through the deep V-neck of his shirt. Tight curls were spread over his upper chest.

The sexy man was a welcome distraction from the clamor of emotions in my head. "Yeah, sure," I said and climbed out of bed. "By the fire."

I dragged a blanket with me to the hearth. It was warm and toasty, and I sat. Taylor did so as well, propping his elbows up on his knees, his lean torso drawing my attention once more.

We gazed at one another. The flames reflected in Taylor's mint green eyes. I tried to wrap my head around the idea we were *married* and in the end, decided the real-Josie was married, and I was just visiting. At twenty-two with no career, I hadn't thought twice about a permanent relationship, let alone marriage.

"You really cared about him," Taylor started.

"Of course I did. He's my father," I replied.

"Truth."

I looked away. "Do we have to do this tonight?" I groaned.

"It's not like he was really your father."

Emotions swirled. I clenched my fists in an attempt to hang onto emotions that were bubbling to be free. "He was more of a father than I've ever had. I shouldn't … care. But I do. Is that weird?"

"No. You're a good person, Josie," he replied and then frowned.

"Is Josie even your real name?"

"Yes. Is yours Taylor?"

"Of course." He gave me an odd look. "You're the stranger here, not me."

"Yeah, right."

His expression softened into compassion. "Are you okay?"

I swallowed the lump in my throat and nodded. "John made me feel found for the first time in my life. He didn't care who I was or wasn't. Just *loved* me." My voice cracked, and I cleared my throat. Surprised by the depth of truth in my statement, I tried hard to push away the feelings making it difficult for me to breathe or think. "Does that make sense?"

"It does." Taylor was gazing at me. "Josie, if you're going to cry … I'm not good with women."

"I don't know what I feel. I just …" Struggling with my feelings, I shook my head. "I don't know. Confused, I think." I laughed. "How about I warn you if I decide to cry."

"Fair enough."

"You could cheer me up by taking off your shirt," I teased. Of the two of us, I was beginning to think Nell needed to give him The Talk instead of me.

"We *are* married."

"You ready for that?"

"Mostly."

Grinning, I studied him. "You're an interesting person, Taylor Hansen."

"As are you, Josie Hansen."

A little raw, somewhat curious, and a whole lot needing to avoid my emotions, I shuffled to him and flung the blanket around his shoulders, too. "Come on. Get close."

He shifted to wrap one arm around my shoulders and pulled me into his hard frame. I sank into him. He was warm, smelled of soap and man, and solid. In college, I'd have jumped at the chance to sleep with him but tonight ... I didn't feel right. I didn't currently care, either, that he was a mystery to me, one I wasn't certain I could trust or wanted to know more about.

I just needed ... this. Someone to ground me from my spinning emotions and confusion.

"John was a good man," he whispered.

"Yeah, he really was." I rested my cheek on his chest and gazed into the fire.

I wish I'd known my father. I had pictures of him at home, but it dawned on me that I couldn't visualize his face at the moment. I saw John's. Why had I never paid more attention to what my parents looked like? *Because looking at the pictures felt like watching John die.* It simply hurt too much.

My breath caught in my throat.

"Do you need me to do anything?" Taylor asked, his grip tightening around me.

"Stay here. Don't let me go until I'm asleep."

"Yes, ma'am." He hugged me to him.

Good man. There was no way a man willing to hold me all night was the bad guy Carter made him out to be. There had to be another explanation.

Chapter Fourteen

THE PHONE BUZZING IN MY POCKET PULLED ME OUT OF A dreamless slumber the next morning.

I awoke with an even worse headache, one brought on as much from my cold as the nightmares. I barely recalled what happened after I dozed off in Taylor's arms, but at some point, the nightmares crept into my slumber. I fell asleep cradled against him and awoke in my bed.

Irritated, I rolled enough to pry the phone free and checked the messages from Carter.

I'm thinking about how to explain space-time theory. Read the first of three messages.

"Ugh, Carter." Not in the mood for science, I pushed myself up and looked around. Tea was waiting for me on the table beside the fire. I crawled out of bed and sat down to drink a cup.

The night weighed heavily in my thoughts, the demise of a good man like John and my shotgun wedding to Taylor. He'd been a gentleman last night and cuddled with me. Some of my suspicions about him melted as I realized how many times he'd had the chance to harm me and had done the opposite.

When my head had righted itself enough for me to return to Carter's texts, I placed my phone on the table.

Short version: Someone is scrubbing his presence in the past from the history books. I do the same for you, which means he's like you. Sent back but not by me. That means the person who sent him is the man trying to undo what I'm doing. Or I'm trying to undo what he is. Whatever. Either way, this Taylor guy is working against you.

I leaned forward and reread the note before going to the third.

So ... I'd say to stay as far from him as possible now that we know the empathic memories can't read him either. He's likely there to stop you on the twentieth fourth.

"That might be an issue." This time, my heart skipped a beat for a reason other than my admiration of Taylor's fantastic abs. I dwelt on Carter's notes, my instincts wriggling.

Taylor was hiding a lot more than how he knew to find me the night I landed.

"The mystery deepens," I murmured and responded with a more pressing question. "*How do you know John, Carter?*" I sent the question.

"You say something?" Taylor called from the bathroom.

"No!" I shoved the phone under my napkin just as he emerged, dressed, freshly shaven and with a wet head. His green eyes were piercing. They traveled from the napkin I clenched to my face.

"How do you feel?" he asked.

"Better, thanks." Not one to blush in front of men, I recalled his kindness last night with mixed feelings. Enemy or ... what the hell was the alternative, if he was a time traveler lying to me about who he was?

The quiet between us was awkward. He cleared his throat finally.

"I'm, uh, headed into town."

"I'll be here," I murmured.

Without another word, he turned and left. I watched him. He had a perfect body down to the tight, round globes of his ass. *At least I married a hottie.* I almost laughed, baffled by the turn of events.

The phone vibrated beneath my hand, and I uncovered it.

"*Long story. Will tell you about it sometime,*" I read the note from Carter aloud. "You have too many secrets, Carter." I hesitated then responded. *Slight problem about Taylor. Think of us as being the only people left on a deserted island. We can't really escape each other. How dangerous is he?*

My insides quaked at the thought of what Carter would say. His assessment of my situation made me wish I had never asked. His response was quick.

Very. As in, if Taylor didn't get rid of your predecessors, his people did. Watch yourself.

"Shit." I lowered the phone to my lap and sat thinking for a minute. Before John's death, I had been on my way to the savages who were going to start a war. But if Taylor was here to prevent me from stopping the war ... "I'm so confused."

Taylor hadn't been the one to take out the girls, though. That much I knew. Intense and able to smell my lies a mile away, he nonetheless was earnest in believing he was supposed to help my predecessors and me, not hurt them. He had also called Carter a madman for implanting chips in my brain.

It made me think whatever was between him and Carter, it was personal.

My thoughts drifted to the well behind the barn.

He hadn't done it. The whispers last time had almost told me who did.

"Nell!" I called.

The servant was never far away. "Yes, Miss Josie?" Nell appeared wearing all black. My spirits dampened.

"I need some air."

"Of course. Your dress is ready. We will lay your father to rest this evening."

I sighed, depressed by the thought.

"Where would you like to go?" Nell asked as I brought in the black dress and corset.

"I feel like I need to be alone. I'm going to the barn."

Nell raised an eyebrow.

"The animals make me smile," I explained.

"Very well, Miss Josie." Nell's normal spark was gone.

I watched my nanny move efficiently as always, in constant motion while her eyes remained so sad. I had the urge to comfort the woman who had been in love with the man who just died but didn't know what to say. Struggling with my own unexpected grief, I ended up not speaking at all as I dressed in black out of respect for my faux-father's death.

Nell didn't dog me out the door like I expected, another sign of her profound grief.

I went to the barn and stepped inside, breathing in the scent of horses, leather and hay. The smells were comforting, and I paused to rub the foreheads of a few horses before leaving the barn and circling it.

I went to the well. Its whispers were faint enough I barely registered them until I was in physical contact with the stone wall. I sank to my knees beside it and closed my eyes, focusing on the images.

Fractured visions floated through my mind, and I grappled with the message the stones were trying to give me. A woman with blond hair falling. The form of a man peering into the well more than once. It was dark when he came both times, his form and features hidden by the night.

One of the women had survived the fall and died slowly, I realized as I watched. There was a stream of memories illustrating the passing of day and night, of shadows that crept down one side of the well as the sun rose and up the other side as it set.

Three nights, I counted. The woman had lasted three nights and days before the memories stopped.

Stricken by what I saw, I took a break to ground myself before I closed my eyes and sought the memories for a second round. My hands trembled, and it took all my willpower not to let my thoughts dwell on what it would be like to lie, broken, at the bottom of a well for three days.

The form of a man was present only one of the streams while the other two girls were pushed from behind and never saw their attacker.

I focused hard on capturing what I could from the image of the man.

It wasn't Taylor. At least, there was no sense of familiarity from the girl peering up at him, and all three had met him. I didn't know why I was so relieved. How he was involved, I didn't yet understand.

Carter's text jolted my out of the recollections of others. I relaxed and wiped my face, exhausted and distraught. I checked my phone.

Then I suggest you run to the other side of the island. Fast. Stay away from him, Josie. He's dangerous.

It wasn't the response I wanted. Carter thought me in trouble of some kind, but I disagreed. If Taylor meant to do me harm, he'd had plenty of opportunities alone with me. There was something about him that made me uneasy, but it wasn't *this* - mortal danger like that which threatened the others.

I hesitated before replying. *What happened to the fifth girl? There are three in the well, me and ... ?*

What if she died in the house, in the room at the end of the hallway?

"They are your friends?" Fighting Badger's voice startled me, and I jumped.

Twisting to see him, I couldn't help the flare of fear that warmed my breast and made my heart race. He squatted a short distance away, dressed in breeches and vest, his long black hair down.

"No," I answered. Sudden interest replaced the unsettled feeling I always got when he was around. "Can you hear them?"

He cocked his head to the side, listening. "Some. They are very faint. Very unhappy."

"The girls in the well are … were … like me. From the future. Someone killed them," I explained. "They've been trying to tell me who hurt them, and I just can't see it." I hesitated then motioned him forward. "Sometimes if you touch something, the memories are stronger." I flattened my palms on the stones.

Fighting Badger took the invitation and sat down beside me, mirroring my movements. We were quiet for a moment. I watched the shadowy images of his twisted mind morph into the memories of the girls at the bottom of the well.

"I see me," he voiced after a moment. "I heard two spirits one night. I did not know the third was alive."

"She suffered a lot," I whispered, stricken by the idea of such a slow death. "Can you see the man who did this?"

Fighting Badger was quiet for a moment. He stood, the bone necklace he wore clinking with his movements. He leaned over the well, straightened then did it again. "A child," he said finally.

"What do you mean?" I asked.

"Look." He took my arm and pulled me to my feet. "Lean over." Uncertain what he was doing, I mirrored his movement. He bent with me over the edge. "A man has a longer shadow." He pointed to me. "A child or woman much smaller. She saw two shadows: mine and one your size."

"A woman," I whispered. My eyes went to the boards beneath my torso. I straightened, pensive. The fifth girl sent back by Carter, someone who might be able to identify other time travelers on the spot.

"Yes."

There were half a dozen female servants in the house and Nell. I didn't see my governess doing this; she had been as ecstatic to see me as John. It made sense the first woman sent back to this era was close, that she might be hiding nearby or within the ranks of servants.

"He knew nothing about you except that you had to be stopped."

I looked up at Fighting Badger's words. "Who?"

"The man who tried to hurt my brother and you. He set fire to the cabin as a warning to my brother."

"So he knew your brother?"

"He said he did."

"What happened …" I stopped. His memories formed once more, and this time, they were absolutely horrifying. "Stop, stop, stop!"

They dissipated into shadows. Fighting Badger smiled.

I released a breath. "Okay. You found the one with blue eyes. What about the other?"

"Other?"

"There were two men in your head that night," I said. "This one and one who was … think about that night again." The memories were faint and very hard to distinguish, given how dark and stormy it had been. "You saw him. I couldn't find him in your head if you hadn't. He was camouflaged, a large shadow, one who had been following you. At one point you thought you heard him?"

"I did," Fighting Badger was hushed. "I saw nothing."

"I saw him, and I think you did, too. I don't think you knew it at the time though."

He snatched my arms suddenly enough that I gasped. "What else? Tell me who he is." His dark eyes burned into me.

"That's all I can see. That's all there is."

Fighting Badger glared at me.

"I wouldn't lie to you," I whispered. "Especially after you helped me."

The fire faded from his dark depths, and he released me.

"Miss Josie!"

"I have to go," I said and stepped back. "You shouldn't be seen here."

Fighting Badger didn't budge. He was still enough to be a statue, his eyes the only part of him that moved. He was watching me.

"Thank you for helping me," I added.

He shifted finally and turned away.

Of all the people here, I understood him the best and least. Our shared skill did nothing to shed light on the source of his depravity.

Hungry and unnerved, I left the well. It was near noon, and I had learned all I thought I would from the dead women in the well. Uncertain what to do with the knowledge of the location of their bodies, I dwelt on their memories while arguing silently with how to help women who were already dead.

At the very least, they deserved real burials instead of being discarded like trash. But revealing that I knew they were there would place me in danger without knowing the threat.

My lunch was waiting for me in my room. I sat down to eat without tasting much. I had the urge to talk to John, even knowing he wasn't there. The house was too quiet with everyone in mourning.

Uncertain what to think about Taylor, I was relieved he'd gone to work rather than stay with me. His home had burnt down, or I'd search it.

Convenient timing. I lowered the glass of water from my lips and gazed at the hearth. My previous suspicions resurfaced: Taylor's connection to the man who burnt down his cabin, his secret about the night he found me, how he knew what he shouldn't about me. He was always around when I needed him most.

Unease stirred within me. He had also rescued me twice, held me when I was upset last night and had multiple chances to do something bad to me.

Stay away from him, Josie. He's dangerous. Carter seemed pretty certain.

The more I thought about him, the more confused I became.

But the real danger was someone else. Someone in the house. That much I felt with certainty.

Sad and distraught, I flung myself onto my bed to stare at the ceiling before I sat up suddenly.

Without Nell looking over my shoulder, I had time to look at the phones the girls had left in more depth. I closed and locked my door before dropping beside the armoire and sliding the bottom drawer open. I carefully pulled the fake bottom of the drawer open to reveal the three phones.

I replaced the drawer and took the phones to the space between the wall and bed, where no one who had a key could enter and see what I did. I started with the oldest phone with the cracked screen. I flipped it on and off and then squinted at the screen to try to read any messages that popped up.

"Nada," I murmured and set it aside. I reread the messages on the other two. Carter had been in a panic when he sent them. Taking a picture of one, I sent it to him with a note. *Why did you tell her to get out?*

The phones were in good shape, aside from the oldest one with a busted screen. There was no indication of who they belonged to, no stickers or personalized covers. Disappointed not to find more out about the mysterious women, I returned them to the armoire and sat back.

"Who the hell put you all there?" I asked the jewelry box with some frustration. "Why only three? Where's the fourth?" And who was the fifth woman?

Would I be able to spot her if we crossed paths, or had she gone native? Determined to find out who wanted me dead before I ended up at the bottom of the well, I left my room.

I wandered the house. I went first to John's room and stood outside it. He wasn't there, but it still *felt* like he was. The enhanced memories drifted to me the way those from the well did, in splintered patches of randomness that were difficult to follow, except when it came to the images of his wife and daughter.

"He loved them so much," I whispered, heart heavy. My eyelids drifted closed, and I watched the joyous memories of the old man that lingered with his energy in the place he passed away. Carrying real-Josie around on his hip, visiting the town square for a parade with his wife, stopping by the market at the edge of town …

I sucked in a breath, touched by the emotion that remained after John was dead. It was beautiful, pure, in a world that seemed to grow darker around me. I made another mental note to ask Carter what exactly he put in my head and how it worked when we met next.

For another ten minutes, I stood outside John's door, the rhythmic tick-tock of his grandfather clock the only sound. I watched the happy memories. Not yet convinced I did the right thing by hiding the truth, I suspected John might've known, since he knew Carter.

I released my breath and left his room.

I could hear the dead. It was a good thing when I sought a missing person. I moved slowly through the house with its multiple parlors and sitting rooms, listening for any whispers or trickles of memories that brushed by me.

Tracking down every servant I could, I greeted them all and watched how they reacted. If time travelers had a tell, I wasn't seeing it.

Hours later, I returned to my hallway and walked down it as well, realizing I had been avoiding the obvious: the source of my nightmares, the room at the very end. A whisper tickled the back of my neck, and I paused at the door.

Something terrible had happened there. The images were blurry, of blood and darkness. Two people ... a fight ... could that be what happened to the missing time traveler?

"Miss Josie!" Nell's call made me jump.

I faced her.

"Why are you not resting?"

"I got bored," I replied.

"That room is forbidden to you." Nell shook her head. "Come. Let me fix your hair before the wake."

I hesitated, intrigued by the idea she didn't want me in the room beckoning to me. It meant she knew something about it. With another look at the door, I returned to my bedroom, where Nell waited behind my chair.

"Why is that room forbidden?" I asked.

"It was your father's direction." She raked the brush through my hair.

I winced. I couldn't imagine her brushing the hair of baby-Josie like this. "You don't know why?"

"It was not my place to ask."

Her thoughts were ... blank. The strange, brief gap fueled my curiosity. She wasn't lying, but ...

I hadn't yet run into something like this. A block, one I didn't think was purposeful, similar to how my uncle's old school record player sometimes skipped.

Half an hour later, I left the house in a heavier than usual gown and black veil that reached my knees. A sleek back coffin was in the back of an elegant carriage, John's best, if I had to guess. I frowned at the final resting place for the kindly man. It wasn't anywhere near what such a beautiful soul deserved.

"Ms. Nell, Miss Josie."

I turned at Taylor's low voice, heart taking off for two reasons this time. He was dressed in a dark suit that appeared new and nothing like what he normally wore. He gazed at me, unreadable. He was sexy as sin in his worn, patched clothing and even more so in a new suit.

More people arrived as I waited, and I found myself moving towards Taylor as much because he cancelled out the memories accosting me as because of how much I admired his striking eyes and the way the suit fit him. I was attracted to him and had been since we met.

Half the town was here, to include Running Bear and several other natives who kept their distance from the others. Without Taylor's presence, I'd be in a puddle on the ground from the onslaught of memories of the people standing so close. As it was, there was something I could almost read from *him* for once. A fuzzy vision of grays and black, of a sky and beneath it …

Almost … I released my breath. One tiny memory was trying to reach me from his mind and failed to make it the last step.

"How was your day?" I asked. I searched his handsome face for some sign of what he hid from me and how dangerous Carter claimed him to be.

"Well." His attention was on the crowd. I had no trouble believing he wasn't one who liked crowds or who knew how to handle his sudden fame in the small town. "Would you care to join me for supper?"

"We're married. Aren't you supposed to order your poor little wife around?"

He chuckled, a flare of genuine warmth crossing his features before it disappeared. "I can. Thought I'd ask first."

"I'd like that," I said, unable to help my smile. *Just don't be the bad guy.* I almost sighed. "We can talk tonight," I added. I didn't have much more time to win him to my side and help me stop the native twins.

"Deal." He offered me his hand.

Together, we walked behind the wagon through the property, trailed by half the town, to a small plot on the backside of a hill in a graveyard. There were five headstones present already with John's grave dug out.

Grateful for the veil, I did my best not to cry too much. I was spent from the night before and just a little afraid of drawing the attention of Philip, who was always within about four feet of me.

I moved away from Taylor to go to the casket. The assault of memories from the townspeople hit me like a stiff wind.

Don't faint. It took a moment for me to steady the foreign, swirling images and emotions in my head. I moved to the far side of the casket, where only the memories of two people were able to reach me instead of the dozen that nearly drowned me.

And then there were *the rest.* I turned to face the other tombstones in the peaceful, well-kept family cemetery.

The dead were talking again. Most were too faint for me to make out, and only one appeared to be … *unhappy,* as Fighting Badger might say. This one was close and, judging by the power of the whisper, somewhat … fresh.

Who would've been buried recently in the family graveyard? I resisted the urge to step towards the whisper. There was no grave where it came from.

"Miss Josie," the preacher said.

Realizing everyone was watching me, I focused on John's casket and bent to lay a wreath of flowers on it. Taylor's arm was around Nell, who wept hard enough for her shoulders to quake.

As selfish as it seemed, I was grateful not to know that kind of pain. I ached for John more than I should, but Nell had no closure with him at all after years spent pining for him.

The preacher began speaking once more. The casket was lowered, and I whispered a final farewell and thank you to the man who showed me what it was like to have a father, even if only for a few days.

The throng of people returned to the area behind the house, where long tables had been overloaded with a feast of food. Bonfires blazed on either side for warmth, and the group sat around the tables, talking and eating.

Sticking close to Taylor so he cancelled out my empathic memory chip, I picked at my food, uncomfortable with Philip seated across the table from me and even less certain what I was supposed to do since Carter hadn't messaged me in half a day.

I had the urge to return to the cemetery once everyone else was gone, to listen to the whisper I'd heard.

It was close to midnight by the time the last guest left, and I made my way up the stairs to my bedroom, trailed by Nell. My nanny helped me change and laid out the slippers once more.

I eyed them. The other thought I hadn't dwelt on as much as I probably should have: what Taylor expected on our second night married. Instead, I was thinking about dead people.

I had slept with men whose names I didn't know the next morning, but something about Taylor was different, and it wasn't just Carter's assertion he was dangerous.

It was the sense of familiarity, the fact I didn't fear him, no matter how many times Carter told me he was a threat. It was almost like some part of me – whether instinct or magical chip – knew Taylor was what he claimed to be: someone who would help me.

The mischievous part of me looked forward to embarrassing him. I slid my feet into the slippers. Nell gave me an approving nod and led me out of the hallway and down John's wing. We passed his room, and I released a breath, relieved we weren't going to the chamber where he died.

Nell left me at the door of Taylor's room, and I hesitated a moment before knocking.

He answered it, dressed in his pajama bottoms and a loose shirt. Stepping aside, he motioned for me to enter.

His room was as large as mine, decorated in manly shades of dark blue and red, with a bed that was closer to a king size than my full bed. I faced him, curious in the tense silence between us. The butterflies were back, along with the distant reminder that Carter seemed to think Taylor was bad.

I just don't see it.

Taylor's eyes swept over me quickly, as if he was afraid to look too long, before he crossed to a carafe of amber liquid I assumed was whiskey. He poured a glass and offered it to me.

I shook my head.

He poured himself one and tossed it back.

"You all right?" I asked.

"I am … new to this."

"To what? Being married?"

His eyes went to the bed in a silent response.

"Wait. You're a virgin?" I asked, astonished.

Red crept up his face. "Not a virgin. No honorable woman will consider someone raised by savages. I've visited the soiled doves once a year on my birthday and …" He drifted off and cleared his throat.

My unease vanished, and I tempered the urge to tease him. He had been uncomfortable but dutiful all evening long. The sight of the uncertainty dogging an otherwise confident man touched me. "I got you covered." I grinned and went to the hearth.

He frowned but joined me. "Where you're from … you're … "

I glanced at him. Every once in a while, he said something that reminded me he knew more about me than I did him. I wasn't always certain what to think about that. "Where I come from, men and women both try on relationships before they're married. It's like pretending to be married to see if it works."

"Does it work?"

"Not usually."

His brow furrowed.

"I'm not a virgin, if that's what you're asking," I supplied. "Have a seat. We can talk."

He left the tumbler on the tray and sat beside me the way he had last night. Apprehension and desire eddied and spun through me. We gazed at each other. I found myself fiddling with the ties of my housecoat, as if it were my first night. I stilled my hands.

"I've never touched a woman meant to be mine," he said softly.

The way he said it robbed me of any shred of amusement I had at being thrown back in time with a near virgin. To him, this wasn't pretending or temporary. It wasn't going to be another one-night stand for me, not when it was *real* to him. I didn't want to hurt him when I left.

I also didn't understand how he could know I didn't belong here – and still believed this arrangement to be real.

"We don't have to do anything," I said. "You don't seem comfortable."

"I want to. I don't know where to start," he admitted. "I've been alone here for so long. I'm not sure what to think about all this." He motioned to the room. "I've never had nothing, Josie, and now I have everything." There was a familiar glow in his gaze, one that reminded me too much of the look John gave me often and stirred my guilt.

I hate lying to good people.

"Maybe I do need a drink," I murmured and stood. I went to the whiskey and poured a shot, gazing absently at my reflection in the mirror of the dresser behind the table on which the tray sat.

How did I tell him not to get attached? He was somehow part of all this yet oblivious at the same time. Unable to make heads or tails of him, I likewise didn't know why I was drawn to trust him.

Taylor rose. "If you're not ready, I understand," he said and ran a hand through his hair. "I'm not sure I am."

And then he said something completely endearing, and I wasn't able to see the danger Carter swore was there. I met his gaze in the mirror and replaced the tumbler. Despite what little I knew about Taylor, no part of me felt like walking away from him tonight.

"We could talk," he offered.

"Oh, hell no. I'm ready, and I'm going to make you blush," I replied with forced cheerfulness. I fumbled with the ties on my housecoat and pulled them free. I let the garb drop to my feet to reveal the near-sheer, sleeveless nightgown I took for being risqué in this era.

His cheeks were pink. Taylor's eyes went down my yoga-toned form. He hesitated and then stepped forward, his heat warming my back. As if afraid to hurt me, he rested his hands lightly enough on my arms to make me shiver.

"It's okay, Taylor. I won't break," I said with a small laugh.

"I know. I want to remember this forever. You only get married once." By the earnestness in his words and face, he was serious.

I'm a piece of shit. Pretending to be one man's daughter and another's wife … I wanted to scream. Instead I drew a breath and closed my eyes, focused on Taylor's caress. I could wear out my attraction to him or better yet, see if sex would motivate him to help me. I hated using people as much as I did lying to them, but if I wanted to succeed and go home, I needed his help.

He ran his palms down my arms and back up to my shoulders. Fingers tickled the sensitive skin of my neck, and I shivered. Fire bloomed in my lower belly. I relaxed and leaned against him.

He traced the tattoo at the base of my neck. "What is it?"

"Pink lotus," I murmured. "I thought it was pretty."

"It's beautiful," he agreed. "You have more?"

"Nope. Just that one."

Taylor's fingers moved to my hair, and I bowed my head so he could undo the simple bun Nell had made. Long, blonde curls toppled down my shoulders. He pushed them over one shoulder and I bared my neck to him, my head resting on his chest. His hand went across my collarbone and around my neck loosely before it strayed to my left shoulder.

His simple caresses were mesmerizing, his intent of memorizing every curve and dip of my body clear in the slow, sensual, light touch. I barely noticed when he pushed the nightgown over my shoulders and down to my feet. His hands traced my sides, hips and across my stomach. He pressed his hips to my ass, his hard erection long and thick enough for me to approve of it even without seeing it.

The brush of his fingertips over my sensitive nipples made my breath catch, and I resisted the urge to shove his hand down my belly to the place between my thighs that ached. I was experienced, but he was just learning.

"You're the most beautiful woman I've ever seen, Josie." he whispered, awe and appreciation mixing with husky need.

I said nothing, lost in the tickling sensations of his hands exploring me. He turned me carefully, and I opened my eyes to gaze up at him. The intensity of his look stripped away my attempt to remain unattached, and I let myself dwell in wonder at the idea of belonging with a man like this, one who treasured every inch of me and wanted our first night to last forever in his memories.

There was nothing standing between us, not two hundred years, Carter or my mission. I was falling into the green depths of his eyes, the tender way he touched me.

But it wasn't enough for me to want to stay.

I hesitated a moment before realizing I was already in too deep to want to walk away without one of us getting hurt. I slid my hands under his shirt and pushed the material up. Taylor's hands left me to remove it before they returned to my hips. He pressed his to mine, and I rested my palms on his chest.

His body was perfect. Thick biceps, rounded shoulders, wiry chest and washboard abs. I traced his skin with the same restraint and gentleness he had mine, admiring the smooth texture and the muscles beneath. I wasn't certain I had ever really noticed a man's body before aside from the part below the waist I was normally concerned with.

"May I kiss you, Josie?" he whispered.

"You don't have to ask, Taylor," I replied and took his planed cheeks. I pulled his face to mine and rested my lips lightly against his. "Just kiss me."

He cupped my cheeks in his hands and obeyed.

I melted into him. Initially unsure, he soon began to descend into hunger. His velvety tongue slid between my lips, and I opened for him readily, returning the kiss with passion. He tasted of whiskey and his own unique flavor. I nipped at his full lower lip playfully. Taking his hands, I slid them down my shape to my ass. He froze for a split second before digging his fingers into my cheeks and pressing me harder against his erection. He trailed hot, wet kisses down my jaw and neck.

"Ah, yeah," I breathed, eyes closing. "I love that you want me that much."

"I do," he replied. "I have since the first day I saw you."

He's a good man. Guilt shot through me but was swallowed by the more immediate urge to feel his naked body pressed to mine. I may have hated lying to good people, but I was no saint. The furnace in my belly was demanding, my core aching with need.

Taylor's ministrations remained measured and slow, rendering me breathless and so turned on, I trembled. My desire soon overcame my patience, and I pushed at his chest in complaint. "Taylor!"

He chuckled. "You've never broken a horse."

"Did you just call me a horse?" I opened my eyes to look at him quizzically.

"No." He was smiling. "The more time you take with a horse, the more rewarding the results."

I started to laugh and then stopped, realizing a near virgin was schooling me on sex. "We'll do it your way," I murmured. A thrill of exhilaration rippled through me. "Break me, Taylor." I grinned.

Lust flared in his gaze. His arms wrapped around me, and he kissed me hard and deep, until I was breathless and held up only by his embrace. Despite his intention to take it slow, Taylor appeared to be struggling.

The wicked side of me wanted to see him lose it. I rubbed his erection through his pants, nipped at his lips, and wriggled against him provocatively, pushing him closer and closer to what I craved.

Taylor responded by slowing his caresses, tapping his fingers against the mound of my pussy without touching the aching nub or dipping into my core. He licked and sucked on the peaks of my breasts and trailed kisses down my neck and back.

When at last he lost his pants and steered me towards the bed, I was close to panting, begging and barely able to walk. He laughed in response and pressed me onto my back, his kisses growing harder and more desperate.

I wriggled beneath him, moaning when his erection brushed the opening of my core. My hands went down his lean abdomen and around to his ass. I dug my fingernails into his cheeks. Taylor captured my mouth and entered me with the same slow control he used to tease every inch of my skin.

I arched beneath him, close to coming from the simple penetration. His dick filled me, stretched my sheath to capacity. Neither drunk sex nor sex with the man I was engaged to felt this incredible. Need and pleasure sizzled across every nerve ending and rippled through me as if this was the first time I had ever truly been aware when it came to sex.

"Yes!" I hissed. "Taylor …"

He kissed my neck. "You feel …" He ended with a groan. "Tight. Jesus. So tight!" His body shook from control and emotion.

"Show me what you got, cowboy," I whispered and then bit his earlobe hard.

His control shattered. Taylor began to thrust hard and deep, penetrating me with desperation I shared. I clung to him, unable to recall when I last experienced sex like this. My orgasm built quickly, and I tensed beneath him as my muscles grew taut.

Even before it hit, I knew it was going to be unlike any other climax. I was too aroused, too aware of Taylor's every breath, too connected to him for it to be anything other than a shattering of my body and heart at once.

My orgasm snapped, and I cried out his name, washed away in waves of pleasure that started in my core and tore through me with intensity that left me breathless, lost.

Taylor came shortly after me. He bucked and plunged into me

several more times before collapsing, his hard breathing in my ears.

I panted and wrapped my arms around him, trembling from the intensity of the orgasm still working its way through my system. My sheath pulsed and rippled around his dick, and I wrapped my legs around his lean hips, crossing them at the ankle to keep him buried deep inside of me.

"Good, Taylor," I whispered. "You can be taught."

He lifted his head. His eyes glowed with appreciation and desire, his penetrating gaze searching my features. He touched my cheek gently and eased off me, a hint of his shyness returning.

"It feels different with you," he murmured.

"I hope so," I said and laughed. "You aren't paying me, for starters!"

He smiled and hugged me against him. We lay in quiet long enough for me to slip into a doze before he began speaking.

"I'll start. I'm from here, or at least, a similar time, which is why I came here to retire. I can't remember how many eras I've visited or how many people I've met along my travels. They offered me the ability to retire where I wanted, and I chose here and now. It's about fifty years before my time, but I wanted to see this era."

I listened, startled he was diving straight into his secrets after avoiding speaking of them since we met. My fingers twirled through his tousled hair absently.

"I believe Running Bear is my grandfather."

"You came back to see your family?" I asked.

"To see the last years of freedom my father's people enjoyed."

"I understand. But I thought you were four when they found you."

"They did. I've lived around ten thousand lives in ten thousand times."

My mouth dropped open.

"Technology has advanced a great deal in that amount of time. Used to, there was no way to bring someone from the past forward. It was a one-way trip, until the secret to moving forward in time was stumbled upon by someone at the agency I worked for. Once they figured it out, the old way of doing business was no longer in fashion," he explained.

"Wow," I breathed. "I don't have any idea what you're talking about, by the way. Carter didn't tell me anything before sending me back. I had no idea time travel existed before him."

"Want me to start from the beginning?" he offered.

"Yeah."

"Time agents are sent back in time to a particular point where there's a disruption or sudden, dangerous change to history as we know it. We go native, as they call it, and are either raised in the era where we land as part of the culture and society or sent back at least five years before to give us time to adjust. The goal is to make us the ultimate sleeper agent who knows the ins and outs of his world. When we're ten, we're granted the memories of our past lives and where we came from. When we grow tired of the travel and relative immortality, we can opt to retire. This is my retirement cycle."

Unable to voice any of the questions pummeling my thoughts, I was silent. Why his story seemed fantastical after knowing what I did already, I wasn't sure.

"Our focus is to prevent men like Carter from modifying history for selfish reasons. There is a time and place where time travel is a way of life. But even if so, there should be no one permitted to change history for personal gain or revenge or any other of those human motivations."

This sank in deeper than the rest. I didn't know Carter's motivation; I assumed he wanted what he said he did, to help people who needed it. "But ... how do you live ten thousand lives?" I asked.

"We technically don't. We live one life. I reached the age of thirty-three in my own time. Let's just say … they sent me back in time on a Friday. I cease to exist in my own time from that Friday onward. But the day before, on Thursday, I'm still there. So the next life, they pick me up on Thursday and take me back in time. For the next one, they pick me up on Wednesday. Three hundred sixty four lives a year. When I arrived here, I was four. It's roughly ten thousand days between the age of four and thirty three, which means ten thousand lives."

"You remember them all?"

He shrugged. "After so many, you tend to keep those you enjoyed the best and forget the rest."

"How is this possible?"

"How are you a hundred and fifty years in the past with an empathic memory chip?" he challenged gently.

I touched my head self-consciously. "You know about that."

"It's either that or you're touched like Fighting Badger. Your language skills were another giveaway. Never met a white man who spoke with your fluency."

"I had no idea there was an entire agency devoted to time travel," I said. "I can't wrap my head around that."

"It's a work in progress. Once they were no longer restricted to traveling strictly from future to past, it opened up the doors to more possibilities."

"Carter … doesn't work for them, does he?" I asked with some reluctance.

"No." Taylor's features grew shuttered for a moment. "The truth is we know little about him or what he wants or why he's decided to use that immense intellect of his to change the past."

Part of me was relieved that Carter wasn't a criminal, while another instinct whispered that the unknown had the potential to be even scarier. "Then who the hell is Carter?" I ventured.

"We don't really know. A genius for certain. He *created* the empathic memory chip, a marrying of technology and human brain power that's theoretically impossible."

My breath caught. "Oh, god. Am I going to explode?"

The sense of disconnect returned. I shook my head, and my ears buzzed.

"Focus," he whispered. He rested his palms on my cheeks.

Just as fast, I was yanked back into reality. I released a breath. I was sitting up, a blanket wrapped around me, while he sat beside me. Enough time had passed for him to put on his pants again.

"I keep getting dizzy," I said.

"Side effect of traveling," he explained. "Look at me."

I obeyed. Taylor's hard green eyes grounded me once more. I took his hands. "You're the only one the chip can't read."

"That I can't explain," he said, taking in my features. "Your nose is bleeding." He rose and went to the basin, dipping a cloth in the water before returning. "Did you tell him about it?"

"Yeah. He's researching it." I accepted the moistened rag. "Thanks." Running through all he'd told me, I giggled at a single thought. "You've probably had ten thousand wives by now!"

"No. Just one."

"Ten thousand lives and only one wife?"

"Yes."

Wow. This was definitely more serious than I wanted it to be. "Taylor," I started, not sure how to say what I needed to diplomatically. "I'm going back."

His eyebrows lifted. "What do you mean?"

"Just that. I'm going back to my time. The twenty first century, where Carter found me."

"Carter didn't tell you."

"Tell me what?" I lowered the rag, gaze riveted to the chiseled features of the cowboy who'd just made love to me.

"My agency has been working to undo what he's doing to history since … well, for a thousand of my lives at least. He's sent back more people than I can count, but Josie, he doesn't have the technology to pull you back to the future. Only we do, and only lately."

"*What?*"

"I know you communicate with him. Ask him. Tell him Taylor told you."

It took a moment for his words to sink in. In a state of complete denial, I couldn't speak let alone refute him.

"I thought you came back to this era by choice. Nearly everyone Carter sends back chooses." The look of pity that warmed his features was too genuine to ignore.

"No," I mumbled and stood. "You can't be telling me I'm not going home! Carter wouldn't …" I was close to hyperventilating and caught myself against the nightstand before stooping to grab the housecoat I'd dropped. I fished out the phone and shot Carter a hasty note riddled with typos I didn't care about fixing. "You'll see, Taylor. You'll see."

Carter wouldn't lie to me.

"There's no way back, Josie. Not for you. There's just *here*." Taylor stood but didn't approach me, his wiry form relaxed.

I stared at him, devastated. No matter what I had begun to suspect about Carter, the idea he'd been flat out lying to me about a way home wasn't something I'd considered.

"I'm not going anywhere either," Taylor said. "We have a place to live our lives comfortably."

What the hell did I say to that? "I need a drink." *Please, please, please answer fast, Carter!*

He did. I had just dumped four shots worth of bourbon into a glass when my phone vibrated. Heart pounding, I checked the message.

He's right. But it's not what you think. I have a plan for you.

"What the hell does that mean?" I demanded of the phone.

Taylor approached, one hand going to my back. He tilted the screen so he could read it. His expression was considering.

"I don't understand," I said. "Taylor, I'm going home! Tell him I'm going home!"

"Josie, you're not going home," he replied gently. "And this makes me think you aren't staying here, either. That chip in your head is rumored to be worth billions. Even Carter can't afford to let you stay, if he's got a reason to use you."

His words warbled. Rather than the usual sense of disconnect, this was an all out break with reality. I was barely aware of collapsing, of Taylor catching me while my mind checked out in the worst way possible.

This must be what Fighting Badger feels like. It was ... chaos. Shadows. Emotions.

Fear.

They were swallowing me, along with darkness I prayed put me out of my misery.

Chapter Fifteen

I AWOKE ALONE AROUND MIDMORNING.

This is wrong. Last night left me befuddled, ready to weep, fragile. I rested my head on a pillow and gazed at the blue sky visible through the window of Taylor's bedroom. I reached for my pocket and the cell only to realize I was naked. Pushing myself up, I spotted my housecoat on the floor in front of the mirror where I had dropped it and stood to grab it.

The cell was cold and heavy in my hands. I'd been debating what to say to Carter since I learned the truth last night. This time, when I looked around me, I didn't see a fascinating vacation spot, but the reality that I might be stuck here.

Are you okay? Carter had texted last night.

"No, I'm not." I fiddled with the phone. *How could you lie to me like this?* I demanded, adding half a dozen frownie faces. It was a rare day when I wanted to call someone instead of text, but today was that day I needed to give him a piece of my mind – and couldn't. Because I was stuck in the past.

There was so much I wanted to say … it was too jumbled for me to sort through. Anger bubbled at the thought of the man who sent me here. Was I so naïve that I let my feelings and the sense of familiarity with Carter blind me to the truth about him? What *was* the truth?

I dressed and padded down the hallway to my room. My breakfast sat waiting in front of the fire, and water dripped from a tap into the warm bath waiting for me.

"I love you, Nell," I whispered. My body was in desperate need of a hot bath.

Carter texted. For a split second, I was afraid to read it. I waited until I'd sunk into the hot water and started to relax before I checked the cell.

I swear, Josie. I would never hurt you. You have to trust me and what I'm doing is for a reason. I put you in the safest, most comfortable place possible this time.

What did he mean *this time*? I didn't get the sense that he was a puppet master when we drank together, but I was starting to think he was one.

What bothered me most: no matter what he told me or how deep his betrayal was, I *wanted* to believe him. It was irrational, even for someone ruled by her heart like I was. I couldn't explain it anymore than how I trusted him from the first time we met and hadn't questioned his motives about sending me here.

There was something about Carter … something that made me want to place my faith in him blindly.

I can't trust you if you keep lying to me, I responded.

At least he was waiting for my texts today. His answer was fast.

"*I didn't know how else to get you on board with what I'm doing,*" I whispered his response aloud. "*I'm sorry. Truth from here on out.*"

Even if I believed him, did it matter if he told me the truth now? He had trapped me in the past, where I'd made a series of decisions based on temporary circumstances. Like marrying Taylor. It was probably the smartest choice given the alternative, but when he realized I wasn't ready to love anyone …

Or maybe it didn't matter. The role of a woman in this time period was restricted enough that I needed either a husband like Taylor or a father like John.

Overwhelmed once more, I hid the phone under my housecoat. Nell was shuffling around in the bedroom. I was kind of grateful for her sorrow; it kept her from hanging around and nagging the way she usually did.

The scent of ham and fresh bread reached me. Without waiting for my nanny, I climbed out of the tub, dried off and put on my housecoat, determined to enjoy breakfast before being strapped into another girdle.

I ate everything. My appetite was gone, trapped somewhere in the darkness I went through last night, and anxiety driving me to eat. Finishing the food, I stared into space. My thoughts were leaden, murky.

"You will want to visit your father's grave this morning, I believe?" Nell still wore black. Her eyes were red rimmed and her features pale.

Graveyard. The unhappy spirit whose whispers disturbed me at John's funerals might reveal what happened to the first woman sent back in time.

Did I want to solve this mystery anymore?

Yes. I wasn't sure why, but I needed to know. I was in danger, and I couldn't take it as lightly as I had before. There was no easy way out of here.

"Yes," I replied. "I think I do."

Nell strapped me into my black gown once more. Usually I barely tolerated the ordeal, but I bore through it in silence this time, aware that I needed to get used to it.

"I'd like to go alone, Nell," I told her gently.

"Yes, Miss, I thought you might." Nell's faint smile was watery.

I felt bad for her. If nothing else, Taylor being here instead of Philip meant she'd live out the rest of her life comfortably. There also might be peace on this little piece of the frontier with him working to bridge the locals and natives.

The morning was cooler than I expected when I stepped outside. I rarely saw the servants of the house; the small army worked in general obscurity. As if needing to catch up after the storms, there were no less than eight men and women hanging linens and clothing on long clotheslines stretching behind the house. A cool fall breeze rustled my dress as I watched the servants pin new laundry up or fold dried laundry.

None of them glanced my way, and I frowned, recalling my former suspicion about someone in the house being behind the murders.

Turning away, I walked towards the small hill that marked the graveyard. I wasn't a melancholy person by nature, and the fresh air, wide-open prairielands and beautiful grounds left to me by John cheered my spirits. I lifted my skirts as I reached the dirt trail leading to the wrought iron gate surrounding the cemetery.

I paused at the fence, a weird sense coming over me, the idea that I'd be buried here, too. Shaking off the dark thought, I opened the gate and walked along the cobblestone path towards John's grave.

As with the first time I visited, the loudest of the whispers was also the unhappiest. It distracted me when I wanted to tune into John's beautiful memories. Trying to ignore it did nothing to quiet the miserable member of the dead haunting the graveyard, and I relented.

Kneeling beside the patch of grassy earth where no grave was marked, I closed my eyes and listened.

My breath caught immediately. The same nightmare I'd been having since I arrived – fire, shadows, voices, blood – emanated from the unmarked grave as well. The visions weren't any clearer, but something else was.

Pleasant memories like John's were mixed in with the scary ones. The incredible bond and love between father and daughter stranded on the frontier. Real-Josie and John had traveled together to see the natives, to town, to the wild lands of the west and the civilized east.

I saw why John wanted so much for me to be the daughter he lost. They hadn't left each other's sides since the death of her mother when she was around eleven. Josie was his source of joy and happiness, and he was hers.

Tears blurred my eyes as I typed a note to Carter. *I found the real Josie.* I didn't know what happened to her, aside from the shadowy, sorrowful memories that linked her grave to the room down the hallway.

Did I want to know? It was clear something horrible had occurred in the house. The idea that her killer, and that of the other Josies, was hidden among the servants returned.

I needed to know, because I had to have a chance not to end up in an unmarked grave or at the bottom of the well.

I climbed to my feet and paused, sensing … someone. It was the same odd presence that tickled my instincts at Taylor's the night his cabin burnt to the ground. It wasn't the man Fighting Badger had tortured and killed; it had to be the shadowy figure following the native.

"Talks to Spirits." There was a note of something in his voice that made the hair on the back of my neck rise.

I turned – and gasped. Fighting Badger's clothing was torn, and he was bloodied. "What's wrong?" I asked immediately and crossed to the fence dividing us from one another.

"There was another man like the first," he said. "Someone who came to find you and do harm. I stopped him and tried to bury him with the first man." He shifted. His mind was its usual tangled mess, but I glimpsed his twin being dragged away while he watched.

"What happened?"

"They took my brother."

"Who did?"

"The men who found the bodies." His gaze went to his feet. "I tried to stop them. I killed three before Running Bear told me to run."

"What men?" I whispered. The vision in his head told me before he spoke.

"White Men. Settlers. They plan on hanging him because of what I did."

I gazed at him. His distress was tangled with his darkness, and it struck me that he had come to me for the reason his brothers both hinted at: he had no one else. As far as the natives and townspeople knew, he didn't exist.

It wasn't just my desire not to see a good man hanged that propelled me to act. It was the knowledge that I didn't know if I could handle the dark mystery awaiting me at the end of my wing after everything that happened the past two days.

Taylor hanged men on Saturdays, which gave us two days to help Running Bear, two days until …

The twentieth fourth. Instincts clamoring, I exited the cemetery. "We have to tell Taylor," I said and hurried by him.

"What do I do?"

I stopped. The angry side of me wanted to tell him to drink his medicine. He'd killed an unknown number of people. If anyone hanged, it should be him.

But I couldn't. He had killed two men to protect me, however misguided that was, which made me at least partially responsible. Coupled with the knowledge he was mentally ill and exiled to die at the age of ten, I wasn't able to summon any kind of condemnation.

"Go to your cave," I answered. "Don't let anyone see you, and don't leave until Taylor or I come find you." Without waiting for his response, I hiked up my skirts and ran back to the house and into the foyer. "Nell!" I called.

"What is it? What's wrong?" came her harried response from the direction of my wing.

"We need to go to town!"

"Now, Miss Josie?"

"Yes!" I didn't wait for her but strode out onto the porch and began to pace.

Nell appeared alarmed as she ran down the stairs and out of the house. "I'll have the carriage brought around."

I glanced towards the carriage house. For once, I wasn't content to wait for the slower pace o this time period. "We're going by horseback," I decided and left the porch.

"Miss Josie, what is it?" Nell asked again.

"Taylor's Indian brother is in trouble."

Nell said nothing. I sensed she wasn't as alarmed as I was, but I didn't care. I would've left her if I didn't think she was too fragile and likely to freak out with me disappearing.

We saddled horses quickly and left the property. The trip to town was about twice as fast on horseback, especially alternating between a trot and gallop, and we reached the town in about twenty minutes.

There was a crowd outside of the sheriff's, one that made me uneasy. They appeared calm, but I doubted even a calm lynch mob was a good thing. I dismounted in front of the mercantile store, a safe enough distance away from Taylor's office. Handing off my reins to Nell, I started through the crowd. A few of those gathered called out congratulations for my marriage while several more shared condolences. I smiled and waved, moving as fast as possible to the door.

A beefy deputy outside the door glanced at me without challenging me, and I entered.

The office was jammed. The native with the silver stripe in his hair, who had been with Running Bear the night they found me in the storm, was present, accompanied by another. The judge was there as well, two more of Taylor's deputies, and my new husband. Running Bear was in a cell with Doctor Green, who appeared to be wrapping an injured arm.

"Josie," Taylor spotted me. "You shouldn't be here."

"I heard the news," I said.

A spark of understanding crossed his gaze. "Peter, hold things down. I'm gonna have a word with my wife."

The deputy he addressed smiled at me.

Taylor waved me towards the cells rather than outside, and we ducked into the far one. He took my cheeks in his roughened hands and kissed me lightly. I smiled, wanting to tease him about how brave he'd gotten after one night together, but didn't. I moved close enough to feel his body heat.

"Fighting Badger came to you?" he asked.

"Yeah. He's upset." I searched Taylor's face. "He said he killed two men who were after me. I know one of them knew you."

"Josie, now is not –"

"Now *is* the time," I said firmly. "You'll forgive me if I'm out of good faith."

Taylor's expression softened. "I know. It's been a rough couple of days. That's why I'm asking you to head home, and we'll talk later."

"No."

He sighed.

"Taylor, what if this – Running Bear's death – is what I'm supposed to prevent? You can't tell me you want your brother hanged!" I whispered insistently. It was a rare day when I was angry, but I was now. I didn't even know whom it was directed at.

"It's much more complicated than that." He shifted back to lean against the wall. "I've settled down the town's folks who want him hanged today. The judge has already decided there won't be a trial, not after the three additional men Fighting Badger killed, and your cousin Philip is threatening to take this to the governor if I stand in the way of a hanging."

"I hate Philip," I muttered.

"He's a thorn in my side but also the least of my problems." Taylor took one of my hands, his gaze going to the ceiling. "I suspect Running Bear is my grandfather. He had no children after his first family was killed. If he's hanged before he can father any more then …"

New fear trickled through me. "How do you know it was him and not Fighting Badger?" I asked. "I know the chances are slim, but there are two of them."

"One of them didn't exist in the original timeline. There's no record of twins anywhere. I suspect Fighting Badger died the first time around, and me being here somehow altered that."

"If Running Bear dies Saturday, so do you," I murmured. "What better sign is there that I'm meant to stop this?"

"Aside from the fact Carter is a master manipulator?" Taylor asked, frustration in his tone. "Josie, there was no event that happened in the original history that would've let you save a million lives. That door closed when the government began taking the land from natives a hundred years ago. Nothing you could do *here* could make a difference. It was a lie, one Carter told you to get you here."

"For what purpose?" I demanded.

"As I said: there's no one who has ever figured out his motivation for anything he does. He's sent back hundreds of people in time, and not one of them can tell us why."

His words stung hard enough that the sense of disconnecting with my world emerged. My eyes closed. The buzzing in my ears grew loud, and I floated in my mind.

"I'm so sorry," Taylor's arms were around me.

The spell passed. I gripped the thick material of his work shirt and breathed in his scent. I was seated on the bunk in the cell, pressed against him. My nose bled once more, and I wiped away the thick rivulet of red.

I wouldn't ... *couldn't* believe that Carter had lied to me about everything.

"The two men Fighting Badger caught and killed were sent from my agency," Taylor added, his warm lips moving against my ear to ensure no one overheard. "My people have dealt with Carter so much that they've taken on the mentality of eliminating whoever he sends back, mainly out of fear of the master plan of his they can't figure out."

"So I was in danger," I voiced.

"Yes."

"All the more reason to stop this nonsense and save Running Bear!" I lifted my head.

"You don't think I want to save him? He's my brother, Josie. He helped raise me." A flicker of emotion touched his features. "You don't think I want to retire and spend the rest of my life with you on John's property, helping the settlers and natives get along?"

"I do." I offered a smile and touched his roughened jaw. "What're we going to do?"

"I don't rightly know."

"We could leave town," I suggested. *You have no idea how good that sounds.* After discovering all the bodies on the property that shouldn't be there, I was beginning to view John's home in a different light. "We have money. We could help him escape and then leave."

Taylor nodded, though he didn't look at all interested in the idea. "My people can find us. They sent back three agents. The third ... Josie, he's the kind of danger I can't protect you from. I don't know where he is, why he hasn't attacked, what his plan is. But he's never, ever failed a mission. If he's here, we're in serious trouble." He paused, troubled, before continuing. "If we ran, it would take a great deal of money to stay hidden and even that wouldn't guarantee our safety."

"Well ..." I drifted off, uncertain I wanted to ask what was at the tip of my tongue. "You said your people have the ability to bring people back to the future now."

"In exchange for what? Me turning over you for them to deal with or leaving my grandfather to hang here?" He shook his head. "It's not an option."

It was selfish, but I wanted it so much to be an avenue we could take. I understood his concern for those he cared about. If I had to risk letting John or Nell die, I wouldn't do it, either.

We sat in quiet.

"Are you ... serious about what you said? That there's nothing I can do here to fulfill Carter's goal?" I was hurting again.

"Not the way you described."

"And if Running Bear dies, then you just ..."

"Cease to exist."

"I couldn't handle that outcome." Not ready for a husband or love, neither was I ready to lose the one man I knew I could trust, who cared about me enough to protect me from his own people.

Taylor was one of the best men I'd ever met. If I had to be stuck in the past with someone, he was a good choice. I could even see myself adjusting to a life here with him.

"Sheriff!" one of the deputies called.

"Josie, please, go home. I'll be back late, but when I am, we'll figure this all out."

I didn't like the answer at all, but I didn't know what else to do. With a nod, I resisted the urge to grab my phone and text Carter. There were too many people milling in the neighboring office.

"Good." Taylor touched my cheek and planted a warm kiss on my forehead. "I'm sending another deputy with you. There's one at the house already."

He rose and went to the door separating the two spaces, speaking quietly to someone. I half expected him to smile or turn back and offer up some sort of better solution than we take everything and run.

He didn't. I knew he had a lot on his mind, considering his own life was at stake. Even so, I needed something more concrete this time. And ... I was burning to tell him about real-Josie, because there was no one else I could tell. The burden of her death wasn't one I thought I could carry alone.

Her death surely had nothing to do with the third agent from his agency that was in town to finish what the other two didn't. Josie had been dead at least a year. I was in danger from two directions, one I knew and wasn't going to prevent without Taylor's help, and the other I hadn't pieced together yet.

I owe Fighting Badger my life. Yet I had no clue if his protection and Taylor's was going to be enough for me to survive the past, especially if Carter couldn't fix the microchip he seemed to think was malfunctioning.

Wanting to talk to Taylor again, I nonetheless decided we'd have a better chance to talk in private later. He had enough going on without worrying about yet another dead body I'd found on John's property.

I left the cells and moved through the crowded office, trailed by a deputy. Nell was at the doorway, waiting. Beside her was someone I didn't have any patience for at this moment.

"My uncle would be rolling over in his grave if he saw your husband stand in the way of justice," Philip proclaimed loudly enough for those nearest the office to hear. Grumbles of agreement went through the mob.

"Let him do his job, Philip," I replied.

"As the man most likely to be elected mayor at the polls next month, I will ensure he does," came the calm reply. "I will also ensure there's a full inquisition into your inheritance, cousin, as well as what was behind this sham of a marriage. You took advantage of a weak old man." He moved closer. "If I have to take my inheritance from you by force, I will."

I had never wanted to hit anyone the way I did him. *Except maybe Carter.* I was too angry to reply and simply strode away.

It wasn't until I reached the horses that I had a retort. Grumbling it under my breath, I mounted and waited for Nell.

She had the glassy-eyed look once more, and her memories were skipping.

"You okay, Nell?" I asked, concerned.

She blinked several times before her eyes found me. Her memories stabilized, revealing she was thinking about Josie and John once more. "Yes, Miss Josie. I am distressed is all."

"Let's go home. You can show me how to make you tea, and I'll take care of you for once." I had never thought the strong willed woman weak or frail, but she looked it.

Nell smiled and mounted her horse. "You always were good to me, Miss Josie. Your father must be missing you in heaven."

I said nothing, aware that, if anything, he had been reunited with the real Josie.

We returned to the house just as another storm breached the horizon. Any hope I had of it being simply a cloudy evening was dashed when I saw the servants bringing in the clothing and linens, rounding up the sheep and tarping down the wells.

Dismounting, I took care of my horse quickly while Nell brushed and fed hers. We met in the middle of the barn.

"I think I want to lie down for a bit," I said, itching for some me-time to text Carter. "Will you be okay, Nell?"

"Of course. Why wouldn't I be?" Nell replied, her spark back.

Weird. But the woman had a brain tumor in addition to being stressed out after the events of this week. She didn't trail me into the house but remained with the deputy in the barn, helping him take care of his horse.

The moment I stepped into my room, I whipped out the cell and stared at it. Carter hadn't texted, as if he was waiting for me to be willing to speak to him again.

With Taylor's words raw in my thoughts, I managed to write out what was bothering me. *Did you lie about why you sent me back?* I hit send and went to the dressing room to replace the bonnet on its stand.

My phone vibrated, and I read his response. *Sort of. Taylor was your real mission. I've been tracking him through several hundred time periods, and this was the first time I was able to catch up with him. Please don't hate me. There's a reason I'm doing this, and when you find out what it is, you'll understand. If it helps, you being there did help a few people.*

"You're crazier than Fighting Badger," I said, astonished he'd think there was any explanation I'd accept for all the lying he'd done. "I didn't leave my life behind to help a few people! I came to rescue a million." And what could he want with Taylor? Before I could ask him, he sent me another note.

BTW- I have a potential solution for the nosebleeds and headaches. You're going to have to turn off the empathic memory chip.

I was close to crying again, shaking with anger and too upset to vocalize let alone type the mess of emotions in my mind. Instead, I wrote back, *Am I doing self-brain surgery?*

I drank a glass of water and worked on calming myself before I dared read his answer.

LOL – no! This is much more ... primitive. It requires a 2x4 board and good aim. A hard blow to the right place on your skull will disengage it.

"Billion dollar technology and you shut it off with a two by four." I gave a choked sob that was half laugh, baffled, and then stopped short when his next message came in.

You'll need to do it soon. There's a chance your brain could swell. It won't be a quick or painless death. I swear, Josie, I want you to be safe and healthy. I wouldn't suggest this if there was any other way.

Tears stung my eyes. So I was trapped in the past, and my head was about to explode, thanks to Carter. I was an absolute fool. Looking around, I realized this place wouldn't be bad, if there was a way to stay with Taylor and Nell.

But without knowing what happened to the other girls – and real-Josie – turning off the brain chip was the third most foolish decision I'd made when it came to Carter. Not to mention that trying to figure out what he wanted with Taylor, or what lengths he'd go to in order to influence the man I was about to spend the rest of my life with, scared me.

First things first – what Carter wanted or did wasn't going to matter, if I died in this house like real-Josie and the three imposters sent back in time. I had to survive that threat, the mysterious third agent sent back by Taylor's agency, and then I could deal with

Carter's insanity.

I'm going to find out what happened to Josie first, I replied to him. I hid my phone in the folded clothing on my bed belonging to Taylor. It was the first time I willingly gave up the phone, but holding it was infuriating me. I wanted distance between Carter and me, and I didn't care if that pissed him off.

I left my room, finally ready and determined to confront the source of the whispers, and the truth about real-Josie, that lingered at the end of the hallway.

Today was the perfect day for more bad news. I was no longer trying to look only at the good in the world around me. Carter's betrayal and the fates of the women who came before me had stretched me to my limit, and I was going to dive further into the darkness to find the final pieces of the puzzle. Feeling a little reckless, a little raw, I checked to make sure Nell wasn't lingering and then started towards the door.

The whispers grew stronger, the images starting to form. I tried the doorknob. Finding it unlocked, I slid inside and looked around. The furniture in the large room was covered with white sheets. It resembled mine, from the familiar wallpaper to the rugs and drapes covered with the exact same stitching. The layout was a mirror copy of mine as well.

In fact, everything was.

"Okay. Weird."

I lifted the sheet off the table near the dead hearth. I had a tray just like the one on its top. Walking to the vanity, I lifted the sheet to see the exact same items organized the exact same way as they were on my vanity. The air of the room was heavy and smelled of must, the memories waiting for me to close my eyes and admit them. Like the well, the visions were harder to capture than those from a person, as if there had to be enough energy lingering in the surroundings to release the memories.

Someone had gone to great lengths to erase real-Josie's existence, down to rebuilding her bedroom from the ground up in a different place. There could be no good story behind the room identical to mine.

"Except for you. You don't fit in." I crossed to the sheet covering a piece of furniture the size of my full-body mirror but in the wrong location. I tugged the white sheet off and stood back. The beautiful wedding gown made of white brocade highlighted with silver threads and handmade lace on the stand was pristine. It appeared to have been recently pressed. There was no dust or sign of wear on it. "Wow. Lucky Josie."

My room. The wedding dress. Nell's tale about real-Josie leaving the night before she married.

A chill went down my spine. I looked around for other anomalies without spotting any. I began to dread learning the truth about real-Josie. The level of effort that went into the reinvention of her room wasn't possible without her father and governess knowing.

If I lost faith in them, too …

Swallowing hard, I knelt, prepared for a longer session than normal, and closed my eyes. "Show me what happened here," I whispered.

Chapter Sixteen

"SHERIFF, I BROUGHT THE DEAD MEN'S BELONGINGS."

Taylor looked up from the tin plate of dinner sitting on his desk. The excitement of the afternoon had worn off. Only four men remained from the original lynch mob, along with Speaking Wind – the elder from his tribe - and four deputies. He had been trapped in his office nearly all day to deal with the complaints from the families whose men were murdered by Fighting Badger.

The beefy deputy standing guard outside his office didn't let the undertaker's apprentice enter. Taylor stepped onto the sidewalk for the first time since he'd arrived that morning. It was dark, and the chilled wind held droplets of rain.

"The others were returned to their families. We didn't know what to do with these," the apprentice said and held out a wooden box.

"I'll take them," Taylor said. Rather than return to the warm office, he sat down beneath the light of one of its windows to sort through the belongings of the two agents killed.

His agency had a protocol forbidding agents from carrying anything that identified them as someone other than who they pretended to be. Despite this, a sliver of desperate hope rendered his fingers clumsy as he sorted through everything. All he needed was one communications device, a single method to contact his agency or better yet, The Mongol, whose presence in town had been whispered about since shortly after Lance arrived.

There was nothing. Disappointed, he pushed the box aside and gazed out at the night. It was his first real breather this day, and he relished the undisturbed moment to think.

As they had since John's death, his thoughts went first to Josie. She'd been upset when she visited earlier. He hoped it was because of Fighting Badger's visit and not because there was something else wrong. He still smelled her scent on his skin, a reminder of the night that was supposed to be the first of a lifetime of peace and retirement.

Instead, his brother – and potentially grandfather – was about to be hanged, leaving Josie exposed to whoever it was that killed the others who came before her or worse, in the hands of The Mongol. Either way, she wasn't going to last long without protection. His best-case scenario: they'd be on the run the rest of their lives.

After all his years of service, *this* was how his agency repaid him?

He suppressed the anger, well aware that his agency had nothing to do with Fighting Badger taking out innocent people. He was torn between gratitude that his brother had saved Josie and regret, wishing she had never crossed paths with the native.

Taylor climbed to his feet and picked up the box. "Donate anything of value to the church," he instructed the deputy at the door and walked back in. Ignoring his dinner, the only meal he'd had that day, he went to the cell where Running Bear was laying on a bunk, recovering from the beating the town's people had given him earlier.

"You all right?" he asked softly with a glance over his shoulder to ensure they had some small amount of privacy now that the crowd was gone.

"I am well." Running Bear sat up with effort and gripped his chest.

Probably broken ribs, Taylor thought. "What the hell happened? How did you get involved?" he asked aloud.

"Our brother was not in his cave when I went to visit him this morning. I tracked him to your new home and then onward to town. He took the life of a man behind the tavern. Someone saw him, and I tried to intervene." Running Bear fell quiet.

Taylor didn't need to hear the rest to understand what happened. "They want to hang you Saturday. I can get you out of here, but we probably can't return to Indian Territory ever again once we're gone."

"No, brother." Running Bear stood and came to the bars of the cell. One of his eyes was swollen shut and his features bruised. "Protect Fighting Badger. He is our brother. I believe he broke his promise to us for a reason. He told me someone was after your wife."

Taylor's hands clenched into fists.

It wasn't Fighting Badger's fault; it was *his.* Fighting Badger acted only to protect those he cared about since he had taken an oath to his brothers seven years before. "I should be in there," Taylor muttered. "I should've protected her or known or ... prevented this somehow."

"We cannot undo this," Running Bear said. "Take care of him and your wife. I will not see you homeless. Our people know what that is, Taylor, to be taken from the home of your ancestors and sent elsewhere. If my life will prevent that and keep the peace, then I will give it freely."

"But you don't deserve to die." Taylor rested his head against the bars, sorrow creeping into his mind.

"The night you fell from the sky, I was supposed to cross the river with my cousins to hunt bison. Instead, I went to the crater and found you, a child, crying and lost."

Taylor smiled at his most treasured memory. Running Bear had gathered him up in his arms and carried him back to their village and his mother, whose shocked expression at seeing her son holding a boy that fell from the sky was Taylor's second favorite memory.

"That night," Running Bear continued, "Everyone in my hunting party was killed when the river flooded its banks and wiped out the wash and all who had taken shelter for the night there. You have granted me twenty-two years of life I would not have had. I wish to give our brother that chance now."

Taylor cocked his head to the side. "I never heard that story of your cousins," he said, his mind leaping in a new direction. "That night, you were supposed to die, and Fighting Badger would've taken the place as shaman instead of you?"

Running Bear nodded. "He had a strong connection to the spirits but was wild. I think he could've been trained."

"Then he would …" *become the man who would be my grandfather.* He didn't know how to take the news that his blood was tainted by the same madness as Fighting Badger. And who would marry the crazy Indian? Did the death of his brother in the original timeline alter Fighting Badger's position in the tribe, his madness?

There was always danger when it came to going native in a new time, the potential for unwittingly messing with the past. He had lived a quiet life here, one without much interaction or impact with the world outside of the town. He was always careful about altering the history of a time period, even one with little to no impact on the course of major events in history. The name of this town didn't make it into history; it was of no real importance, a quiet hamlet where he could retire and get to know his family tree without worrying about altering the past.

"I am not worried, Taylor," Running Bear said. "You must do what you must. We must preserve the peace, and my death will do that."

"I won't let this happen," Taylor told him firmly. "Speaking Wind is staying here tonight, along with the deputies I trust. You'll be safe. I need to talk to Josie about what we can do."

"Very well, but I believe the spirits have spoken."

Taylor shook his head and strode away, unwilling to accept Running Bear's offer to go quietly to his death. Troubled, he gathered his things and left with a nod to the deputies. By all rights, he should've stayed in town until morning in the hopes the latest autumn storm cleared up.

But he was edgy, worried about Josie and Running Bear, and didn't fully believe the deputies he sent to look over Josie were any match for The Mongol.

Wired with urgency he wasn't able to control, he raced home.

Chapter Seventeen

IT TOOK EFFORT AND MORE TIME THAN USUAL FOR THE IMAGES to crystalize out of the abundant whispers. The room grew cooler, and I opened my eyes once to see the sun was setting before closing them to focus once more on my task.

The elusive visions formed after some time. I clutched the material of my dress, unable to believe what I saw, unable to stop the visions or stop watching.

A burning hearth ... a cool fall day. The wedding gown was in its place by the window.

John was pacing near the fire. He was angry, yelling. It was the night before the wedding just after the largest feast he'd ever given.

A woman who could've been my doppelganger screamed back at him.

The picture did our likeness no justice, and I stared at the woman who could've been my twin in astonishment. Aside from our hair – real-Josie's was straight – there was virtually no difference.

"No wonder he didn't know the difference," I murmured. In one year, John had gone from robust, healthy and a little overweight to the shell of a man I mourned.

Unable to hear their words, I could at least see what happened.

Real-Josie was screaming and crying, and John's face grew redder, his eyes flashing in a way I wasn't able to imagine after my brief interaction with him.

By the way both gestured to the wedding dress, it was as Nell suspected: Real-Josie didn't want to marry the man chosen for her by her father.

Josie rested a hand on her stomach, and John froze, staring at the spot with a mix of horror and fury. Real-Josie laughed and spun away from her father. He grabbed her arm and hit her once. Stunned, Josie stared at him.

Reeling from what he'd done, he took a step back.

"Walk away, John," I whispered tightly. "Please walk away." Tears warmed my cheeks. There was one reason I could think of that this room had been preserved from that night and recreated for the daughters that kept showing up at his door. I saw John mouth the words *with child*, and my heart sank. If an unwed woman going out alone was an issue in this era, an unwed woman who was pregnant had to be the ultimate gossip-worthy transgression.

Real-Josie laughed again, this time gesturing at John angrily. She grabbed the wedding dress and tore it off its stand, flinging it and the priceless heirloom jewelry that rested on it all over the room.

John picked up the bracelet that landed near his feet, his expression one of great sorrow and anger.

I didn't have to guess who the piece had belonged to. John held such reverence and emotion for his wife and daughter alone. I saw the shift in his expression, the moment he lost control, and began crying, not wanting to witness what the man I had found a way to love had done a year before.

He grabbed Josie again. This time, he didn't hit her once, but over and over, even after she had fallen to the ground. He beat her stomach and face, shouting, rage on his face and controlling his actions.

Nell rushed into the room and tackled him.

He threw her off and turned on her, fist raised to crush her head the way he had his daughter's. Sobbing, Nell cowered and pointed.

John turned, and realization replaced his enraged trance. He looked over at the bloodied, battered, unrecognizable face of his daughter and dropped beside her. Horrified, he picked her up in his arms and began rocking, his lips forming her name over and over.

"Stop," I whispered. "Stop, stop, stop!" I clutched my stomach, the images nauseating me. John's unquestioning acceptance of me, of the three other girls who shared my room, became clear. Unable to live with what he'd done, he went mad trying to believe it didn't happen.

Was that why the room was recreated? To dispel the memories and start over? To give him hope and bury the past?

"Miss Josie." Nell's hushed whisper came from the doorway.

I looked up. The lanterns in the hallway were on, framing my nanny against them.

"Miss Josie. You shouldn't be in here." Her voice shook.

Nell knows. She had always known. I struggled to gain control of myself. Wiping away tears, I climbed to my feet despite the desire to curl up somewhere and sob.

First Carter. Now John. My faith in those I trusted was shattering.

"I'm sorry, Nell," I managed. "I have bad cramps."

Nell had no way of knowing about my empathic chip.

I continued to hold my stomach as I moved into the hallway and past her. I made my way slowly towards my room.

"Miss Josie."

"Yeah?"

"You didn't ask whose room this was."

I stopped, my instincts tingling. This time, the memories came from Nell.

While her master wept, she dragged the body down the hallway and out of the house, all the way around the property to the graveyard. She buried real-Josie in the moonlight and then collapsed onto the grave, weeping for the woman she loved as a daughter.

"It doesn't matter, Nell," I replied, pitying my governess. Retreating to my room, I leaned against the door.

Did Carter know? Was this the latest truth he kept from me? I went to my bed and plucked the phone from its hiding spot in the folds of Taylor's clothing. Unable to stop my tears or the pain in my breast, I sent him a message.

Did you know John killed his daughter and her nanny (now my nanny) helped him cover it up?

It was dark out and I was claustrophobic again. One Josie was buried in the cemetery and another three thrown in the well. Where would I end up?

Wiping my face, I pulled on my coat and went to the door. Carter's message stopped me before I opened it.

Nanny? Josie, I know you're upset right now, but I need you to answer this question now. Who is this nanny? Name? Description?

I hesitated, not wanting to fall for another of his tricks. Certain he could have nothing bad to say about John's long time servant, I responded and tucked the phone away.

This time, it was the flow of memories that made me pause.

Nell hadn't left. She stood outside my door, her memories jumbled, shadowy, and then clearing to form images I didn't expect.

She opened the door to the bedroom made anew and saw Josie on the bed, smiling. The blond woman wasn't a perfect match by any means but she was close. John would be happy with this one, happier than he was with the last one.

My breath caught. The memories skipped and broke, and another one formed, this one powerful.

Nell watched the blond woman at the well. It was dark. This Josie had disappointed John, told him the truth about who she was, and John was hurt again, the way he had bee the night his daughter died.

Moving quietly, Nell approached her from behind and gathered her strength. She pushed hard. The woman went into the well without a sound, and Nell pulled the woman's devil's box from her pocket to shine the light down into the well.

The blank blue eyes of the broken woman below stared up at her.

"It is done," she whispered.

John could not be disappointed.

I couldn't move, couldn't breathe. I fumbled for the lock to my door with one hand before recalling that Nell had a key.

The memories flowed, repeating the scene and what happened next. Confused, I watched Nell push each of the time traveler Josies into the well then cover it with wood. Nell had returned to John and told him his daughter fled. She then recalled greeting the newest Josie with hope that this one would make John happy again, the way he was before he murdered his daughter. When the other Josies admitted the truths about their identities to John, Nell acted. Three times this had occurred before I arrived.

I almost told him. Horror choked me while tears streamed down my face. Had I been saved because I chickened out at the last minute?

How close had I been to my own death the entire time I was here?

"Miss Josie? Are you awake?" Nell's voice was strangely flat. She tapped on my door.

Oh, god, what do I do?

I didn't answer. Nell tried the door and finding it locked, walked away, the floorboards creaking beneath her steps. I released a breath.

Then heard the door to the dressing room open.

Fumbling with the lock, I whipped open the door to the hallway and sprinted. My heart slammed into my chest and filled my ears as I flew down the stairs and wrenched the front door open.

"Josie!" Nell called, much closer than I expected. The old woman was fast.

I bolted into the wind and rain towards the only safe place I could think of: the barn. Tugging the heavy wooden door open, I snatched a saddle and bridle off their pegs and went to the stall of the horse I usually rode just as Nell pounded on the front door. I ducked down inside the horse's stall.

"Josie! I just want to take you to see your father!" she cried, the soft bump of the wooden door closing behind her.

The woman's lost it.

Her memories were on the other Josies. She hadn't flipped back, as if the woman who cared for me and the one who wanted to kill me were two different people with two different sets of memories.

My phone vibrated. I tensed, hoping the sound was swallowed by the rain on the rooftop. Easing away from the side of the stall, I pulled it out.

The name of the original governess assigned to Josie was Catherine, an Englishwoman. Nellie Bitters was the name of the first woman I sent back to try to find Taylor. I try to screen travelers for any physical or mental weaknesses that might make time travel less than ordeal, but there's always a chance someone ... unfit makes it and can't handle the change.

I wanted so much to smack Carter.

Until that moment, I had never thought twice about how accommodating Nell was. John had an excuse; he was senile and so guilty, he wanted to believe he hadn't done what he did and probably ignored anything that seemed different about me. But Nell ... she'd walked me through every part of this world, answered questions that should've made her suspicious, and even recognized the phone.

It was more than guilt about real-Josie in her case, more than love for John that drove her into madness. It was Carter who pushed her over the edge by sending her back.

"Miss Josie?" Nell's voice was close.

I held my breath and shoved the phone back into my pocket. Seated on the saddle, I waited to hear what she'd do.

The slide of a shotgun's fore stock and the chambering of a round told me how serious she was. My mind raced. There was no way I was going to get the horse saddled and out of the barn before she got off a round or two. I needed to distract her long enough for me to get the hell out of here.

"Nell. Can we talk?" I ventured.

There was a pause. "You must join your father, Josie."

Swallowing the urge to cry, I wiped tears from my face shakily.

"Father … father told me something before he died. Something he wanted you to know," I lied.

"What did he say?" Her response was fast and anxious.

"Don't shoot. Okay?"

There was a pause, then, "Okay, Miss Josie."

Jesus please let this work. I stood uncertainly.

Nell stood in the middle of the barn, shotgun lowered and attention riveted on me. "Can I ask you something first, Nell?"

She said nothing.

"You came from the future, didn't you?" As I spoke, I moved slowly towards the door. Lightning lit up the gaps around the closed windows and thunder made the ground rumble.

There was a hesitation then a brisk nod.

"You were in love with John from the beginning."

Another nod.

"Why did Carter send you back?" It was probably the least of my worries right now, but after hearing Taylor say no one understood the mastermind Doctor Who behind this adventure, I had the urge to know.

"To look over Josie. Make sure she was safe. And … to find Taylor Hansen." The emptiness in Nell's eyes bothered me. "John … was the best man I had ever met. I couldn't stop him. Couldn't save her. Couldn't do anything to help him when it was done."

Split personality or something. Nell's mind had snapped in two: the time traveler sent on a mission and the guardian of a woman she helped raise whose brutal death broke an already fragile mind.

The explanation that she was supposed to take care of real-Josie made little sense to me in light of my purpose here, unless it was like my original mission: the lie Carter used to get her to agree to going back in time.

"Were you a … governess in your time?" I asked.

"Yes. He said I was going to a place where a little girl needed me."

I didn't want to know how wrong I had been about Carter. Taylor was right; whatever cards Carter held, they were almost impossible to guess. What kind of man abandoned innocent people in the past to end up either dead or crazy?

"What did he say, Miss Josie?" Nell asked, inching closer. She brought the shotgun up to her shoulder. "Don't you move."

I had almost reached the door and stopped cold. "Why are you doing this, Nell?" I whispered, fear doing frantic cartwheels in my mind and tightening my chest.

"You made John happy. He's gone now, and you need to be with him to keep him happy."

"So your plan is to shoot me and tell Taylor what?"

"I won't be here when he's back. *Both* of us will be with John again."

This keeps getting worse. I needed more time to figure out what to do. "I don't want to be shot. I'd rather join the others at the bottom of the well."

Nell appeared to be considering my words.

"Please," I added.

"Very well, Miss Josie." She strode forward and took my arm. "Open the door."

I obeyed. A gust of wind swept by us, and I closed my eyes to the pelting rain. We plunged from the warmth and light of the barn into the cold, dark night. Nell tugged me towards the back of the barn. Her grip was tighter than I expected from someone who looked ready to collapse earlier today.

There was a smaller barn beside us. Behind the horse barn were the sheep pens and half a dozen piles of straw and hay covered with tarps. My best bet was to run once we reached the back and hide behind the tarps, to see if I could make my way around the other side of the barn and back around to grab a horse before she could follow.

We reached the back corner, and I prepared to shove her and run. Someone was in front of the well.

We both froze, unable to make out who it was in the dark.

"Their spirits," Nell said hoarsely. "They've come back for me!"

It wasn't a spirit. That much I was able to tell, but we weren't close enough for me to see the face.

"Talks to Spirits," called Fighting Badger.

Oh, no. I held out hope of this ending in some way that didn't involve Nell killing anyone else or dying herself.

"Indian?" Nell raised her shotgun. "You're trespassing on John's lands!"

I shoved her hard enough for her to fall to the ground and darted towards Fighting Badger. "We need to leave!" I cried, grabbing his arm. "Now!"

The first blast of the shotgun went off like a mini-explosion. I braced myself but didn't feel it hit.

Fighting Badger dropped, nearly taking me with him. I released him with a quick look towards Nell. He struggled up. A flash of lightning revealed the hole in his abdomen, and I froze, horrified.

"I'm sorry, Miss Josie."

My gaze flew up to see her aiming the weapon at me this time. "Nell! You don't want to do this!" I cried. "I didn't even tell you what John told me."

"I'll ask him myself when I see him again."

"Wait, Nell. Just … wait!" I was starting to cry again, my hot tears mixing with the cold rain. I needed time … my mind wasn't working. I didn't do well with stress when it came to tests and I did even worse with a gun pointed at me. "Can I have a minute to … pray?" *Think, Josie, think*! I screamed at myself.

Fighting Badger pushed at me, wanting me to run.

God, how I wanted to. But how did I leave the man who took out two people to protect me? How did I keep them from killing one another?

"Very well," Nell said without lowering the weapon.

"Thank you." I wasn't religious at all; I was desperate. I was stuck in the past, almost two hundred years from home, living in a house where four people had been murdered, John had died, and in a time where people like Nell and Fighting Badger existed.

I had never known how dark the world could get, and it hurt me to acknowledge it. Even so, I wasn't going to let Fighting Badger die alone or end up tossed in a well. In a place without much good, what little comfort or light I could provide was needed.

And I couldn't think of anything else to do right now. I was about to hyperventilate, two seconds from breaking down into sobs.

Kneeling beside him, I peeled off my coat and pressed it against his abdomen.

"You … must run," he wheezed.

"No. You helped me. I'll help you." *Maybe I can give him the peace he's never known, if only for a minute or two.*

"You have 'til the count of ten, Miss Josie," Nell warned.

If I were a braver, stronger, smarter person, I'd charge her or run or figure out how to do *something*. I shifted uncomfortably next to Fighting Badger, stifling sobs while mentally running in circles. Cold rain drenched us while lightning lit up the skies.

My cold hand hit one of the wooden boards Nell had pried off the well in anticipation of tossing me in. Choking on a sob, I moved my weight off it and lifted it. It wasn't going to help me with what I needed – a distraction – but if I had the chance –

"Josie!" Taylor's voice followed a crack of thunder. "Josie, where are you?" He sounded like he was headed towards us from the direction of the house.

Oh, thank god. He was always there when I needed rescuing. "Here, Taylor!" I shouted. "It's Nell! She's got a gun!"

Nell whirled to face him. Staggering up, I lurched towards her with the board and lifted it. She started to turn just as I smashed it into her head.

"Josie!" Taylor rounded the corner.

Nell dropped, and the board fell from my hands. I'd never hit anyone in my life, and in that moment, no part of me regretted it.

"Taylor!"

He flung his arms around me and hugged me hard, his familiar scent and heated strength overwhelming. For once, I didn't care if I could breathe in the damned girdle. "Are you okay?" he asked urgently.

"Yeah," I breathed. "I'm so glad to see you!" In that split second, I loved him enough not to care about spending my life in the past with him. I knew it was adrenaline speaking, that I wasn't in love with him, but I'd never been as grateful or happy to see anyone as I was Taylor.

"What the hell happened?" he demanded. "I found both deputies dead in a stall when I took my horse in and –"

"Nell was a traveler like us. She went a little crazy when the real Josie died, and killed off the other girls who came before me."

He drew away. "The real Josie is dead?" he asked, startled.

I didn't tell him. The story was too sordid for me this night. "We can talk about it later," I said. "Fighting Badger is hurt bad." Twisting out of Taylor's grip, I hurried back towards the native bleeding out next to the well. "We have to get him inside!"

The man was still conscious and wheezing. I squeezed his arm in reassurance before checking his wound. From what I could make out, it was bad.

"Taylor?" I called and looked over my shoulder.

He had frozen in place, staring towards us.

"What's wrong?"

He moved slowly at first then closed the distance between us with haste and knelt.

"Brother," Fighting Badger whispered. "I was … concerned for … Talks to Spirits."

My throat tightened. My internal debate about whether to regard him as a psycho or a hero was nowhere near settled, but all I could think about was saving him.

"I need …sleep," the native murmured. He sagged against the well.

"Don't worry, Fighting Badger," I told him. "We'll get you fixed up."

Taylor took my hand and squeezed. I smiled and glanced up.

Lighting lit up his face. He was pale, his gaze haunted.

"What's wrong?" I asked, alarmed by the expression.

"Josie, I want you to know I care about you, and I'm sorry if I caused any of this," he replied.

"You didn't, and I do know you care," I said and started to shift away.

Taylor caught my arms and tugged me closer. "Josie, I …" he stopped.

Concerned, not understanding what was wrong when we needed to help Fighting Badger, I searched his face. "What is it, Taylor?" I asked, resting my cold hands on his warm cheeks. "Are you okay?"

"Just know you gave me – and Fighting Badger – the peace we otherwise never would've known. You made a difference."

I smiled, puzzled. "Okay. Be sad later. We have a lifetime to talk." I kissed his warm lips lightly and pulled away. "We have to hurry. He's bleeding out. Take his arms, Taylor. If we can get him to the barn, we can figure out how bad it is, and I'll send for Doctor Green."

I stood and moved to Fighting Badger's legs.

Taylor moved into position. "You remember what I told you about what happened if my grandfather died?"

"Yes. But we're going to fix that and free Running Bear, after we get Fighting Badger inside."

A groan came from behind me.

I whirled in time to see Nell climbing to her feet, the shotgun clutched in one hand. I gasped then shouted a warning to Taylor.

Vaguely, almost too briefly for me to capture, I sensed the presence again, the shadowy figure that had been following Fighting Badger for days. He melted from the shadows of the barn, too large to be anyone I had met here and moving too fast for me to see what exactly he did in the murky night.

One minute, Nell was raising the shotgun at me. The next, she was on the ground with the immense shadow standing over her. Lightning did nothing to shed light on his hooded features, but it showed me he was dressed like no one I had ever seen before in leather and fur that appeared ancient. He had to be a man by his size, and he was big enough I'd never mess with him. He bore a *sword* of all things. It was thick and curved and wet with Nell's blood.

He fled just as quickly as he appeared, vanishing into the shadows of the night with speed that made me think I hallucinated.

"Taylor, what the hell was that?" I called. My phone vibrated. Instinctively, I pulled it out while turning back towards Fighting Badger.

Don't freak out. We need to talk about this.

I really hated Carter at the moment. Shoving the phone away, I knelt once more by Fighting Badger's feet then sat back.

"Taylor?" I called.

He wasn't anywhere around us.

"Taylor!"

What is he doing? His brother needed help! I bent over Fighting Badger to feel for a pulse.

There was none.

"Oh, god." I sank to my knees beside him, shivering in the cold rain. He'd come to help me and ended up dead.

His memories whispered to me, and I closed my eyes to hear them. He had died thinking of happier times, of his youth and hunting.

My phone buzzed again. I looked around, not understanding where Taylor had gone and why when his brother lay dead beside me.

"Taylor?" I shouted once more.

Another vibration rocked my pocket. Irked at Carter, I pulled it free.

Taylor doesn't exist. His grandfather is dead. He was never born.

I stared at the note. Taylor had mentioned something like that before Nell awoke. But it wasn't possible for someone who existed to suddenly … not.

History should be changed. Both twins are dead, Carter had messaged.

I sat rereading his notes, the sense of disconnect strong. Sagging against the well, I felt both nostrils ooze with blood this time, and the sharp headache accompanying them took my mind off my shock.

Taylor didn't exist. Nothing was making sense, and my emotions were at a stand still, too lost to know how to react.

"Then how can I remember him?" I typed back to Carter.

He responded, *Because you and I exist outside time. Like how Doctor Who and his companions remember saving the world but the world doesn't remember it was in danger, because they stopped it before it happened? To the rest of the world, he never existed.*

New tears choked me. I had thought spending my life here in the past disappointing, with Taylor providing the only potential ray of light. But alone? In a home where a father killed his daughter, a nanny killed three women only to die herself and ... *I* just became the reason Taylor didn't exist?

Everyone was gone. John, Nell, Taylor, Running Bear ... even Fighting Badger.

I sent you back to remove Taylor from history, Carter added. *It was necessary to reset events I have an interest in changing.*

"Oh, god." I hunched over, dry heaving, unable to fathom the idea I'd helped murder someone I cared about.

Taylor had claimed to have been working against Carter in multiple time periods. Carter had outsmarted him in the cruelest way possible.

I lay in the cold rain for what felt like hours, close enough to Fighting Badger to feel his body cool. The sense of disconnect crippled me, and there was no Taylor to pull me out of it. When I could finally move on my own, I pushed myself up into a sit. My nose streamed blood, my head pulsed, and I could barely see straight from the physical pain.

It was nothing compared to the anguish building inside me. Taylor had lived ten thousand lives ... ten thousand missions to help people ... and I just helped erase all of them.

Everyone was gone but Carter. I picked up my phone with numbed fingers, unable to process anything.

I can't stay here. You have to send me home. I texted.

I was shaking with cold but not wanting to leave this spot. I had last seen Taylor here, and it didn't ... *couldn't* be real that he was ... gone. Not dead, but *gone.* It made no sense. I still smelled him on my skin. How did he never exist if I remembered him?

I can't, but I'll take care of you. Trust me, said Carter's text.

I began to cry too hard to read the next one that came through.

The shadow emerged again, and I froze for a split second before all out sprinting away. I tore past the barns, caught myself from falling in the mud between the barns and house and raced up the stairs. Tearing the door open, I didn't bother to close it but bound up the stairs to my room and slammed the door.

It was warm, quiet and cozy, and I immediately began to calm. I could almost pretend nothing had happened, that Nell was bringing me tea and Taylor at his office in town.

The storm beat against the house and roof. I stood for a long moment in the center of my room, wishing it was the first day here again when I viewed this as an adventure.

Better yet, wishing I was visiting the house as a tourist in the twenty first century.

I flung the phone onto the bed and wriggled and tore my way out of my clothing until I stood naked in the middle of my room. I opened every drawer and wardrobe, seeking what had to be there. Nell hadn't thrown away the phones of the girls who came before me; she must have kept my clothing, if not the clothes of all of us somewhere.

It took an hour of searching, of tossing my room and smashing one wardrobe against the floor. I found my yoga pants and tank top hidden in a cubbyhole in the wall behind the wardrobe, along with the clothing of the other visitors from my time.

Reclaiming my only connection to my world, I collapsed on the ground, hugging them.

They were real. They were mine.

Holding them helped stabilize my reeling emotions, and I sat on the floor of my dressing room, listening to the storm outside. Somehow, the clothes made returning home seem possible. Or maybe it was my desperate attempt to rationalize all that happened, to hope, to not break down into the madness that claimed Nell and John.

The clock struck three in the morning. Cramped and miserable, I calmed enough to stand and returned to my bedroom.

More texts lit up my phone screen. *It's your choice. You can stay there or I can send you somewhere else,* claimed the first.

"I want to go home, Carter," I whispered hoarsely. At the mercy of a madman who thought he was Doctor Who and that I wanted to tag along on an adventure, I sank onto my bed once more and stared at the phone. I debated destroying it and living out my fate the best I could after the crushing events of the past few days. If it meant Carter was out of my life, that I was of no more use to him now that Taylor was gone, it'd be worth it.

"Josie, are you well?" Philip's voice came from the hallway. "I've been patient with you since your father died so recently. But tonight, we *will* consummate the marriage."

I hate that man. Without Taylor to save me, I had apparently been forced to wed Philip in the new history created by Taylor's death. I still wore the ring Taylor placed on my finger, though I guessed in the new version of things, it had been Philip who did it.

I wanted to change history. I had no idea that meant changing my fate as well. Gaze lingering on the door, I sought some response that would buy me time.

"I want to take a bath first," I called.

There was a pause, then, "Very well. Send Nell to fetch me when you are done." The floorboards creaked as he retreated.

Any thought I had about remaining here dissipated in light of being married to a man who was going to kill me, if Taylor's people didn't get to me first.

I unlocked the screen of my phone and scanned through Carter's messages.

I can send you somewhere further back in time.

You have to trust me. Please, trust me, Josie, PLEASE!

Are you there? Are you mad?

"I hate this man, too." Swiping away tears, I realized there was blood on my face. My nose hadn't stopped bleeding.

I cleaned up quickly and changed back into my own clothing, boots and an ankle-length wool coat. If Carter got me out of here, great. If I was stuck with Philip, I'd rather throw myself into the well or better yet – steal a horse and run away like the real Josie should have.

Tell me what to do about my empathic memory chip, I ordered Carter. *I'm bleeding again, worse than before,* I texted him.

Oh, good. You're okay. You need to go back to the well. Fast, before we lose the lightning.

It was the last place I wanted to be. The mention of lightning reminded me Carter needed it to fuel sending me back in time, the way he had the night I arrived. I looked around my room with dread and regret.

I really did like it here. I had seen the possibility of remaining here with Taylor, too. The thought of him made my heart and stomach twist hard enough for me to ache. I could stay here, where we had hoped to make a home …

But with all the memories that now haunted me … with Philip waiting in the shadows …

The urge to run and never look back filled me with scared energy that replaced my exhaustion. I didn't even ask Carter where he planned on sending me. I didn't care, so long as it was far, far from here, somewhere where I could forget about Taylor and how I'd probably un-created the only good man left in the world.

I left quickly and quietly, hurried down the stairs of the brightly lit house and fled out the front door.

With some dread, I returned to the gruesome scene behind the barn then texted Carter. *I'm here.*

The massive man I'd seen before disengaged from the shadows of the smaller barn. Clutching my phone, I resisted the urge to run. He'd protected me once, and Carter swore he wanted me alive for some reason.

"Kneel," the man ordered in a voice low and gruff enough to be thunder.

Swallowing a sob, I obeyed and closed my eyes, shivering as much from cold as emotion.

Just know you gave me – and Fighting Badger – the peace we otherwise never would've known. You made a difference. Taylor's parting words echoed in my thoughts. They were generous, considerate, an attempt to comfort me in the face of being uncreated, erased from history, the universe.

You made a difference.

I didn't deserve the words or the emotion behind him, as if he truly believed I'd helped him and Fighting Badger. Only I would mourn the man who didn't exist. Only I would remember him. Only I would know there once was a good man named Taylor Hansen, whose sole wish in life was to retire and live in peace with me.

He deserved so much more, and I had taken everything from him.

The tears began again. I made no effort to stem them this time.

The shadowy figure pressed a large thumb to the back of my neck. I waited for the brilliant light or maybe, for him to chop off my head the way he had halved Nell.

Something smashed into my head instead, and I slid into darkness.

Chapter Eighteen

Gradually, I became aware once more. I was engulfed in brilliant light and heat, caught between the sensations of moving rapidly and floating in place, distantly aware of sonic booms and cracks, as if traveling between times required ripping the fabric of the universe.

This trip was smoother than the first and felt shorter. Seconds after the sonic boom, the light cleared, and I was left on the ground once more, in the dark.

It wasn't rainy – but it was *freezing.* Bone-deep cold air gobbled up the heat generated by time travel, and I began shivering before I opened my eyes. Sunspots blinded me for a moment. I tested out my body as I waited for my vision to clear. I was uninjured from the travel, simply disoriented.

How many times did Taylor travel like this? I almost sighed. I'd hoped Carter would wipe my memory, if that was even possible. I was hurting once more, unable to stop thinking about my first trip through time and how I was the sole person left standing when it ended.

The empathic memory chip was strangely silent, and I realized how much chatter had been going on in the back of my mind. Now there were just my sad thoughts and the dread of guessing what Carter had in store for me next.

I sat up. Moldavite chunks steamed around me in the crater. I wore the same clothes I'd changed into before leaving the eighteen forties and gazed at the sky. The stars were brilliant and bright, the moon a sliver and sky completely clear. I'd never seen a night like this with all the light pollution in my home of southern California. It was too stormy for me to notice the sky in Indian Territory. But this ... this was absolutely breathtaking.

And cold. Jesus – had I ever been this cold? It hurt my nose and lungs to breathe. I wrapped the riding habit around me more tightly and tucked my face into the tall collar. Making my way to the edge of the crater, I climbed out onto what looked like the steppe: a wide, open land of short cropped, verdant grass that glowed silver in the moonlight. In the distance were mountains, and between them and me ...

Nothing.

"It's freakin' cold here!" I muttered. The air was still but had begun to penetrate my wool coat.

There was no Taylor to rescue me this time. The reminder left me feeling more desolate than the steppe stretching out before me.

The sound of movement and shuffling reached me, and I turned, letting out a startled gasp.

An army of forms on horseback extended behind my crater towards another set of mountains, as far as I could see. The men were watching me in complete silence that defied the size of the force. No one stirred. I doubted anyone was even breathing. They were as still as statues, until one of them dismounted.

He dropped all sizes of swords and knives on the ground at his feet before approaching me. Removing his helmet, he stopped a good six feet away, his gaze on the distance between us. He seemed to be thinking about whether or not he wanted to get any closer.

I took in his appearance and dress, trying to place where –and when – I was. His face was round, his eyes almond shaped and skin tone pale olive with ruddy cheeks. He wore layers of clothing: thick, bulky wools and fur-lined leathers over loose trousers and a wide belt cinched at his waist.

I'd never seen anyone like him. Of everything about him that intrigued me, his hair was what I fixated on. Beneath the bowl-shaped helmet, he wore two long braids of grey that marked his seasoned age, one on each side of his head. The rest of his head was shaved.

"Father Sky sent you to bless our battle," he spoke.

Father Sky. At no point in college had I studied ancient religions, so placing the reference was beyond me. I had no idea where I was. Somewhere in Asia, maybe. Not China, not India, certainly not Europe or the Middle East. Like many Americans, I could probably find India and China on a map, but I had no clue what countries lay in the vast space between them. It would be just my luck to end up in one of those places.

"The moon guides us with its white path," he continued with a low bow. "It is an honor to be blessed by Father Sky in such a way."

I understood half of that. "Nice to meet you, too," I managed awkwardly.

A ripple of whispers went through the first several lines of horsemen able to hear me. The man before me broke into a wide smile. "We have milk and meat for you, Goddess of the White Path. You will eat with us this night, and tomorrow, you will accompany the silks and slaves to the Great Khan, so that he may witness this honor."

Great Khan. Now *that* I recognized. Alarm ricocheted within me, and something Carter said when we first met blared through my memories.

Tell that to Genghis Khan when you meet him!

"Oh, Carter. You did *not* send me back to the era of Mongol conquest," I whispered.

"Bring my finest horse!" the man ordered over his shoulder.

If I thought peeing in a bordalou was bad, I didn't want to know what awaited me here.

Exclusive Excerpt from

Black Moon Draw

By Lizzy Ford

Chapter One

THE SHADOW KNIGHT OF BLACK MOON DRAW LIFTED HIS boar's head to the sky, worn yet energized by the day at battle. As the battle-witch had promised, he had won shortly after sunset and stood, triumphant, over the body of his slain enemy. The battlefields were littered with the dead and dying, enemies slaughtered by his bloodlust and brute strength, and the bodies of men who served him. He counted the dead then nodded in satisfaction.

It was a good day. Except he needed a new witch. His lay among the corpses, her purple robes fluttering in the late summer breeze.

With six kingdoms conquered and three remaining to oppose him, he did not have time to celebrate his victory with a feast. The end of the era was coming, and with it, the fulfillment of a thousand-year curse that gave him little time to find the last great battle-witch he had sought for ages. The Heart of Black Moon Draw was depending on him. There was no way he was going to fail.

My phone rings, jarring me out of the reading zone where I've been hiding from reality all day. I blink at the words on the screen of my laptop to help me return from the world of Black Moon Draw and then snatch the cell phone on the desk beside my mouse.

"Hello," I answer groggily. Sitting back, I wipe my nose with my palm. The tears stopped a while ago. My nose is still running.

"Hey, baby. Saw your Facebook post," my mother says. "Sorry to hear about Jason."

"Shit happens, Mom," I mumble. "Real life's so much stranger than fiction."

"Is the wedding really off or is this something you're both working through?"

I flinch, lost for a moment. I've spent the past year preparing to dedicate my life to the man I thought was my true love, only for him to tell me he's found someone else, a week before the wedding.

Someone more *grounded*, he claims.

I hope she's ugly. It's a terrible thought, but I can't help it.

"It's off, Mom," I answer. "He says I spend too much time with fictional people when I should be in the real world with real people."

My mother is silent.

I know she's working hard not to utter an *I-told-you-so*. Jason isn't the first person to try to pry me out of the land of the nonexistent and he isn't the first to leave my life over it.

Probably not the last. I'd like to think I *have* to lose myself in books. I've been a librarian for a year now and one of my tasks is to help identify great books to feature at the library. It's a perfect job. All I do when not behind the desk at work is read. If I don't keep reading, how will I know if I've found the next great thing? There's some vindication for a bookworm who reads an awesome book before it's mainstream.

"He was good for you," my mother says. "But what's important is your happiness. Maybe this will encourage you to try to get out more?"

"I don't *want* to get out more. I'm happy being an introverted hermit. I don't care how poor or anti-social I am! If that's not good enough for him . . ." I fight back tears.

"Okay, baby." My mother clears her throat. "Anything I can do for you?"

"No. Thanks, Mom."

"Let me know if you want to go out for a cinnamon roll or something."

"Okay. I'll call you tomorrow." I hang up, tired of being upset. My eyes blur as I stare at the screen of my laptop.

Black Moon Draw is the name of the story that's waiting for me, an unfinished fantasy novel I found on Wattpad, a site where authors write books in real time by uploading a new chapter every so often.

I discovered it this morning, after finishing everything in my Kindle on my to-be-read list and then surfing the net for more books by my favorite author, a mysterious figure who goes by the initials LF. There's no website or bio anywhere for this author and I was thrilled to discover this partially finished story after rolling through her catalog over a period of three days. I assume LF is a woman – most romance writers are.

This book was written for my shitty week.

It features the ultimate, non-redeemable character, the Shadow Knight of Black Moon Draw, whose soul is so black, the sun can't warm its depths. The violent, half-man, half-beast knight rules a kingdom where there is no daylight, only the perpetual fog and grayness of twilight. He spends his lifetime in battles and steamrolls over everyone in his path.

There's no peace, no love, no hope in Black Moon Draw. Only death and destruction and a knight who doesn't know mercy or forgiveness.

"I love this. I wish I could chop off people's heads with one strike," I murmur, rereading the last little bit before the chapter ends. "Freaky but cool."

The book speaks to me, which is why I keep hitting refresh on my browser in the hopes that the author has updated in the time it took me to read. Thinking about the knight makes me shiver. He's sexy in a very caveman way. Definitely not civilized, which fits my brittle mood today.

I glance at the television and sit up straight, exhausted after spending the day alternately crying and reading. I've had my four all-time favorite movies – *Labyrinth, The Princess Bride, The Neverending Story,* and *Pride and Prejudice* – playing on a loop all day. I'm on vacation this week and supposed to be in the final stages of planning a wedding, not stuck in my house.

Now I'm just gonna spend what's left from the wedding fund on books to help me escape my miserable life.

Pushing away from the desk, I go to the bathroom and stare at my bleary appearance. My hair is in a lumpy ponytail, my eyes rimmed with red, and nose red as well. I've spent the day eating ice cream and am almost surprised it doesn't already show on my otherwise trim body. A true bookworm introvert who hates to leave the house, I've done a thirty-minute yoga video religiously every day in my living room for the past three years since leaving my mom's house. With striking blue-green eyes and dark hair, I'm pretty but also plain.

According to Jason. What a bastard. I can count the number of compliments he's given me since we met on one hand. Our relationship is always like a rollercoaster: brief periods of euphoria followed by months of despair.

I wash my face before returning to my desk.

"Take me away, mysterious LF," I tell the laptop.

I go down the checklist I made of essential characters that appear in every one of LF's books. Part of the fun is figuring out who is whom before the author reveals it.

"I've got the Fool, the Betrayer, the Devoted-but-Doomed guy, the Red Herring, the Loyal Second-in-Command, Beautiful Maiden, Love Interest, Villain, a bunch of minions . . ." I pause. My thoughts go to the Shadow Knight. "The Hero. Hmm. Can the biggest, most violent, mysterious, and relentless badass - with no possibility of redemption - be a hero?"

I lean back and sigh.

"No, he can't," I answer my own question. "And a . . . creature like him can never have a love interest. No one in their right mind would want to be with him." Normally I'm able to spot the end game of a novel a couple of chapters in, but this is something different entirely. "How can a book have no hero or love story? What the hell is LF doing?"

The Shadow Knight is unlike any of the characters LF has ever written about. He doesn't fit any of the profiles of the characters LF includes in her books and thinking about him makes me feel . . . edgy. Scared or uneasy because he seems so real. When I read his passages, I can almost hear his deep, gravelly voice and smell the scent of horse leathers.

Which is silly. It's the sign of a great author, not me going crazy. Besides, what reader fears fictional characters?

"So we have a romance with no hero and no love story." I rest my head on my desk, exhausted. "I didn't think that was possible. At least he's sexy."

Unable to see how his mind works like I can the other characters, I've been locked in a silent battle with him since starting the first chapter. I want to hate him for being what he is, but find myself compelled to reread every one of his passages instead.

Fed up, I close the laptop. The *last* thing I want today is a story I have to dissect. I need a distraction, not another stupid man intent on infuriating me.

"You're giving me a headache. You and every other man on this planet," I mutter to the imaginary knight. "What the hell are you waiting for? Why don't you just tell me your story the way every other character does? And why is it taking LF so long to upload a new chapter?"

A fictional man, of course, can't answer.

"At least you're mortally wounded at the battle of Brown Sun Lake, you bastard. I'm hoping she leaves you that way. I can't believe she misspelled *coincidence* twice in the first two chapters, either. Ever heard of spell-check, LF?" I ask no one in particular. "You're stressing me out! You know what will make this easier? Wine."

I've got a couple of nice bottles I had been saving for the wedding rehearsal. I'm halfway to the kitchen when I realize there's something else I've been saving for that occasion.

The gorgeous, purple dress my mother bought me.

Halting, I debate whether or not drinking wine in a fancy dress at home makes me desperate or is a reasonable way to cope.

One of my three cats meows from his spot on the kitty jungle gym in one corner. My shoulders slump.

"You're right. I really am gonna end up a crazy, single, cat lady," I whisper, new tears forming. "Why can't the heroes in books be real?"

My cat blinks at me, but doesn't answer.

"I hate my life. There's no happily-ever-after in the real world." I'd give anything for a do-over, another chance to be someone worthy of a fictional Hero instead of a wallflower with insecurity issues.

Pretty certain I'll die a crazy old maid, I decide to wear my prettiest dress, break out the wine and chocolate and watch *Pride and Prejudice*. Maybe when I wake up in the morning, there will be a new chapter waiting for me.

Chapter Two

THE SHADOW KNIGHT PACED ACROSS BLUE STAR BRIDGE, THE wooden and stone walkway that arched across the river dividing his kingdom, Black Moon Draw, from his eastern neighbors of White Tree Sound.

He stopped in the middle, listening to the sounds of night. Somewhere, an animal splashed into the shallow waters, probably chasing its dinner, while the calls of owls and other night birds rose from the forest at his back. He didn't register the night chill that skated across his muscular form. Built with the power of a bear and the agility of a panther, he was poised and ready to fight. The sword at his back was taller than a full-grown woman and the axe, daggers, whip, and other weapons at his belt were polished and waiting for their next kill.

Ignoring the nervous band of White Tree Sound sentries that stood on one end of the bridge, he swung his massive boar's head around to observe his surroundings. Moonlight trickled through the fog shrouding Black Moon Draw and reflected off the slow moving river below.

"M'lord," a quiet voice said from behind him. "You will cross Blue Star Bridge this night?"

The bridge was the established border of his lands. He had paid little heed to the kingdom on the other side, with whom he had a truce born out of necessity rather than desire. He had too many other battles to fight to worry about this peace-devoted enemy. He alone could take the forty sentries bunched around the end of the bridge, but the army beyond the forests would require some planning and more men than he had to spare in order to defeat them.

"Not tonight," he said in his low, deep growl. "I need a new battle-witch."

"And you think to find one here?" His most trusted advisor, the man who trained his armies, drew abreast of him. He wore the head of a wolf, the silver eyes and sharp fangs gleaming in the night.

"In my dreams, this is where she appears." There were no sounds other than those he expected to hear, no unusual scents picked up by his sensitive boar's nose.

"Perhaps the Red Knight of White Tree Sound has her." His master-at-arms eyed the restless men belonging to the neighboring kingdom.

"No. She has not come yet."

"From where do you expect this battle-witch to come?"

"From the edge of the world." The Shadow Knight flipped a dagger in his hand, caught it, and sheathed it once more. "Come. She is not here."

"Did these dreams say when she would come?"

"Dreams are like shadows. Even I cannot capture them fully," the Shadow Knight replied. He pulled himself effortlessly onto his massive steed with one arm.

"Except the one about your battle-witch." His second mounted his horse as well.

"'Tis how I know it's different. She will be here." His gaze lingered on the bridge. "'Tis my destiny to reclaim the lands lost by my bloodline before this era ends."

"We have less than a fortnight."

"She will come," he said, resolute.

"I know the value of a good battle-witch. We can post a sentry, if it pleases you."

"Aye. A dead battle-witch does me no good." The Shadow Knight pulled off the Heart of Black Moon Draw – a medallion carved from a rare, black gem and containing the magic of the kingdom – from around his head and tossed it to his master-at-arms. "Instruct our scout to claim her on my behalf."

"Aye, sire."

The Shadow Knight wheeled his horse to face the forest. Squeezing his calves against its belly, he raced into the trees, towards the army preparing for tomorrow's battle.

Chapter Three

*O*H, GOD. MY HEAD!

I'm afraid to move, knowing once I do, the world's worst hangover will kick my ass. The dull, brain deep throb is already there, waiting to explode when I try to stand. Instead, I listen for the familiar sounds of my apartment in the morning: the neighbor's annoying alarm, the honking of traffic, shuffling of people down the hallway as they leave for work . . .

. . . the gurgle of a stream?

I smell flowers that aren't anything like the vanilla plugins in my bedroom, and something is tickling the sensitive inside of my forearm.

Spiders!

Only such an irrational fear could make me snap up into a sitting position without considering my head.

I groan, gripping it.

I blink, trying to focus, to see my bedroom wall instead of the dead forest where the wall should be. Squeezing my eyes closed, I open them again. My hands drop to my sides and I stare.

The trees are still present, their bare, sagging branches rattling in a cool morning breeze that makes me shiver. Wildflowers litter the grassy area around me, dancing in the wind. Fog clings to the branches of trees and covers the sky.

I slap my cheek lightly to make sure I'm not stuck in a dream. This . . . place certainly seems real. The source of the gurgling is a wide stream whose banks are connected by a graceful, arching stone and wooden bridge. It feels like morning, but is gray out, like the period of graininess between sunset and night.

Where the hell am I? I could have drunk myself to death and maybe the bridge leads to heaven.

Do people in heaven get hangovers?

My head hurts too badly for me to freak out. It's definitely a fitting ending to my week. I'm wearing my pretty purple dress, my feet bare, and dark hair hanging around my shoulders. At least I left the earth dressed decently.

"Oh, my poor mom!" Deep sorrow is building within me at the thought of not saying farewell to my mother and I shift onto my knees. Branches snap from somewhere across the bridge. I concentrate on controlling the headache. My stomach hurts and muscles ache, like I spent the night in some awkward position sprawled across the couch watching my favorite movies.

"Are you the witch?" The male voice makes me jerk.

I face him – and scream. Crouched ten feet from me is a creature with a man's body and a panther's head whose golden eyes are watching me like he's hungry. The unholy combination of man and beast is terrifying.

"Stay away from me!" I shout.

Maybe this isn't heaven. I stagger to my feet, smash to my knees, and then stumble up again.

I fling my arms out to either side to help me balance. The ground isn't moving, but it feels like it is. When my head stops spinning, and I'm fairly confident I won't fall, I look again at the half-man . . . thing. He's dressed in brown leather leggings and a long shirt cinched at his waist by a thick belt. A sword dangles from the belt.

From the neck down, he's a man in every way I can see, from his very human hands and fingers to normal shaped feet in boots.

But his head . . .

"What *are* you?" I ask.

He's watching me closely with his round panther eyes, his jaw open in a noiseless pant. He hasn't moved out of his crouch, as if he's trying to figure me out the way I am him. "You are from the edge of the world?"

"I'm pretty sure I'm not from here." I gaze around in confusion. "This isn't heaven, is it?"

He laughs, a strange, half-growl, half-guffaw.

I take a step back.

"Black Moon Draw has never been mistaken for heaven," he replies.

Black Moon Draw?

"Oy!" someone shouts from the bridge.

I turn, gripping my head again at the sudden movement. A man – a *normal* man – is standing in similar clothing in the middle of the bridge. His tunic is white and bears the symbol of a tree on it.

"Will you be claiming that witch?" he calls to the man with the panther head. He has a Cockney accent I have trouble understanding.

"She's on our land!" The panther-man snarls, standing. "You would be wise to heed my warning. If you cross that bridge, none of the gods will stand between you and my master!"

The other guy is hanging out in the middle of the bridge. It's clear he's not going to cross it and I don't blame him one bit.

"Did you say Black Moon Draw?" I ask the panther-man.

"Aye." He glances at me then returns his golden glare to the man with the tree on his shirt.

"No, really. Black Moon Draw?"

"Aye."

"Terrifying, isn't it?" the man on the bridge calls. "White Tree Sound is at peace and ruled by a man nothing like the beast of Black

Moon Draw."

"My master is not a beast!" Panther-man retorts.

My ears are buzzing and I'm starting to think I either didn't wake up or I woke up in hell.

"Is your master the Shadow Knight?" I ask. "The one with a boar's head who knows no mercy and chops off the heads of pretty much everyone he meets?"

"Aye." Panther-man says with a hint of pride.

"He'll deflower and kill you. Come to us and we will treat you well. Our last battle-witch was made a lady and died of old age," the man on the bridge yells.

At least, I think that's what he says. His accent is heavy enough I'm filling in some of the words.

Black Moon Draw. Shadow Knight. Battle-witch.

I rack my brain. There must be a reasonable explanation for what's going on. Perhaps I didn't wake up from a weird dream? Or did my misery turn into an all-out break with reality?

It's all I can think of. I can't remember most of last night after cracking open a second bottle of wine. This place certainly seems real, from the cool mist settling into the trees to the freak show beside me.

But it *can't* be real. If I were going to be dropped into a book, it'd be *Pride and Prejudice* or, better yet, *Fifty Shades of Grey*, both of which contain civilized worlds with Heroes who only need their Heroines to make their lives complete. From what I read, this nightmarish world is plagued by death and war. Why would I be here of all places?

The two are arguing. I'm having difficulty making out their words and more trouble standing. I sink onto the ground and stare, dazed, confused, horrified. There's a tiny voice in my head telling me that if I thought my life was bad before, it just got a helluva lot worse.

Panther-man clasps my shoulder and kneels before me.

I blink his animal face into focus and recoil.

"I claim you in the name of the Shadow Knight of Black Moon

Draw. Do not cross Blue Star Bridge. They will deflower and kill you." He places something heavy and cold in my hand. "This will grant you safe passage through our kingdom, should you need it. I will not be gone long." He stands and leaves.

It takes me a minute before the sensation of wanting to faint passes. I'm clutching a black jade or obsidian medallion with strange carvings strung on a thick, worn piece of leather. Studying it, I'm trying not to be weirded out by how heavy and real it feels, as if this whole place isn't a flimsy dream that'll dissipate soon.

How can this be real? I'm perfectly sane, or thought I was. Psychosis brought on by mental trauma sounds more likely than I'm stuck in a *book.*

"M'lady." Another voice calls from the bridge.

Looking up, my gaze lingers.

Wow. Dressed in a rich red cloak lined with fur, the brunet man on the bridge has the chiseled features of a model. He's smiling, a perfect, white, even grin, that renders him boyish, charming.

"I'm the Red Knight of White Tree Sound. I rule all of this." He motions to the forest beyond the bridge. "I would like to invite you into my lands and home."

I really hope Prince Charming has a castle. It figures I have to go to a fictional world to find the perfect man.

"I think I'll stay here," I reply. "In case I can go home."

His eyebrows lift. "Home is Black Moon Draw?"

"Oh, god, no. Never. From what I know of that place, it's hell."

His brow is furrowed.

I swallow hard. I'm not going to cry, at least, not until I'm fully convinced this isn't a dream or psychotic break.

"I would encourage you to cross the bridge," he says. "Before the Shadow Knight comes to claim you. We are in need of a battle-witch. You will be safe and protected."

"Battle-witch?" I'm thinking hard through my headache to recall what LF wrote about the mysterious women that the warriors of this world believed could predict and influence the outcome of battles.

"Every knight-ruler in the realm has heard of your coming. The last great battle-witch," he replies. "Come. We have food and clothing to warm you."

It's kind of hard to say no. Jason definitely wasn't a looker and I've never had a man this handsome give me the time of day. While I know nothing of his little kingdom, I do know that I don't want to be here when the violent Shadow Knight shows up.

Getting to my feet, I make my way through the grasses to the stone path leading across the bridge. I pull on the medallion Panther-man gave me, just in case.

Just in case WHAT? I wake up in a different book? Get lost in the forest?

Nothing is making sense right now, except that I'm definitely hungry and could use a blanket or warmer clothing.

"No tricks? I'll be safe?" I ask, pausing at the foot of the bridge.

"You have my word," the Red Knight responds quickly.

Why not? Maybe this man is the elusive Hero I hadn't yet discovered in LF's book. Or maybe he's the Red Herring meant to lead me astray or the Betrayer . . . How the hell do I figure it out?

The panic bubbling within me makes my head pound worse. Whatever I think of the Red Knight, I at least know the Shadow Knight will probably behead me if he finds me.

I walk and join the Red Knight in the middle of the bridge, pausing to gaze up at him. My god – he's utterly beautiful.

"You will need new robes," he observes, gaze lingering on my breasts. "You are in the correct color, but not the correct cloth."

Purple. I'm remembering more details now. The battle-witches of this world wear purple. The color is rare and only the elite seers wear it.

What happens when they realize I'm not a battle-witch?

The thought makes my head pound. I touch it gingerly.

"You are unwell?" the Red Knight asks.

"Drank too much wine last night."

"Ah. A common ailment." He waves over one of the three men waiting in the area between the bridge and forest. "Come." He starts down his side of the bridge.

I glance over my shoulder, noticing for the first time how the mists hanging in the branches of trees on the Black Moon Draw side of the bridge are absent in White Tree Sound. There are birds on this side of the forest, and it smells of pine. The forests are different – one alive and one dead – yet divided only by a stream. It's sunny on this side of the stream, too.

This is too weird. I need time to think or maybe to get rid of my headache first because thinking is too difficult right now.

Trailing the Red Knight off the bridge, I pass the three guards waiting for him and follow him onto a deer trail. We don't walk far and stop on a rustic road hedged by trees. A shoebox looking, wooden wagon with four horses out front and a driver waits in the middle of the road.

Another guy in white opens the door for the Red Knight, who sweeps off his cape before climbing in. I get in as well and sit opposite him. There's a trunk between the two benches and a lantern hanging from the low ceiling in the center whose light doesn't reach the corners of the wagon.

The wooden benches are covered by pillows. It's warmer in here and I rub my upper arms to help warm me.

"'Tis a half day ride to my hold," he tells me. "You are hungry?"

I nod.

He taps the trunk. The top slides off as if by magic and he reaches into its depths to lift a tray of food: jerky, cheese, bread, and whole fruit. A pitcher and two stocky goblets are present as well.

Another tap and the trunk slides closed.

"Eat," the Red Knight urges me. "The moon apple is a specialty of my lands." He holds up a white apple.

"Thanks." I accept it and put it in my lap. I'm not much of one for apples. Bread, though, is my weakness, as evidenced by my thighs, and I grab a piece. "You said you've been waiting for me?"

"Battle-witches are rare. The knight-rulers of our realm are sent visions or dreams when a new one is to come," he explains with another charming smile. "The Shadow Knight has been eyeing my lands for many years. We are at peace, but I'd like to be ready."

What do I say to that? "I don't blame you," I reply awkwardly. I take a huge bite of bread and then a sip of wine. The bread is dry and hearty, the wine a little stronger than I'm used to.

The carriage jolts into movement and I rock back, catching myself on a pillow.

"His was recently killed," he adds. "I know he is looking for a new one."

"What happened to yours?" I ask.

"'Tis the fate for any battle-witch captured by an enemy. Deflowering and death. But mine died of old age since there has been no war in years."

"Deflower? You mean rape?"

"Rape or seduction. Most battle-witches are young like you and fall for a handsome knight who brings them flowers. I barter such services to any kingdom that needs it. It's how my coffers stay filled with gold and I stay on good terms with all."

He's a damn gigolo. Why am I not surprised?

"Why not just kill her?" I demand, not understanding the need to seduce a woman before lopping off her head.

He laughs, like I've asked the stupidest question on the planet. "Because your kind can't die! If I chop off your head, it'll grow back by tomorrow morning. But you can lose your powers, if you are no longer pure, which makes you vulnerable."

I lower the wine. Do I make a joke about it being too late to be pure and risk him beheading me to prove a point, or do I play along and hope

I'm never challenged to prove I'm a battle-witch?

You wake up. That's what you do. I close my eyes and will myself out of this mess.

"They say if an ordinary man even kisses a battle-witch, his man parts will fall off. I have a certain immunity to such a fate," he adds.

Are these wacky rules made up by LF? Because they don't make much sense to me. Have these people ever chopped off the head of an alleged battle-witch to test their theory?

Opening my eyes, I'm not surprised to see I haven't been magically transported back to my home. I start eating again. I'm guessing sleeping with the fine specimen of a man before me is off the table as well, though I'd rather not sleep with a man-whore in the first place.

Unless he *really* knew what he was doing in bed, à la Christian Grey and unlike Jason.

"The guards said you appeared last night," the Red Knight says and leans forward, as if he doesn't want anyone to hear his words. "You were not there and suddenly you were. From whence came you?"

I sip my wine, once again at a loss as to how much I should say. The Red Knight is waiting patiently, his friendly, open features encouraging me. He's not giving me the vibe I'm used to, that I'm about to be judged or made fun of.

"From another world," I reply honestly. "I don't know where or how. I went to sleep there and woke up here."

"Someone sent you here," he guesses.

"Yeah. How'd you know?"

"Let's just say you're not the first who's been sent." He's frowning, his eyes moving to stare at some point in the distance.

Is it possible the people of this world are aware of mine? How crazy would that be?

"My head hurts so bad." I can't even entertain such a deep thought.

He's too distracted. "This world, is it magical?"

A glance around reminds me these people don't know what

electricity is let alone the Internet. "You can say that."

He sits back, pensive.

I eat quietly, uncertain what's bothering him. The cheese is awesome, much better than the bread and wine. I'm not a fan of jerky and quit after choking down one piece.

"What is your name, witch?" he asks finally.

"Naia."

"Naia." A flicker of surprise crosses his features. He shifts forward again. "You must not tell others of this magical world from whence you came or the person who sent you or even your name."

"Why not?"

"A battle-witch, such as you are, is expected to have knowledge of the unknown and magic. But another world?" He shakes his head gravely. "You will be flogged or worse, put to death, for even mentioning it. And . . ." He pauses, as if not sure he should continue, before he does. "I'm going to track down the person who sent you. I don't need others getting in my way."

Ummm . . . yeah, right. No book character can find its author, because they aren't real.

Listening and growing more confused, I'm surprised by the severity of his expression and the sudden way he's looking at me as if he wants to feed me to Panther-man after all.

It hits me then that this man, the Red Knight, is a warrior, one trained to lead men into battle and kill, even if his kingdom is at peace. It's not like he's a Starbucks barista or coworker at the library. He's armed with a sword and knife and friendly – but dangerous. If he wants to track LF down, I doubt it's to thank her for creating his world.

"If you find that person, tell her to send me home," I reply finally.

"I shall," he said. "In the meantime, listen to me carefully. When asked, battle-witches always say they are from the edge of the world. You and I know differently. No one else can know."

"I'm sorry." It seems like the right thing to say. "I didn't know. I won't say anything to anyone." I want to ask him if he knows he's just a fictional character. By the look on his face, it's not a good time to point that out.

"And if you are asked by anyone, you are to tell them you were found on my side of the river. Do you understand?" His gaze is piercing, his face stony.

"I think so."

"You must *know* so. I will ensure you never return home if you admit the truth to anyone."

Things just got real a little too fast for me. I nod and then find my voice. "I understand." My heart is slamming into my chest, adrenaline racing through me as my instincts warn me of danger. It's hard to keep in mind that none of this is real when he looks like he's ready to stab me with a knife.

The intensity around him fades and the smile returns. "I have never found a new battle-witch. I am eager to learn how well you predict battles."

"Yeah." My head is feeling better from the food. My appetite has fled. "Me, too." It seems like the only safe answer and I start to retreat into my shell, the way I do around anyone else in the real world. I know the world of this book is dangerous. I'm starting to think it's dangerous to *me*. "Um, do you know how I'm supposed to predict battles?" I venture.

"My last battle-witch would look at her hand. When there was aught to share, she shared."

I glance down instinctively at my hands. To my surprise, there's something on my right palm, written sloppily in a maroon Sharpie.

"Can you see it?" I ask, holding out my palm to him.

"I cannot. What does it say?"

Maybe I am a battle-witch. How weird would that be? Squinting, I study the writing. It appears to be moving, scrolling like the ticker at the bottom of a news station. Beneath it is a digital clock marking days, hours, minutes, and seconds.

"There's some sort of countdown," I say, watching the seconds tick down. "What happens in about ten days?"

"The end of this thousand-year era," he replies.

"Is that good or bad?"

"It should be neither." He's rubbing his jaw, gaze growing distant. The tension is back in his frame, a sign I take as bad.

"Should be," I repeat.

"If it 'twere any other era, aye."

If television and movies have taught me anything, it's that countdowns are never good.

"What else is there?" he asks.

"It says there are others seeking me who will attack you before the fork." I reread it, puzzled. "Does that make sense?"

Across from me, the Red Knight has gone rigid, one hand on the hilt of his sword. "Are you certain?"

"Yeah. Why? What's wrong?"

He reaches back and slaps the wall of the carriage twice. "The fork is less than a candlemark from where we found you."

I have no idea what a candlemark is – a measure of time? distance? – but judging by his reaction, it's close, and that's bad.

The wagon stops quickly enough that I barely catch the cheese that comes hurling at me.

"You mean they're coming now?" I ask in alarm.

"Stay here." He shoves the door open to the wagon and leaps out, slamming it closed behind him.

Black Moon Draw

is available in ebook from your favorite ebook store and paperback from Amazon and special order from your local bookstore!

About The Author

Lizzy Ford is the award winning, internationally acclaimed author of over thirty five books written for young adult, new adult and adult romance readers, to include the internationally bestselling Rhyn Trilogy, Witchling Series and the War of Gods series. Lizzy has focused on keeping her readers happy by producing brilliant, gritty romances that remind people why true love is a trial worth enduring.

Lizzy's books can be found in every major ereader library, to include: Amazon, Barnes and Noble, iBooks, Kobo, Sony and Smashwords. She lives in southern Arizona with her husband, three dogs and a cat.

Connect with Lizzy:

WEBSITE:
www.LizzyFord.com

FACEBOOK:
www.Facebook.com/LizzyFordBooks

or find her on TWITTER!
@LizzyFord2010

Also by Lizzy Ford ...

History Interrupted
West
East
North
South

Non-Series
Black Moon Draw

Sons of War
Semper Mine
Soldier Mine
SEAL Mine

Starwalkers Serials (with Julia Crane)
Severed
Trapped
Exiled
Revealed
Escaped

Heart of Fire
Charred Heart
Charred Tears
Charred Hope

Rhyn Trilogy
Katie's Hellion
Katie's Hope
Rhyn's Redemption

Rhyn Eternal
Gabriel's Hope
Deidre's Death
Darkyn's Mate
The Underworld

War of Gods
Damian's Oracle
Damian's Assassin
Damian's Immortal
The Grey God

Damian Eternal
Xander's Chance
The Black God

Anshan Saga
Kiera's Moon
Kiera's Home (novelette)
Kiera's Sun

Santa's Ninja Elves (short stories)
Natasha
Hunter

Non-series titles
Star Kissed
A Demon's Desire
The Warlord's Secret
Maddy's Oasis
Rebel Heart

Published by Evatopia Press

WITCHLING
Dark Summer
Autumn Storm
Winter Fire
Spring Rain

INCUBATTI
Zoey Rogue
Zoey Avenger

BROKEN BEAUTY NOVELLAS
Broken Beauty
Broken World

VOODOO NIGHTS
Cursed
Chosen

... and many more coming soon!

With so many books, it's hard to know where to start! Here's a quick list of suggestions!

FAN FAVORITES (paranormal): "Katie's Hellion," "Dark Summer," "Damian's Oracle"

ABOUT A READER WHO GETS SUCKED INTO A BOOK: "Black Moon Draw"

CONTEMPORARY ROMANCE: "Semper Mine"

SPICY URBAN FANTASY/PARANORMALS: "Zoey Rogue","Charred Heart"

SWEET (FADE TO BLACK SEX SCENES) PARANORMAL ROMANCE: "Damian's Oracle," "Katie's Hellion," "Xander's Chance"

NOVELLAS: (paranormal) "A Demon's Desire," (contemporary romance) "Maddy's Oasis"

TEEN PARANORMALS: "Dark Summer," "Cursed"

TEEN LITERARY FICTION: "Broken Beauty"

LIZZY'S FIRST BOOK EVER: "Damian's Oracle"

TIME TRAVEL: "West"

SCI-FI ROMANCE: (dystopian) "Rebel Heart," (alien) "Kiera's Moon," (futuristic) "Star Kissed"

FIRST BOOKS IN EACH SERIES
"Damian's Oracle" (War of Gods)
"Katie's Hellion" (Rhyn Trilogy)
"Gabriel's Hope" (Rhyn Eternal)
"Charred Heart" (Heart of Fire)
"Dark Summer" (Witchlings)
"Zoey Rogue" (Incubatti)
"Hear No" (Hidden Evil)
"West" (History Interrupted - standalones)

"Semper Mine" (Sons of War - standalones)
"Severed" (Starwalkers)
"Cursed" (Voodoo Nights)
"Broken Beauty" (Broken Beauty Novellas)
"Xander's Chance" (Damian Eternal)
"Elle's Journey" (The Foretold Trilogy)
"Kiera's Moon" (Anshan Saga)

Made in the USA
Charleston, SC
26 July 2015